Dear Reader,

No matter how busy your day, there'll *always* be time for romance. TAKE 5 is a new way to indulge in love, passion and adventure—and still be on time to pick up the kids! Each TAKE 5 volume offers five condensed stories by top Harlequin and Silhouette authors. Now you can have the enjoyment and satisfaction of a full-length novel, but in less time— perfect for those days when it's difficult to squeeze a longer read into your hectic schedule.

This volume of TAKE 5 features five tender love stories...five *sweet* escapes! Day Leclaire delights readers with the tale of an amnesic bride in *One-Night Wife* and *Who's Holding the Baby?* features a pretend engagement turning into something more. A husband for a day is needed in *New York Times* bestselling author Kasey Michaels's *Compliments of the Groom.* In *A Secret Valentine,* *USA Today* bestselling author Dixie Browning tells of a teacher who finds it hard to resist the one man she *has to,* and opposites attract in Browning's *East of Today.*

Why not indulge in all four volumes of TAKE 5 available now—tender romance, sizzling passion, riveting adventure and heartwarming family love? No matter what mood you're in, you'll have the perfect escape!

Happy reading,

Marsha Zinberg
Senior Editor and Editorial Coordinator, TAKE 5

Kasey Michaels is the *New York Times* and *USA Today* bestselling author of more than sixty books. She has won the Romance Writers of America RITA Award and the *Romantic Times Magazine* Career Achievement Award for her historical romances set in the Regency era; she also writes contemporary romances for Silhouette and Harlequin Books

Day Leclaire and her family live in the middle of a maritime forest on a small island off the coast of North Carolina. Despite the yearly storms that batter them, and the power outages, they find the beautiful climate, superb fishing and unbeatable seascape more than adequate compensation. One of their first acquisitions upon moving to Hatteras Island was a cat named Fuzzy. He has recently discovered that laps are wonderful places to curl up and nap—and that Day's son really was kidding when he named the hamster "Cat Food."

Dixie Browning is an award-winning painter as well as a writer, mother and grandmother. Her father was a big-league baseball player, her grandfather a sea captain. In addition to nearly eighty contemporary romances, Dixie and her sister, Mary Williams, have written more than a dozen historical romances under the name Bronwyn Williams. Contact Dixie at www.dixiebrowning.com, or at P.O. Box 1389, Buxton, NC 27920.

TAKE 5

Quick Reads. Great Escapes.

**NEW YORK TIMES
BESTSELLING AUTHOR**

Kasey
Michaels

Day
Leclaire

Dixie
Browning

HARLEQUIN®

TORONTO • NEW YORK • LONDON
AMSTERDAM • PARIS • SYDNEY • HAMBURG
STOCKHOLM • ATHENS • TOKYO • MILAN • MADRID
PRAGUE • WARSAW • BUDAPEST • AUCKLAND

ISBN 0-373-83501-9

TAKE 5, VOLUME 5

Copyright © 2002 by Harlequin Books S.A.

The publisher acknowledges the copyright holders of the individual titles as follows:

COMPLIMENTS OF THE GROOM
Copyright © 1987 by Kathie Seidick

WHO'S HOLDING THE BABY?
Copyright © 1994 by Day Totton Smith

ONE-NIGHT WIFE
Copyright © 1995 by Day Totton Smith

A SECRET VALENTINE
Copyright © 1983 by Dixie Browning

EAST OF TODAY
Copyright © 1981 by Dixie Browning

This edition published by arrangement with Harlequin Books S.A.

® and TM are trademarks of the publisher. Trademarks indicated with ® are registered in the United States Patent and Trademark Office, the Canadian Trade Marks Office and in other countries.

Visit us at www.eHarlequin.com

Printed in U.S.A.

CONTENTS

COMPLIMENTS OF THE GROOM

Kasey Michaels

"*I won! I won! I won!*"

Amanda Elizabeth Tremaine danced around the room, alternately laughing and shouting.

Jeanne Tisdale, head instructor of the Happy Days Nursery School for more years than she cared to count, was accustomed to the exuberance of her young assistant, and now simply sat back in her desk chair and waited for the whirlwind that was Mandy to blow herself out.

Mandy was now standing in front of her, palms flat on the desk. "Well? Why aren't you dancing with joy?"

"Amanda," Jeanne said calmly, looking up into the younger woman's widely smiling face. "I'm forty-three years old. I just spent three hours with Justin Brosious, Todd Terrance Tillson, Sean 'Mad Dog' O'Connor and a dozen other damp-bottomed terrors. I couldn't dance with joy if Robert Redford waltzed in here and threw himself at my feet. Would you settle for a small whoopee—once I find out what I'm celebrating, that is?" she urged.

"Oh, I'm sorry," Mandy exclaimed penitently, running a hand through her short crop of burnished curls. "You remember how the stereo broke last month, and how we haven't been able to afford a replacement?" she began. "Well, I happened to hear about a contest on WFML—you know, that hard-rock radio station they play in the coffee shop across the street—and, surprise, surprise, they were having a contest to give away CD's, T-shirts, and, oh, all sorts of prizes, with the top prize to be a state-of-the-art stereo system." Mandy once more looked like she was about to erupt. "And I won *first prize!*"

"But, Mandy, dear," Jeanne said, "don't you want the prize for yourself?"

Mandy waved a hand in dismissal. "Mrs. Thorton would throw me out on my ear if I played the thing above a whisper. I'll just reserve the right to play some of my own music on it after school hours."

Jeanne looked intently into Amanda's face. "What did you have to do to win?" she asked at last.

"I didn't have to do anything except complete a sentence. You know—one of those twenty-five words or less things."

Jeanne saw Mandy lower her dark lashes to hide eyes that couldn't conceal a lie, and a strange, nervous churning began in her stomach. "What was the sentence, Amanda?" she prodded gently, not really wanting to hear the answer.

"Well," Mandy began, her voice so low Jeanne had to strain to hear her. "It was just one of those silly things. You know-like, um, like, oh, I eat this cereal *because,* or I like this car best because, or we make love best to music because—"

"What!" the older woman shouted.

Mandy rushed into speech. "It was a contest for newly-weds. I just made up some drivel and sent it in." She tilted her head and smiled reminiscently. "Though actually, it *was* rather good—all that malarkey about moonlight and bearskin rugs."

"Oh, good grief."

"I just—er—I just sort of *smudged* my 'Ms.' on the entry so that it looked more like a 'Mrs'"

"Oh, I see. Innocent dishonesty," Jeanne answered dully, pressing her fingertips to her suddenly throbbing temples.

"I have the day off tomorrow anyway," Mandy said. "All I have to do is show up, identify myself as 'Ms-rs' Amanda Tremaine, and pick up my prize. See? It's that simple."

THE OFFICES of WFML—both the radio and the television stations operated out of the same building—were situated atop a medium-size hill just outside the city of Allentown.

She'd explain her reason for the fib she had told on the entry form and then throw herself on the deejay's mercy.

Surely Vic Harrison would understand and give her the stereo anyway. After all, hers *was* the best entry.

"Amanda Tremaine," the receptionist said unemotionally, holding a red-tipped nail against a line of typing that was part of a long list of names. "Down the hall to your left, you'll see the freight elevator. The lobby elevator is being serviced. Second floor, three corridors down to your right, third doorway. Don't go in if the red light is on."

The elevator door took its own sweet time in opening. Mumbling and grumbling to herself, she kept her head bowed and stepped inside. She pushed the button for the second floor.

The machine began its ascent with a jerk. But just as quickly the elevator gave another jerk, breathed a loud wheeze and then settled itself firmly between the two floors.

"Oh, Lord," Mandy exclaimed aloud. "God's getting me for lying!"

THE MAN leaning a shoulder lazily against the rear wall of the elevator had lifted his brows in silent approval of the feminine form that stood before him, then realized he had been so preoccupied with his own thoughts that he had somehow forgotten to get off at the first floor.

After inspecting the female all the way down to her slim, well-turned ankles, he allowed his assessing gaze to return to the top of her frame, to linger on the riot of curls that he was sure had earned her the nickname of Carrot Top in grade school.

"There's nothing to be alarmed about," he began in his most bracing voice, only to be cut off by Mandy's high-pitched yelp.

"Where—where did *you* come from?" she asked, whirling around to notice the other occupant of the elevator for the first time.

His deep blue eyes crinkled a bit around the corners as he smiled a wide, lopsided grin. "Well, first, or so they tell me,

I was nothing more than a gleam in my father's eye. Then—''

''Stop that!'' Why do I have to get all the weirdos? Mandy asked herself, running a hand through her hair.

Lord, but she was a looker, the man thought. I especially like the turned-up nose. And the freckles, yeah, they're just the right touch.

''I'm being punished,'' Mandy said, distractedly looking around her and seeing nothing but her prison—four walls of pea-green chipped paint—and her fellow prisoner, a first-class nut case. She closed her eyes and gave a defeated sigh. ''I should have known this was going to happen,'' she moaned. ''Now the elevator is going to fall and I'll be killed.''

''Are you hysterical or is that outburst supposed to be in aid of something extremely deep?'' her companion asked, leaning his broad shoulder against the elevator wall, all thoughts of his luncheon meeting forgotten as he watched the woman's antics with growing good humor.

Mandy ignored his teasing sarcasm. Hugging her arms around herself, she suddenly whirled away from him. She muttered fatalistically, ''Oh, what difference does it make. I'm being punished, that's what it is. It was only a *little* fib, hardly even worth stopping an entire elevator for, for goodness' sake. *When* will I ever learn to look before I leap?''

The man, who seemed utterly invulnerable to any hints he should mind his own business, placed himself directly in front of her. ''Here's where I either kiss you senseless or throw cold water in your face. Which do you prefer?''

''What?''

''You're hysterical, lady,'' he told her calmly. ''Haven't you ever been to the movies? It's standard Hollywood practice. You have your choice of treatment. Either that or you stop babbling about God getting you and tell me what has you in such an uproar.''

Mandy took another look at the tall, dark, terribly handsome man smiling down at her before launching into a garbled version of her descent into sin.

"Is that all?" the man asked incredulously once she was done. "God, lady, if you're going to hell for that, where do you suppose they put Al Capone?"

"Don't try to cheer me up," Amanda said, causing her companion to issue a sharp bark of laughter.

"Just go in to this Harrison guy and brazen it out."

"You really think so?" she asked, impulsively grabbing his muscular forearm. "After all," she went on, "it wasn't like I was planning on robbing the crown jewels or something. Or trying to take something just because I wanted it for myself. I mean, it *is* for the chil—"

A firm hand grasped her chin and turned her toward him, their gazes meeting and locking as he whispered huskily, "Lady, did anyone ever tell you that you talk too much?" Then he leaned forward and joined his lips softly with hers.

It was just the faintest whisper of a kiss, but Mandy thought she could feel the earth moving beneath her.

It wasn't until an amused male voice penetrated her distracted thoughts that she understood that the elevator had at last completed its journey to the second floor. "Well, *hello* there," the voice sang out mischievously. "I wondered where you had gotten to. Helen didn't say you were bringing the lucky hubby along, Mrs. Tremaine. No wonder he's grinning like that—that was some letter!"

The man who had taken advantage of her agitation by kissing her now stood up and held out his hand to the leering Harrison.

"Mr. Harrison?" he said cordially in his deep, husky voice. "I'm Mr. Tremaine. You'll have to excuse the wife here. We haven't been married long, you know, and she still gets a little flustered whenever I kiss her. You understand how it is," he ended, winking at the disc jockey in a way that had Mandy aching to choke them both.

"Follow me, Mr. and Mrs. Tremaine," he said, starting

off down the hallway. "I tried to get hold of you this morning to let you know about a change in our plans, but then I decided it would be more fun to tell you two in person. It seems we have a little surprise for you two!"

Mandy shot her pseudo-husband a questioning look, but he merely shrugged his shoulders and took her hand. "By the way," he whispered, leaning over so that his warm breath caressed her ear, "what's your first name?"

"Mandy," she squeaked. "Amanda Elizabeth Tremaine, actually."

"Very nice, Amanda Elizabeth," he told her, giving her trembling hand a reassuring squeeze. "Just call me Joe and we'll be fine. Just fine. Trust me."

Mandy groaned and allowed herself to be led down the corridor to her fate.

"YOU'RE GOING on a *what!*"

Mandy pushed Jeanne back into her chair and cautioned her to remember she was an old lady of forty-three. "I said, I'm going on a honeymoon in Atlantic City for five days so the station can film us for their nighttime-magazine television show. Joe says if we ever tell the truth they'll arrest me, and maybe him, too, and so I have to go through with it—surely you can understand that."

Jeanne Tisdale, not saying a solitary word, and looking neither right nor left, stood up and walked toward her classroom full of terrible twos. At the moment, they seemed to be the lesser of two evils.

*

THE MAN Mandy still knew only as Joe Tremaine walked briskly down the tiled corridor and pushed open the door that led into the executive offices of WFML. It was after hours and the secretary who sat behind the desk, guarding the new owner's private sanctum, was gone for the day.

Without stopping to knock on the double wooden doors, he entered the executive office and headed straight for the tiled shower that was part of the suite, dropping his sneakers, jeans and T-shirt haphazardly along the way.

He wasn't usually sloppy but tonight he was in a hurry. He had a date with his "wife."

A scant fifteen minutes later he was dressed in white duck slacks and a faded sea green collarless Panama Jack shirt that he knew looked good with his tan. He was just putting his billfold in his front pocket when the door from the secretary's office opened.

"Going out on the town, Josh?" the older man who had entered asked, lowering himself gingerly into a chair. "I should have known it wouldn't take you more than a day in town to get yourself lined up with one of the local beauties. Lord, it's been a long day. I'm bushed. I just thought I'd stop by to hear your first impressions before heading back to the hotel. So? Do you think we made a good deal? I've always wanted to own my own television station. The radio end of it was just a bonus."

The whole time the older man had been talking, the man he had called Josh was busy, combing his hair in front of the mirror that hung over the credenza. "I like the station fine, Dad," he said. "In fact, I think I like your 'bonus' best of all. I find I have to be out of town for several days starting Saturday. Do you think you can handle the paperwork on this project yourself?"

The older man, who looked much like his son except for the gray hair at his temples, stood tall. "I've been handling things since before you cut your milk teeth. This whole investment is small potatoes and you know it. I just thought I needed a hobby, that's all."

Josh looked around the expensively decorated office. "Some hobby. It's a good trick you didn't decide to dabble in railroads. I don't think even Phillips, Inc., is up to turning a profit from Amtrak.'' Joshua Phillips walked toward the door, picking up his silk sports jacket as he went. ''Put a candle in the window, Dad, I may be late.''

THEY WERE seated in a cozy wraparound corner booth in the restaurant.

''You're right,'' Mandy said, ''we have to discuss this stupid fool stunt you talked us into.''

''I talked us into!'' Josh exclaimed, causing a few heads to turn in their direction.

Mandy turned her head to look at him accusingly. ''*You're* the one who jumped in with both feet, smiling that sickening smile and saying, 'Hi, I'm Mr. Tremaine' and then *winking* in that horrid way like you and Vic Harrison had some dirty secret between you.''

Mandy closed her eyes and tried to concentrate on the memory of the delighted children who had danced and sung all that afternoon to the tunes that filled the playroom courtesy of the new stereo. It was worth it, she told herself over and over in a soundless chant.

She shook her head. ''I can't go through with it.''

Josh took one look at Mandy's tear-bright eyes. What had begun as a lark had become a deadly serious project on Josh's part. No way was he letting Amanda back out now.

He reached over and took her hands in his. ''Amanda, I— I need your help,'' he improvised wildly. ''There are things—faintly shady things—that can go on in radio and television stations. Things that groups such as the FCC investigate.''

''You're a government agent?'' she asked in a breathy whisper, already caught up in the thrill of the thing. She leaned back in her seat, giving him a superior smile. ''I thought that Vic Harrison guy had shifty eyes when we met him. What is it—bribes, payola, kickbacks?''

My, what a great big imagination you have, Grandma, Josh

thought, barely keeping a straight face. He never said he was an agent, he just said there could be problems with stations.

No matter how hard Mandy pushed, Josh refused to say anything else, reminding her that secret government assignments were always on a "need-to-know" basis.

"You'll be less liable to slip up if you keep thinking of me as Joe," he told her.

Josh had said that the small station's only mobile cameraman, the one sure to be sent on this assignment, could be the subject of some investigation. It was a stroke of inspiration that finally satisfied Mandy and had Josh silently pitying the poor cameraman, who was sure to be confused by Mandy's interest in his every movement.

Mandy leaned back against the seat and put a hand to her stomach. "That steak was so good. Burnt on the outside, nearly raw on the inside. The chef did it perfectly. Grandfather always said I was a cannibal, but to me Pittsburgh-rare is the only way to eat good steak."

"Grandfather?" Josh repeated casually. "Does he live in town?"

Instantly Mandy was on the defensive. "Why do you want to know? You're investigating WFML, not me."

Easy, Phillips, easy, he cautioned himself. Flicking Mandy's cheek playfully, he said, "I just wanted to know if I was going to end up looking down the business end of a shotgun before this honeymoon is over. After all, grandfathers tend to be very protective of their unmarried granddaughters."

Her shoulders visibly relaxing, Mandy forced a smile. "No, Grandfather doesn't live around here. But if he did, you wouldn't be the only one in trouble. My helping you to uncover something illegal going on at the station would get his blood boiling." Mandy laughed shortly. "When it comes to business dealings, well, let's just say Grandfather believes in the old adage 'all's fair in love and war.'"

He allowed a companionable silence to continue while he

drove the car around the block and headed west. He turned the radio on.

"Where are we going?" Mandy asked at last, suddenly coming out of her reverie. "I thought you were taking me home."

Mandy could barely make out Josh's profile in the dim light of early evening. "You don't want to go back to that hot apartment yet, do you? I want to see a bit of your fair city while I'm here. What's that over there?"

"That's Wild Water Kingdom. We took the nursery-school kids there already, and I think I had even more fun than they did. And got a sunburn that tormented me for a week!" she added, touching her shoulders gingerly in remembrance.

Josh turned his head to look at her. "Tender skin, Carrot Top?"

"Carrot Top! Don't call me that!" she warned, jabbing his shoulder with her hand. "I've killed for less."

Pulling into the parking lot in front of a candle shop that was closed for the night, Josh stopped the car and turned off the ignition. "And hot-tempered, too," he teased, knowing he was pushing his luck but loving every minute of it. "Don't you ever worry that you might be considered a stereotype?"

"Don't you ever worry that you might one day use that smart mouth of yours to bite off more than you can chew?" she shot back.

Leaning back against the car door, Josh gave a low whistle. "Hey, I like red hair. I even like freckles." Easing himself across the bench seat to sit next to her, he slid an arm around her shoulders. "I could even learn to like green eyes, given half a chance."

Mandy could feel the heat radiating from his body, he was sitting so close beside her. "I am not a stereotype. I'm me. *You're* the stereotype."

"Me? A stereotype?"

She saw him wince, and knew she had scored a few points of her own. "Your hair is perfect. Your teeth are perfect.

Your tan is perfect. Everything about you is perfect.'' She threw up her hands as if the enormity of his perfection was just too much to be borne. ''You're just too darn perfect to be real, that's what.''

''There's one thing about me that's not perfect,'' Josh interrupted. ''I'm not a perfect gentleman.'' So saying, he positioned his hand firmly on the back of Mandy's neck and as his lips met hers, he effectively cut off her cataloguing of his sins.

THE NEXT DAY it was back to WFML and another meeting with his father, who was beginning to ask a few pointed questions.

''I checked with your mother, and she said she hasn't heard from you about your going home,'' the elder Phillips began clumsily. ''Your secretary doesn't know anything, either. So where are you off to, son, some decadent singles cruise in the Caribbean?''

''Dad, I'm thirty-two years old,'' Josh said, shaking his head in mock sorrow. ''So why do you persist in making me into the reincarnation of Don Juan?''

Matt Phillips sat down on the edge of the desk and grinned. ''Because it keeps me young.''

''You've struck out this time. This trip is strictly business.''

''You're in business with *me*. So how come I don't know anything about it?'' Something was in the air, he could smell it. ''Don't you think I can be trusted?''

Josh reached up a hand and rubbed the back of his neck, wincing slightly. ''It's not my secret to tell, Dad, I'm sorry. I've just got two favors to ask of you, okay?''

''I'm listening.''

Josh scribbled a name and address on a slip of paper and passed it to his father. ''Tell Vic Harrison, the disc jockey on the afternoon shift, to have a duplicate first-prize stereo and honeymoon trip awarded to the first runner-up in last week's contest.'' Again Josh wrote something down and handed it to his father. "Here's a telephone number where I can be reached. Don't use it unless there's an emergency. It's a hotel. Ask for Joe Tremaine when you call, and for God's sake don't give your own name if a woman answers the phone.''

"You've got that wrong, son. It's 'if a man answers, hang up.''' Matt stared down at the telephone number. "Who the hell is Joe Tremaine?''

"I am, Dad, at least for the next five days.''

The older man's eyes narrowed as he struggled to understand. "Are you in some sort of trouble, son?''

Josh gave his neck a last rub. "Do you remember a guy named Alexander Tremaine?''

"Tremaine. Of course! Now I know why that name sounds so familiar. Lord, that was all so long ago, three, maybe four years. Nasty business.'' He felt a sinking feeling in his stomach as he remembered Josh's reaction at the time. "Josh, what in blue blazes is going on?''

"I've been waiting a long time to see Alex Tremaine brought to his knees. And I think I've finally found just the way to do it.''

"Dave Benjamin was a good friend once, Josh, and I know his breakdown threw you. But do you really think even Dave would want you to do this—whatever it is you're planning?''

Josh's face took on a closed expression. "*I* want to do it for Dave. I can get him, Dad, I know it.''

"Legally?''

"Legally, Dad, honest.''

"Morally?''

Josh's eyes shifted away from his father's piercing gaze. "Nothing's black-and-white, Dad, you know that.''

Matt's blue eyes stared back levelly. "Revenge has the tendency to be a double-edged sword. Be careful you don't find yourself ending up as the injured party.''

Suddenly, unbidden, a vision of Mandy's guileless face

floated in front of Josh's eyes. "Yeah, Dad, I think I'm already figuring that one out for myself."

*

JOSH SAT slouched in the corner of the back seat of the plush navy blue limousine. From a poor beginning, Saturday morning had progressed steadily downhill. Mandy had greeted him with a scathing look and had stomped off barefoot to her bedroom to get dressed, telling him his coffee was ready and waiting for him on the kitchen counter. It had been cold, too, as if she had planned it that way.

Then the film crew had shown up, ten minutes ahead of schedule and so full of early-morning cheer that he had entertained the thought of slowly strangling all three of them.

Chaos had instantly ensued, what with the technician grousing about the lack of electrical outlets for his precious equipment, and the director—some sorry-looking blonde named, of all things, Lois Lamour, and reeking of perfume— fluttering around telling them how "terrifically exciting" it was going to be to film in Atlantic City.

"Get me some coffee," Josh had said to Mandy when he could get her attention.

"I did get you some already, darling," she had chirped, wifelike, smiling at the cameraman, who had been inspecting her through the opening made by his cupped hands as he held them out in front of him like a camera lens.

"But it's cold, *sweetheart*," Josh had returned, smiling at the cameraman as he spoke through gritted teeth.

He never had gotten his coffee, he remembered now, looking across the expanse of the wide back seat at his pretend wife. Mandy was sitting primly in her corner, talking to the director, who was perched on one of the jump seats like an overage canary.

He remembered Mandy's prediction that God was getting

her for thinking about doing something wrong. Was it possible Josh was being punished for what he was about to do? It was beginning to seem possible.

"Have you been directing long, Lois?" Mandy was asking as the limousine purred its way along the Atlantic City Expressway. "It seems so glamorous."

Lois patted her bony chest and boasted: "I've been at WFML for three years now," she said proudly. "I'm also the director for the weather segment of the evening news."

Oh, so Lois Lamour was responsible for the weather segment, was she? Josh thought evilly. Sitting forward, he leaned over a bit to gain the director's attention. "It's such a pity about the weather girl. Gee, if only you could ditch that dame."

"That's my sister, Lana," Lois replied, her bottom lip jutting out dangerously. "I handpicked her myself. The name Lana Lamour *means* weather, in Allentown!"

Placing a hand on Josh's forearm, Mandy dug her nails into his bare flesh. "Joe is such a tease." She turned to glare at Josh, who was sitting there, his blue eyes as wide and innocent-looking at a choirboy's on Christmas morning.

He directed his cherubic gaze on Lois. "I was being silly, Lois," he said dutifully. "I really like the weather girl."

"Joe feels rather strange about this honeymoon, Lois," Mandy broke in before Josh could say anything more.

"Yes, Lois," he said, using his left hand to pry Mandy's fingers off his forearm. "I guess this whole television thing is going to take a little getting used to. Mandy entered the contest without my consent, you know, and I really don't know if I like having our honeymoon filmed for television. It's so—so *public,* you know."

"But we just *love* the stereo, don't we, honeybun?" Mandy put in hastily.

Here was his chance to pay her back for the cold coffee. "It's in our bedroom. Right beside the white bearskin rug." He turned to Mandy, running a finger down the length of her throat and enjoying the slight wiggle of her body as she re-acted to the shivers his teasing stroke had caused. "You read my wife's winning entry, didn't you, Lois? Need I say more?"

Look at him, Mandy thought wretchedly. His smile is pos-itively obscene, she told herself, wishing she could crawl into a hole.

Herb, the technician, who was still grumbling about trying to work around an inadequate electrical supply, perked up his ears from the front seat. "Yeah, I heard from Vic it was a real scorcher, Lois. What did it say?"

Joe looked over at Mandy, who was glaring at him in helpless rage and embarrassment, and waggled his eyebrows at her. "I think I just might have a copy in my coat, Herb," he said helpfully.

"I'll order a huge pot of hot coffee every morning from room service the moment you wake up," Mandy promised rashly in an undertone.

Josh looked at her for a long moment, deciding whether or not he felt satisfied. "Drop the 'honeybun' business and you've got yourself a deal," he bargained quietly, reaching for his coat, which was draped over the other jump seat.

"Done," Mandy promised, then sighed in relief as Josh searched through his coat pockets before apologizing to Herb.

"Can't seem to find it. Sorry, fella," he said, leaning back once more and sliding an arm around Mandy's shoulders. "Hey," he added, looking out the window, purposely chang-ing the subject, "I think we're almost there. Lois, did you say the Tropicana is right on the boardwalk?"

As the director pulled a brochure out of her briefcase and began reading aloud about the hotel, Mandy leaned closer to look up into Josh's face and whisper, "Truce?"

Josh looked down at her, seeing the apprehension in her innocent green eyes. Apprehension, and something else. Un-less he missed his guess, Amanda Elizabeth Tremaine liked him in spite of herself. He suppressed a wince as his guilty conscience gave him a sharp poke right between the shoulder blades.

He had to keep it light, keep their relationship strictly on the surface. Mandy was better off fighting with him than she was believing he was one of the good guys. "Truce?" he repeated, leaning down to whisper in her ear. "Not by the hair of my chinny-chin-chin, sweetheart."

Watching as her green eyes clouded over with pain, Josh was at a loss to explain why he suddenly felt more than a little injured himself.

THE CONCIERGE suite at the Tropicana was everything Mandy had expected, and quite a bit more. It was on two levels, for one thing, consisting of a formal sitting room that connected with the bedroom area by way of a spiral staircase. With the couch on one floor and the king-size bed on another, Mandy could see no reason for any problems, if only Joe would promise to behave himself.

She walked around the two-level suite, admiring the floral carpets and inspecting what looked to be original oil paintings hanging in a cluster above the couch. Wait until he sees the bathroom, she thought, standing in front of the huge wall of windows that overlooked the boardwalk. A person could float a battleship in that tub. Not that Joe would think that. Oh, no, he'll probably make some ridiculous suggestion about bathing together to save water or something like that.

She walked over to the credenza to inspect the cleverly arranged fruit tray the hotel management had sent up along with a complimentary bottle of wine. "Have an apple, Mandy," she suggested. "Maybe an apple a day will keep the bully away."

"Ah, yes, Amanda Elizabeth, but will it keep the wolf away?" She whirled around sharply, her movement jostling the fruit on the tray.

"Oh, look what you made me do!" she accused as the fruit went tumbling to the floor.

Josh's shoulders shook with silent laughter. "Just having a little Mandy-to-Mandy chat, were you? Did you ever consider outside help?" he asked, bending down to pick up an orange before walking over to stand in front of Mandy. "Yours, I believe."

Mandy snatched the orange out of his hand and angrily slammed it down on the silver tray, which immediately flipped into the air like a giant silver tiddlywink before doing a graceful swan dive to the floor, giving Joe's ankle a glancing blow on its way down. "Damn it all to hell, woman," he swore, falling to the carpet at her feet, "are you trying to kill me?"

Mandy just went on picking up the fallen fruit and piling it on the fallen tray.

"Well? Are you?" Joe repeated.

She looked up, blinking her wide green eyes. "Sorry. I had assumed it to be a rhetorical question."

Josh narrowed his eyes and made a respectful grimace. "Touché, Amanda. I guess I've been coming on a little too strong today, huh?"

"Do the words 'Mack truck' ring a bell with you?"

He put out his hand. "I was doing it for your own good, you know." He looked down into those damned innocent green eyes and felt his stomach sink to his toes. How could he tell her she had to remain immune to him or else he couldn't be held responsible for the consequences once the two of them were alone in the hotel room for the next four nights?

Josh closed his eyes for a moment, racking his brain for an easy way to say what must be said. "I don't want you to like me too much," he blurted out at last.

Josh's words stopped Mandy dead in her tracks. Her gaze traveled from his face to his toes and then back up to his face.

"You overestimate yourself, Joe," she said finally, just as

he thought she was either going to laugh in his face or deliver a sharp slap to his cheek.

With that, Mandy walked leisurely to the stairs and climbed to the balcony bedroom. After a few moments Josh heard the soft closing of the bathroom door and finally let out the breath he had been holding for what had seemed to be forever.

"I think she took that fairly well, considering," he told the oil portrait over the side table. "My God," he then exclaimed, shaking his head in disbelief as he realized he had just talked out loud to himself. "Now she's got me doing it!"

Upstairs, Mandy was standing just inside the bathroom. A thought struck her. "If he doesn't want me to become too involved with him, he should *chase* me, not *fight* with me. He's going about this thing all wrong!"

*

"How COULD YOU do that to me!"

The door had just closed on the television crew and Mandy turned to attack.

"Do what?" Josh asked innocently, moving away to turn on the television set.

"How could you order me *well-done* steak, that's what! It was like shoe leather! And I had to eat it, didn't I? It was either that or let Lois and the rest of them know that my dearest 'husband' doesn't have even the faintest idea as to how I like my steak cooked." Mandy stomped over to the couch and threw herself down in a huff. "I know what you were doing, you know."

Josh turned to peer at her inquisitively. "You do, do you?"

"Yes, mister smarty-pants, I do." Mandy was marvelous in a fury. "You were punishing me for trying to learn something about Herb over dinner. You remember Herb, don't you? The cameraman you told me you were here to investigate? What's the matter? Didn't you think I could even ask him a simple question without giving the game away?''

"You're feeling insulted, aren't you, Amanda Elizabeth?" Josh deduced maddeningly. "I know!" he announced, beaming at her cheerfully. "I'll go down to the hotel shops and buy you a trench coat. Would you like a thirty-eight special, too? No," he said quickly, as Mandy's eyes seemed to shoot daggers at him, "I don't think you'd look good in a shoulder holster. It'd give you bulges in all the wrong places. I like your bulges where they are now."

Jumping to her feet, Mandy began pacing rapidly around the room, her arms flapping like the wings of a flightless bird in her agitation. "That's right, make jokes. Ha, ha, very funny. You ought to go on the stage, Joe whatever-your-name-is, you know that? You could—"

Josh cut off her tirade by going up to her and physically trapping her arms at her sides. "You're getting hysterical again, Mandy, just like in the elevator," he told her as she tried to wriggle out of his grasp.

"So? What are you going to do about it, big man? Give me that tired old 'that's how they do it in Hollywood' line again?"

The movement of her body against his chest was making a mockery of all his good intentions. He bent down and effortlessly hoisted her into his arms. The two of them landed on the soft cushions of the couch a second later, Mandy clinging tightly to his neck as he followed her down, capturing her mouth with his own.

She was sweetness; she was fire; she was as intoxicating and addicting as strong drink. His mouth moved over hers; his lips drank from hers; his tongue tasted hers. He wanted more, still more. He wanted it all—everything she was willing to give.

And she was giving and taking with all the passion her red hair and fiery nature allowed.

"You drive me crazy, lady," Josh confessed.

Mandy looked up into the eyes scant inches from her own. Clearly she had better get this situation back under control. "I drive you crazy?" she quipped, turning her head away. "I'd be flattered, if I didn't know that it's such a short trip."

His maddening lopsided grin came into view as Josh slowly disengaged himself from Mandy and slid away from her.

"Where—where are you going?" Mandy asked as Josh got up and started across the room.

"I'm going to take a shower," Josh growled. "A cold shower."

She watched him until his legs disappeared at the top of the stairs, then sat up, guiltily straightening her wrinkled skirt and blouse. "Good thought," she mused aloud. Then she spied the complimentary bottle of wine, still cooling in the ice bucket and, although she rarely drank, decided it was as good a time as any for a medicinal dose of alcohol.

MANDY STOOD quietly before the huge windows in the living room, pretending to enjoy the sunrise, but her eyes were closed against the pain she felt clutch at her chest. Josh was making no bones about the fact that once the honeymoon and his investigation were over he planned to walk away from her, heart-whole and guilt-free.

At least he was being flattering, letting her know that he was attracted to her, even if it was only a physical attraction. After all, what else could it be? she reasoned sadly, considering the fact that he didn't hide his opinion that she didn't really have both her oars in the water.

"He's not exactly my fantasy prince come riding into my life on his snow-white stallion, either," she explained ruefully to the rising sun. "He's rude, arrogant, conceited, a terrible tease—and much too secretive. Even if he does have the sexiest blue eyes I've ever seen." She was silent for a moment. "Even if his kisses turn my whole world inside out and his body—oh, damn, that must be the coffee!"

The firm rapping on the door of the suite interrupted Mandy's musings.

"*Good* morning!" the waiter exclaimed cheerily, carrying in a heavy silver tray. "Hey, you're the newlyweds who won that contest, aren't you?" he asked, snapping his fingers as if he'd just remembered that fact. "I saw the film crew come in with you yesterday. What a break. I'm an actor, you know. If I had known I could get television exposure as easily as you have, I'd have dragged my girlfriend Sylvia off to City Hall in a flash. I'm Rollie, by the way."

His enthusiasm was infectious, and Mandy found she was smiling in spite of herself.

"This could be your big break, you know, if you work it right. With that red hair and those great legs, hey, you could be the next Lucy. Can you take a pratfall?"

Mandy screwed up her face in confusion. "A pratfall? I'm not sure. What is it?"

Rollie ran up several steps of the spiral staircase. He turned and assumed an air of sophisticated elegance. Head held high, he then began his descent, before seeming to slip on the third step from the bottom, a hilarious look of astonishment widening his expressive eyes. He somersaulted comically down the remainder of the stairs.

"*That's* a pratfall," he announced, glowing. "Pretty good, huh?"

Above their heads, Mandy could hear the sound of running feet, and within seconds Josh was racing down the stairs, a huge bath sheet wrapped around him from his waist to his ankles, his face covered neck to nose with a heavy coating of shaving cream. "Mandy!" he shouted. "Are you all right, honey?"

Mandy opened her mouth to answer him, but suddenly Josh lost his own footing, and within the blinking of an eye he was somersaulting down the last three stairs, doing a grand imitation of Rollie, if only he knew it.

"Oh, Joe," she wailed, falling to her knees. "Are you all right?"

"Never mind me, damn it. Are *you* all right? That's the only thing that's important."

He was so serious, so very concerned, that it tugged on Mandy's heartstrings. Unfortunately, he was also the funniest thing Mandy had seen in years.

She tried to speak. "You thought...and then you...oh, you look so *funny!* I didn't think it was him," she said between bouts of laughter.

"Who him? Him who?" Josh looked up, suddenly aware that they were not alone. Rollie gave Josh a wincingly bright grin and a jaunty salute.

Josh closed his eyes and counted to ten. He had been right: God *was* getting him.

"Rollie's going to be an actor, you see," Mandy pressed on, her words tumbling over themselves. "He showed me a pratfall. That's the noise you heard. You did it just like him." Mandy began giggling all over again.

Josh shrugged Mandy's arm away and stood. "Rollie," he said with great dignity, considering he was standing in the living room looking like a clown who had run amok in a nudist camp. "Good luck with your career. Come back later, and we'll see if the director can find a place for you in the filming, okay?"

Rollie's jaw dropped open. "You're kidding!" he exclaimed, hardly believing his good luck. "No, you're not kidding, are you? Hey, you're all right, sir." He fairly danced his way to the door, laughing as he declined the tip Mandy was holding out for him.

Once the door had closed behind the ecstatic waiter, Mandy turned to look at Josh, who was already on his way back up the stairs. "Hey," she called, stopping him in his tracks. "You're all right, you know. Under those designer clothes you wear beats a heart of pure marshmallow."

Leaning on the banister, Josh let his chin drop onto his chest in relief. Relief and the sudden realization that Mandy's words made him feel that the whole incident had been worth it, just to have gained her approval.

BY MIDAFTERNOON Mandy was thoroughly disenchanted with the wonderful worlds of acting and television. Filming, she had discovered to her dismay, consisted more of standing around and waiting than it did of actually performing in front of the camera.

"Mandy," Lois said, waving her on her way without even turning around. "You need some more makeup, unless you want to look like a ghost on camera."

"Put the makeup on until you think you should be out walking the streets, Mandy," Herb put in encouragingly.

In the end, Lois had to wield the makeup brush herself, as Mandy still hadn't made her cheeks pink enough to suit the director. The filming, which consisted of nothing more than a repeated panning of the room as Mandy and Josh sat on the couch holding hands and smiling like village idiots, was at last completed.

"That's it?" Mandy squeaked incredulously as the hot lights were finally turned off. "All that carrying on for five puny minutes of film? I don't believe it!"

"Now, now, darling, temper, temper," Josh soothed. "Go upstairs like a good little bride and scrub that gunk off your face so I can take you to dinner."

The phone in the suite rang then, causing Lois to say that it must be her station calling her about something important. But the call was for "Joe Tremaine."

Mandy went part of the way up the stairs before she heard her "husband" say into the phone, "Joe Tremaine here," and was struck by a sudden curiosity as to the identity of Joe's caller. Racing up the rest of the steps, she threw herself down on the large bed, took a deep breath, and carefully lifted the receiver of the bedside phone.

"So, *Joe,* how's it going?" she heard a deep, skeptical voice ask.

"The weather's quite warm here, Dad, and I believe it may even get hotter." Mandy made a face at the receiver. "Dad!" she mouthed silently. What a ridiculous code name for an investigator.

"How much longer do you intend to be gone?" the man asked. "Vic Harrison has been asking some pretty probing questions around the studio. As a matter of fact, I have a few rather probing questions of my own for you, *Mr. Tremaine.*"

"Give me a couple more days, Dad, then I'll have everything I need to take care of that little business we talked about in your office the other night, okay? Just cut me some slack. If there's no emergency, you shouldn't have called. Bye now."

"Don't you hang up on me, you scoundrel!" the other voice yelled into the phone. "Josh? Answer me, damn it! Josh!"

Mandy set the phone down quietly. "Josh," she breathed softly. "I like it."

THE FOOTAGE of the two happy newlyweds strolling down the boardwalk that night gazing soulfully into each other's eyes had required an hour of set-up time and seven takes.

But finally the filming was over. Josh had waved the crew on their way.

He looked down at Mandy, his warm breath fanning her cheek. "You want to go back to the hotel?"

Mandy closed her eyes a second, savoring his closeness. "No," she answered. "I want to walk along the boardwalk."

And walk they did, up and down the crowded boardwalk. They stopped several times to look into shop windows, selecting outlandish presents for everyone they knew.

At midnight, they walked across the width of the boardwalk to stand at the railing along a deserted stretch of the beach, looking out over the ocean.

"What have you found out so far about Herb?" Mandy asked. "He seems rather closemouthed, doesn't he?" Her voice lowered to a conspiratorial whisper. "Do you think Vic Harrison is involved? I know you denied it before, but then when I heard—" Mandy stopped talking, cutting off her words in mid-fantasy.

"Mandy?" he said, noticing her tightly closed lips. "You were eavesdropping from the bedroom earlier when I talked to my—"

"*Dad?*" she said on a sneer. "Really, Joe, surely you could have worked out a better code name than that."

Josh raised his eyebrows and stared at her, hardly believing his luck. Bless her beautiful, twisted logic.

Mandy whirled on her heels and made to walk away from the railing, but Josh was too quick for her, gathering her into his arms and pulling her back against the railing. "I think I'm beginning to fall in love with you, Amanda Elizabeth Tremaine."

Mandy melted against his lean, hard frame. "You—you don't really know anything about me. And, well, you can hardly say I know anything about you. I *like* you, honestly I do." She closed her eyes with a sigh. "Very much. But I wasn't born a nursery school teacher, you know."

He could feel her stiffening in his arms before she actually pulled away.

When Mandy turned around, tears were standing in the corners of her eyes. "Until we can be completely honest with each other, I think it's best if we continue on as we were."

Mandy was right, he was going too fast. It wasn't just *his* past that concerned her; of that he was sure. Maybe she was just as disenchanted with her grandfather as he was—after all, she had run away from their home more than three years ago without leaving a trace. It had been the talk of the town for a while, Mandy's disappearance. That, and the incident with Dave Benjamin that had occurred the same week.

He shook his head, looking away from the dark ocean and straight into her eyes. "You're right," he confided softly. "I think it's time we called it a night."

MANDY LAY in the middle of the huge bed as moonlight streamed in through the large picture windows.

"I think I'm falling in love with you," Josh had said, and she could still hear his low, husky voice.

Love didn't grow in such a short time, did it? Especially love between two people who really knew less than nothing about each other?

And if he did know everything about me, about Grandfather and my involvement with Dave, would he still think he loved me then? A tear rolled down her cheek. Because I do love him, very, very much. Would he be happy that I loved him, or would he run from me as fast as his legs could carry him?

While Mandy wrestled with her demons in the dark bedroom at the top of the spiral staircase, Josh lay on the pulled-out couch in the living room, trying to decide what he should do next. "Making a clean breast of things might not be such a bad idea, Phillips," he mused aloud.

"Then what, Phillips? You'd still have to tell her about the plot to revenge yourself on old Alexander Tremaine for what he did to Dave Benjamin. How you were going to send old Alexander Tremaine a videotape of you and his missing granddaughter cavorting in sin in Atlantic City, just so he could sit in his castle and turn purple with rage. How were you planning to drop that little bomb and still convince her you love her?

*

"No, no, *NO!* Mandy, you're still doing it all wrong. You're too tense." Lois Lamour waved her hands in barely controlled anger.

"I'm really sorry, Lois," Mandy said, swallowing down hard on her anger. "It's just—it's just so *staged*. I mean, whoever heard of a couple having breakfast in bed while a waiter hovers over them?"

"Hey, I'm playing my role right!" Rollie protested, straightening his bow tie as he stood beside the bed, coffeepot at the ready. "Besides, Mr. Tremaine here promised me this part."

"Yes, darling," Josh said as he sat close beside her in the middle of the bed. Josh withdrew his hand—the one that had just slipped under the covers to reach over and tickle her rib cage. Josh looked at Mandy's flushed cheeks and sparkling green eyes. "And Rollie's looking for an Academy Award," he added, a smile hovering on his lips.

The scene was finally completed without a hitch, and Josh actually found himself looking forward to the filming inside the casino.

Lois agreed that the Fruit Market seemed an ideal location for the scene she had planned, and soon Josh and Mandy were standing side by side in front of two slot machines, large cups full of quarters at the ready.

Mandy dropped quarter after quarter in the slot and watched the pictures of fruit spinning around dizzily before coming to a halt.

A ringing sound caught her attention and a yellow light on top of her machine began blinking as it registered a win. Then she heard the clinking of quarters as the metal tray located at the bottom of the machine began filling with coins. "Oh, my God," she shrieked excitedly, looking down at the cup, "I won!"

As she spoke she was scooping the quarters into her cup,

her fingers trembling with excitement. "I'm on a roll, I can feel it."

She grinned at Josh playfully, then slipped five more quarters into her machine.

Mandy and Josh played the slot machines in the Fruit Market until Lois at last thought they had gotten enough good film to call a halt. "Mandy," Josh urged, when she didn't seem to hear Lois's okay to stop the action, "you can stop now, the camera's off. Mandy. Mandy?"

But Mandy wasn't listening. Her entire being was concentrating on feeding quarters into the machine.

"Looks like she's hooked," Herb offered.

Josh thanked the technician for his warning, then waved the crew on their way before turning back to take hold of Mandy's arm just as she was about to drop another load of quarters into the slot. "You want to walk around for a while?"

Picking up both of their cups, Josh nodded his head encouragingly in the direction of nearby Jackpot Lane.

Mandy played the slot machines at random as they walked along, laughing at the comical graphics that took the place of whirling fruit on the "knockout jackpot" machines in Cherry Court, and making jokes about playing the "lazy man's slots" as she fed quarters into the automated machines that had no pull handles to test her strength.

"They make losing your money too easy," she decided after putting a few dollars into a video poker machine in Tropicana Gardens.

"Had enough, Miss High Roller, or do you want me to buy you a green visor so you can try your luck at the blackjack tables in the main casino?" he asked.

Mandy looked at Josh consideringly. "You've had enough, haven't you, Joe? Why didn't you stop me?"

He pulled her close to give her a quick hug. "I've had a great time watching you have a great time, my love, that's why. I wouldn't have missed it for the world. Happy?"

"Very happy," she breathed, fascinated with the way Josh's tanned skin crinkled so sexily at the corners of his eyes when he smiled. "I honestly can't remember the last time I had this much fun. You know, I've hardly been any- where in years," she mused, almost to herself. Then, as she saw the question coming into his eyes, she rushed on, "I mean, I've been so busy at the nursery school, you under- stand, that—"

"That even a pretend honeymoon with a make-believe husband, all put to music with a hovering film crew and a secret investigation, is to be considered a treat," he ended, slowly losing his smile.

He wasn't ready to hear why she was living in such strait- ened circumstances in Allentown when she could be riding high on the hog in Southampton with Alexander Tremaine. He'd rather concentrate on the Mandy Tremaine who lived in a third-floor walk-up apartment and taught nursery school.

They stood close together in the middle of the wide bal- cony as hopeful gamblers and casino personnel detoured around them unnoticed. "I can't think of any place I'd rather be, or anyone else I'd rather have here with me, *Josh*." Her emerald eyes opened wide as they searched for his reaction.

"You know who I am?" he asked, his arms tightening about her waist.

"After you hung up the phone yesterday afternoon the man you called Dad said your name—he yelled it, actually. I don't think he's too overjoyed with you right now, Josh," she ended, slowly sliding her hands up around his neck.

"Why didn't you tell me?"

"Why should I tell you? You've never asked for my life story."

"You're one remarkable lady, Amanda Elizabeth Tre- maine," he whispered.

Mandy closed her eyes. No, I'm not, she wanted to scream. I'm only being this way because then I won't have to return the favor and tell you all about *me*. About my past—about my grandfather's destruction of Dave Benjamin, or the part I played in the whole sordid mess. Oh, Josh, why can't we just stay here in Atlantic City forever, and let time stand still? "You're not so bad yourself, fella," she murmured against his chest while she blinked back tears.

And then, in the middle of the Flight Deck, with hundreds of people passing by on either side, they shared a kiss that proved not all the ringing bells and flashing lights in Slot City came with a price tag attached.

Or did they?

I don't think I'm falling in love with her, he told himself with a vehemence that startled him, I *am* in love with her. I, Joshua Mark Phillips, am hopelessly, madly, and passionately in love with Amanda Elizabeth Tremaine. I am going to throw her over my shoulder and carry her off to the nearest justice of the peace just as fast as I can.

And what about your plans for the videotape? his conscience asked, stopping him in his tracks. Are you going to tell her how you planned to send a copy of it to old Alexander Tremaine to punish him with the certain knowledge that you, one of Dave Benjamin's friends, was bedding down with his only granddaughter?

I'm also going to cross my fingers and lie like hell, hoping she'll never learn about those other plans.

THE LIVING ROOM was in darkness. Mandy could smell his spicy aftershave, feel the strong, even beating of his heart.

Josh had been holding her in a loose embrace, enjoying the faint tickle of her burnished curls as he lowered his head slightly to bury his face in their silky warmth. Josh was lost, totally and completely lost. His entire world consisted of the beautiful woman he held so tenderly in his arms: Mandy of the emerald green eyes and the innocent, trusting heart. He wanted to pull her hard against his chest and crush her mouth with his own.

Josh took Mandy's hand and held it close between them

as he drew her more firmly into his embrace. "Alone at last," he breathed into her ear.

Her moist lips slightly parted. "And do you plan to have your wicked way with me then, sir?"

The slow, lopsided grin she had learned to love appeared then as Josh let go of her hand, slipped his arm under her knees and lifted her high against his chest. "Shut up, woman, and point me toward the stairs," he answered, nuzzling her neck.

Mandy's arms held him tightly as she buried her flaming cheeks against his shoulder. "I love you, Josh what-ever-your-name-is," she whispered.

Josh stopped, his foot on the bottom step of the spiral staircase. "It's Josh Phillips, Ms. Amanda Elizabeth soon-to-be Phillips. And I love you, too—more than I thought it was possible to love anyone."

"If that's a proposal, Mr. Phillips, I accept," Mandy answered quietly, leaning forward to press a soft, tantalizing kiss on his neck.

Josh moved to ascend the staircase.

"WHAT IN BLUE blazes is going on in here? Joshua! Damn it, Josh, where are you?"

Josh froze in his tracks. It couldn't be his father. Not now, for God's sake. His arms tightened instinctively around Mandy.

Matthew Phillips located the switch just inside the door, and the living room was flooded with light. His gaze caught sight of the redheaded young woman clinging fearfully to his son.

"I can only hope I got here in time. I'm Matthew Phillips, Ms. Tremaine," he offered, holding out his hand as he crossed the room. "Joshua's father, I'm ashamed to say. I think it's time we all had a little talk," he urged, holding out his arm and gesturing toward the couch on the other side of the room.

Mandy slipped from Josh's arms and went to perch nervously on the edge of the couch. Josh looks just like him, Mandy thought numbly. Is this how Josh will look in thirty years?

"You've got the floor," she heard Josh say in a strange, tight voice.

"Mr. Phillips," she cut in nervously, "is it something about the investigation? I know Josh didn't get too far with it here in Atlantic City, but he really has been working hard."

"I'll bet he has," Matt slid in nastily.

Mandy ignored the interruption to continue: "Josh thinks Herb is only a small part of a larger plan, and as soon as we return to Allentown he'll be able to locate the higher-ups. Isn't that right, Josh?" she asked, turning to him, hoping he'd say something—anything.

"*Investigation*, Josh?" his father repeated, at last dropping into a chair. "My, you have been a busy fellow haven't you, son?"

Mandy's heart sank to her toes. "There isn't any investigation, Josh, is there?" she asked brokenly. "Herb's just a cameraman, isn't he?"

"Who's Herb?" Matt put in, then waved his hand to negate the question. "Never mind, I don't want to know."

Josh crossed the room and sat down beside Mandy, taking her suddenly cold hands between his own.

"WILL YOU KINDLY move your miserable, lying self out of my way, please?"

"For crying out loud, Mandy, stop this," Josh pleaded, going over to the bed and the open suitcase that lay there, closing the case with a determined snap.

Mandy picked up the suitcase and began filling it with toiletries. "Tell me, Mr. Phillips of Southampton, Allentown and all points east, did you have Herb set up a secret camera in here, just so you could be sure to catch *all* the action?"

She looked around the room, hunting for a hidden camera hanging from the ceiling.

"You know damn well I wouldn't do that!"

"How should I? I really don't know anything about you, Josh, do I?" She went over to the dresser and opened the top drawer, filling her hands with delicate undergarments. She began slamming the clothing into the suitcase. "I do know you're a low, conniving, lying—"

Josh grabbed up the undergarments, flinging them across the room.

"Mandy—darling—listen to reason," he begged as she crouched on the floor, picking up the clothing he had thrown. He swung away from her to slam a fist against the wall. "I could kill my father for telling you the way he did. If he had just phoned and confronted me with what he thought, I could have told him that I never would have used that tape. It was a stupid idea in the first place—I wasn't thinking clearly. I'd never consciously hurt you, Mandy, please believe that."

She pulled the second dresser drawer out entirely and walked to the bed, dumping the drawer's contents into the suitcase, then dropped the drawer an inch from Josh's foot. "Believe that?" she snorted.

Ever since his father had explained how he had finally made the connection between the extra first prize in the contest and the telephone number of the Tropicana, Mandy had not been thinking, she had been reacting. Not that Josh could blame her.

Giving Josh one last scathing look, she took up her purse and rapidly descended the stairs to the living room, leaving Josh where he stood.

"Hello, room service? This is Mrs. Tremaine," Mandy was saying into the phone as Josh came within earshot. "I desire a bottle of your finest champagne—no, make that *two* bottles—well chilled, and your best imported caviar," she commanded regally. "Just make sure Rollie Estrada brings it, do you understand?"

A small smile curved her lips. "Thank you *so* much," she replied coldly before slamming the phone back down on its cradle.

"Mandy—" Josh began, only to be interrupted by a loud knocking at the door. "Damn it!" he swore, throwing his hands in the air. "Nobody can move that fast!"

"Open this door, Joshua!" came the muted shout from the hallway. Josh spread his hands wide, palms up, as if to say, "Why the hell not?" and went to throw the door wide open.

Matt Phillips stormed into the room looking slightly disheveled.

Josh angrily ran a hand through his hair and flung himself down into a chair. "What are you back for, anyway? Haven't you done enough already?"

"Stop feeling sorry for yourself," Matt commanded sternly, looking at Mandy and realizing the slender hold the young woman had on her emotions. "Mandy?" he asked softly, taking a tentative step in her direction. "Is there anything I can do? Any place I can take you?"

Mandy looked at each of the Phillips men in turn, her narrowed eyes two chips of emerald ice. "I wouldn't cross the street with either of you!" she spat, going to answer the jaunty rapping at the door to allow Rollie, pushing a trolley holding two silver ice buckets and a huge domed serving platter, into the room.

"You guys planning on having a party or something?"

Josh rose to go over and put a detaining hand on Mandy's arm as she hoisted her purse to her shoulder, clearly intent on leaving. "Mandy, you can't just walk out on me like this," he implored, keeping his voice low.

"Just watch me, buster," she shot back, shrugging off his hand. "Your celebration feast has arrived—ordered by the victim herself. Have a ball!"

Pulling her stiff, resisting body into his arms, Josh went on, unheeding. "I gave up the idea of revenge almost as soon as I thought it up, Mandy, I swear it. I love you. Deep down inside—under all that hurt you're feeling right now—you know I love you. Please don't leave, Mandy, please."

With a heartrending sob, Mandy tore herself out of Josh's arms and ran for the door. "Rollie!" she called to the waiter, who was just uncorking the first bottle of champagne. "Take me to the nearest bus station. *Please!*"

The door to the hall had already closed behind Mandy, and Josh knew she wasn't coming back. Reaching into his pocket, he drew out a small stack of bills and thrust them into the waiter's hand. "Stay with her until the bus leaves, Rollie. Can you do that for me, friend?"

Rollie saw the naked pain in Josh's eyes. "Sure thing, buddy," he told him solemnly. "She'll never be out of my sight for a minute, I promise."

Josh stood looking at the closed door.

*

IT WAS DARK in the back of the bus, so dark that few people noticed the young woman huddled in the window seat, her legs tucked under her as she sniffled quietly into her handkerchief.

The full load of casino-goers exchanged stories of their exploits in the various casinos as the bus rumbled along the Atlantic City Expressway, either bragging of their winnings or complaining over their losses.

"Hey, little lady," said one of the happier gamblers, leaning across the aisle to get Mandy's attention. "Nothing can be that bad, can it? You saved enough for the bus ride home, didn't you? After all, how much could a little girl have lost in one trip, anyway?"

"Not much," Mandy whispered, too quietly for the man to hear her. "Only my heart."

THE ONLY SOUND that broke the silence of her apartment on the long, lonely nights was the sound of her own weeping.

She had tried filling a few of those long evening hours by looking through the newspapers that had accumulated in her absence, only to open the financial section in one of them to see a grainy picture of Matthew Phillips staring out at her. Phillips, Inc. Opts For The Media the headline read, with the copy beneath the picture detailing the company's purchase of WFML's radio and television stations and giving both Matt's and Josh's names as the chief stockholders.

The story must have been released sometime after they had left for Atlantic City, she realized. Phillips, Inc. maintained holdings in Basking Ridge as well as just outside Southampton, Long Island and many other towns in New Jersey, New York and Pennsylvania. Josh had been working alongside his father ever since his graduation from Yale.

Dave Benjamin had gone to Yale, although he had dropped out in his junior year. Maybe that's when he and Josh first met, she had thought as she read the story.

The friend he had cared about enough to concoct his scheme for revenge had nearly died because of her.

Mandy shook her head, bringing herself back to reality. She gathered up the small mountain of papers and shuffled barefoot toward the garbage can in the kitchen. She stepped on the foot pedal that controlled the top of the can and dropped the papers inside, then let the lid drop with a bang.

That's funny, she thought, sniffling self-pityingly as she stared at the lid. I didn't think it made that thumping sound when it closed.

As she began to make her way to the living room, she heard the thumping sound again. Slapping a hand to her head she skidded around the corner and flung open the door.

"Josh," she breathed, closing her eyes in mingled apprehension and relief. She motioned with a wave of her hand that he should come in and sit down. "I thought you were the garbage-can lid."

Seating himself on the couch, Josh looked up at her, a sad smile on his face. "Why do I get the feeling Sigmund Freud would have a field day with that comparison?"

Mandy looked down at the floor, nervously kicking the fringed end of her small imitation Oriental carpet with one bare foot.

"Rollie damn near took my head off for making you run away. They all like you a lot, Mandy. Herb said to tell you that you looked great on tape."

Mentioning the videotape was a truly brilliant move, Phillips, Josh told himself angrily as he watched the deep pink flush creep up Mandy's neck and into her cheeks.

"Look, Mandy, I didn't come here to talk about the film crew. I came to apolo—"

Mandy cut in hurriedly. "There's really no need, Josh. I understand why you did what you did. I'm just sorry that you did it all for nothing. Grandfather couldn't care less what I do, or who I do it with. You see, he disowned me more than three years ago."

Josh's mouth dropped open in surprise. "Disowned you? What the hell are you talking about, Mandy? He couldn't have disowned you. You disappeared without a trace. Tremaine made a big thing about it at the time, said he had private detectives out looking for you."

Mandy gave a wry laugh. "He knows where I am, Josh."

Josh ran a hand through his hair, trying hard to understand. "I don't get it. Why?"

This is it, Mandy, she told herself. This is where you watch Josh's love for you turn into ashes. "Grandfather disowned me because I accused him of trying to kill Dave Benjamin, even if I knew it wasn't entirely true." She took a deep breath and said the rest in a rush of words. "You see, Josh, *I* destroyed Dave, just as surely as if I was the one who ruined his company."

Mandy went over to stare out of the window overlooking the street, unable to look at Josh.

"Mandy, darling," he began hesitantly, "Dave Benjamin tried to commit suicide when his business went sour. You didn't have anything to do with it."

She whirled around to face him. "Oh, no? My grandfather purposely set out to ruin Dave because he didn't think Dave was good enough for his precious granddaughter. Dave told me all about it." She laughed almost hysterically before ending with a sob, "And I didn't even love Dave. I never intended to marry him. It was all for nothing."

She shook her head, her eyes shut tight against the condemnation she was sure she would see in Josh's face. "I couldn't face it, so I ran away with my tail between my legs. Grandfather's last words to me were to warn me not to come back until I grew up. *Oh, God!*"

Josh drew her unresisting body into his arms, cradling her against his chest as she broke into loud sobs. He didn't understand this, didn't understand it at all. Dave had never mentioned Mandy to him when they had occasionally met for lunch before his college friend had suffered his breakdown. Dave had only ranted and raved and cursed the greedy, power-mad Alexander Tremaine for deliberately running his company into bankruptcy.

Surely Mandy was blaming herself for something that wasn't her fault. And had been blaming herself for more than three years, he reminded himself with a grimace.

Still holding her tight against him, he walked toward the couch and gently helped her to sit down. "Mandy," he urged, trying hard to lift her head from his chest, "you didn't destroy anybody. What did your grandfather say when you asked him about Dave?"

Mandy sat up and sniffed a time or two. "I—I never did ask him," she admitted, blowing her nose. "I only saw him once after Dave's breakdown, and that was to tell him that I knew what he had done. He didn't deny it, Josh." She looked up at him with tear-drenched eyes.

"So you ran away," Josh ended for her, using his own handkerchief to dab away her tears.

"And I ran away from you five days ago. I guess I'm consistent. Right?"

Josh looked down at her, his slow lopsided grin making her heart do little flip-flops in her breast. "And here I was wondering how I could bring up the subject without having my head handed to me on a platter. You do know, Amanda Elizabeth, that the time has come to stop running?"

Her heart skipped a beat. "Meaning?"

"Meaning, my dearest love, that you and I are going to drive up to Southampton tomorrow to beard old Alexander Tremaine in his den. It's time you laid all your old ghosts to rest so that we can get on with our lives—together."

Putting a finger under her chin to lift her head so that she was looking straight into his eyes, Josh said solemnly, "Now, come here. We have some catching up to do. I believe we were in the middle of something rather important when my dear father interrupted us."

*

ALEXANDER TREMAINE had built his estate on the near outskirts of Southampton. "I still think we should have phoned ahead," Josh said, looking at his watch and seeing that it was only four in the afternoon. "He may not be home."

Mandy giggled nervously. "Grandfather will be home. He hasn't stayed at his office past two-thirty in twenty years. Since my parents died, in fact."

Alexander Tremaine really built himself quite a house, Josh thought as he pulled the car to a halt in front of the great oaken door of the Tudor mansion. It was only as he was extracting the key from the ignition that he realized that Mandy still hadn't unbuckled her seat belt. She was sitting rock still, staring at the concrete steps in front of the mansion.

"That—that's where I found Dave," she told him softly, before averting her eyes to stare straight ahead. "For a moment I thought I could still see him lying there. Silly, isn't it?"

Josh went around to open Mandy's door. Holding out his hand to her, he silently bid her to come with him.

"Miss Amanda," the middle-aged man Josh took for the butler said when he answered their knock, showing no surprise at her presence after such a long absence. "Mr. Tremaine is in his study, as you'd know."

"Yes, thank you, Farnsworth," she answered, reaching for Josh's hand as she began walking toward the back of the house.

Then they were at the end of the hall and the butler was holding the study door open for them so they could enter. Mandy went first, stopping only a few steps inside the door, Josh close behind her.

The room looked like the law library of some old established Philadelphia firm, Josh decided, his gaze traveling over the book-lined walls to finally focus on the huge mahogany desk that sat in front of the velvet-draped windows.

The man who sat behind the desk just looked old, old and wrinkled and tired.

"I told you I didn't want that damned medicine, Farnsworth," the old man growled without looking up, "so you can just take it back to wherever you got it from."

"It's not Farnsworth, Grandfather," Mandy explained, moving another tentative step into the room. "It's me, Mandy."

Alexander Tremaine looked up over his half-frame reading glasses. "Who's that with you?"

"My name is Joshua Phillips, sir," Josh explained, stepping past Mandy to walk over to the desk, his right hand extended. He held it out long enough to count slowly to ten, and then let it drop to his side.

"I know who you are, Phillips, *and* what you and my

granddaughter have been up to," Tremaine informed them, leaning back in his oversize leather chair. "According to this report in front of me, it would appear Amanda is just as naive and foolish as she was the day she left me—*here*." He looked Josh up and down. "Playing house with my granddaughter, were you? How much will it cost me this time?"

Mandy forgot her fears as she raced to Josh's side. "Josh and I are going to be married, Grandfather," she put in firmly. "I won't allow you to talk to him that way, do you understand?"

"You *won't allow* it, will you, missy!" Tremaine exploded, rising to his feet. "Do you have any idea what it cost me the last time? Half a million dollars, that's what, and then the cowardly fool goes and pretends to blow his head off on my doorstep when it wasn't enough, so that I've been footing the bill at that fancy private hospital for three years while he chases the nurses. Not that I care about that, because I don't. But he really made me pay, didn't he, when you left me?"

Mandy stood there wide-eyed, slowly shaking her head back and forth, as the truth finally hit her. "You *paid* Dave Benjamin to stay away from me? But I thought you forced him into bankruptcy. Grandfather, I don't understand."

Josh stood quietly beside Mandy, thinking hard. "Dave was lying all along, wasn't he, Mr. Tremaine? He lied to you about the depth of his involvement with Mandy, and to Mandy about the reason for his money problems. And when the money you gave him still wasn't enough, he faked a public suicide so that he could be put in an institution away from his creditors. What was it—gambling?"

Alexander Tremaine looked at Josh with dawning respect. "Maybe you're not as dumb as you look, pretty boy. Although only a woman would believe a person could try to blow his brains out at point-blank range and end up with a flesh wound that didn't even need stitches! Dave Benjamin is about as crazy as a fox."

"Yet you're paying for his hospitalization," Josh remarked, winking at the older man. "Why do I get the feeling you're not as bad as your press paints you?"

"My investigator says you're half of Phillips, Inc.," Tremaine said, changing the subject. "Tell me, do you hold up your own end, or are you just another daddy's boy?"

Josh smiled broadly, slipping his arm around Mandy's shoulders and pulling her close. "I can run rings around you any day, old man, if you push me. Does that answer your question?"

The older man threw back his head and laughed a dry, papery sound. "Mandy, I think you can keep this one," he said approvingly.

But Mandy was still trying to understand exactly what had happened three years ago.

"Why did you let me leave?" she asked finally, putting her thoughts into words. "I know you never liked me much, but I didn't think you hated me."

"You were *sulking,* child, just like you always did, turning the whole sordid mess into trashy melodrama, with yourself cast in Joan Crawford's role." He turned to Josh, confiding good-naturedly, "She was always a dreamer, weaving fantasies in her head. I was the Black Prince, I believe, ever the villain. But she's got a good head on her shoulders. I knew she'd be back one of these days—when she grew up."

Mandy walked around the desk. "Grandfather," she asked, her voice low with intensity, "did you ever love me—even a little?"

Josh thought Alexander Tremaine looked more old than ever as he tentatively put out a hand and stroked Mandy's cheek. "I love you enough to be willing to put up with a bunch of carrot-topped great-grandchildren, Amanda Elizabeth, if that answers your question. Hey, stop that," he warned happily, "I'm too old and frail for such treatment. Amanda Elizabeth, stop hugging me at once, do you hear!"

"Your medicine, sir," came Farnsworth's superior tones from somewhere behind Josh.

Josh looked at the butler, standing stiff and straight, a small silver tray in his hand, and then over at Mandy and her grandfather, locked together in a healing embrace. He turned to Farnsworth, a rueful smile on his face. "Mr. Tremaine has already got his medicine, Farnsworth."

ROLLIE ESTRADA softly closed the door to the Concierge suite at the plush Tropicana Hotel, his wide toothy grin very much in evidence as he pocketed the large tip Josh had just handed him. "I do love a happy ending," he said to no one in particular before placing the Do Not Disturb sign on the doorknob.

WHO'S HOLDING THE BABY?

Day Leclaire

Grace Barnes stood in front of the door that read *Luciano Salvatore, President* and took a deep breath. She could do it. Sure she could. All she had to do was knock. The man on the other side of the door would say, "Come in." She'd open the door, step into the office and her deception would begin. After that, she only had to keep her job with this man for one year and she'd receive the financing necessary to start her own business. What could be easier? She lifted her fist to knock, but before she could, the door opened.

And that's when she saw him for the first time. In that instant, she realized how badly she'd misjudged Dom Salvatore and how foolish she'd been not to give him credit for knowing his son. He'd warned her. Oh, he'd definitely warned her. Every assistant Luc hired fell in love with him and ended up making a mess of the work situation. But she'd thought Dom had exaggerated. He hadn't.

Luc Salvatore was the most gorgeous man she'd ever set eyes on. High, aristocratic cheekbones and a square cleft chin complemented a striking masculine face. Thick, dark brown hair fell in careless waves across his forehead, emphasizing eyes that held her with almost hypnotic power. He filled the doorway, and unable to help herself, she took several hasty steps backward.

"Well, well…" he said, folding his arms across his broad chest and leaning against the jamb. "Who have we here?" Although he didn't have his father's Italian accent, there was a similar underlying lilt to his deep, husky voice that brought to mind exotic climes and sultry nights.

"I'm…I'm Grace Barnes," she said. To her horror, she sounded almost timorous. This would never do! What was wrong with her?

Slowly he straightened and walked toward her. She stood

rigidly, not daring to speak, not daring to so much as move. For some inexplicable reason her heart pounded and it became a struggle to draw breath. *Think of Baby Dream Toys,* she told herself. *Think of Mom planning for the day we'd open our own business.*

Utilizing every ounce of control she possessed, she held out a hand. "I'm Grace Barnes," she repeated in a cool, strong voice. "Your father hired me as your new assistant." To her relief, her fingers were rock steady.

He took her hand and shook it. "It's a pleasure to meet you, Miss Barnes. Or is it Mrs.?" He released her right hand and lifted her left, studying the glittering diamond decorating her finger. "Miss Barnes. Spoken for, but not yet taken. Our loss is…" he tilted his head to one side and lifted an eyebrow "…whose gain?"

She froze, staring up at him, staring into eyes that made her think of hot, liquid gold. She prayed her tinted lenses concealed her panic. She hadn't anticipated the question and she should have. "Will… William," she replied, picking the first name to pop into her head.

His mouth curved, his expression wickedly amused. "Our loss is Will-William's gain. Come on into my office. Let's get acquainted. Would you care for a drink? Coffee, tea? I even have freshly squeezed orange juice."

She followed him, trying to gather her composure. "Nothing, thank you," she said, once again affecting a calm, collected guise.

"Sit down. I assume my father told you I was out of the country during the interview process. Explain why he chose you from all the other applicants."

She didn't dare tell him the truth. Dom had specifically asked that she not mention they'd met through Salvatore's annual young-entrepreneur contest, a contest designed to help young businesspeople start their own companies. She'd hoped to win first prize—a monetary award that would have enabled her to open Baby Dream Toys. Unfortunately, she'd placed third, a mixed blessing. Though that prize wasn't sufficient to enable Grace to open her shop, it had, fortuitously, brought her to Dom's attention and given her the opportunity to fulfill her dream…if in a rather roundabout manner.

"I gather from what your father said that you've had trouble keeping your assistants," she finally replied. Which kept Dom from fully retiring, a situation he was desperate to correct. "He felt that wouldn't be a problem with me."

Luc's eyes narrowed. "Really? And why is that?"

"Because I'm serious about my work."

And because all she needed to do was keep her job as Luc's assistant for one year—and unlike his previous assistants, maintain a strictly professional relationship—and she'd be given the financing to start her own business. There wasn't a chance she'd fall for Luc's charms and sacrifice her dream. Not a chance.

Luc inclined his head. "Let's hope so." He leaned back in his chair. "Tell me more about yourself."

Hesitantly, she complied, outlining the résumé that rested on his desk. And all the time she spoke he watched her. She wondered if he saw through her disguise, realized her blond hair had been tinted drab brown with a temporary rinse, that she'd dressed in oversize, unattractive clothes, that her tinted glasses had nonprescription lenses. And what about the engagement ring? It rode her finger, an unfamiliar weight as well as an uncomfortable fabrication. She stirred uneasily. For a minister's daughter, duplicity came hard.

But she wanted to attain her dream. She wanted it more than anything in the world. And this temporary deception would get it for her.

"So," she concluded her recital, "I worked there for one year before being offered this job." With nothing left to say, she fell silent.

At long last he nodded. "Welcome aboard, Miss Barnes. As usual, Dad has shown excellent judgment. Let me show you to your desk." He stood and led the way into the outer office. "Here's your new home. Have a seat."

He held her chair out for her with a natural, unconscious ease. "Thank you," she murmured.

"Get familiar with the setting, take some time to explore the office area, have a cup of coffee or tea and report to me in an hour. Then we'll go over office procedures, and I'll explain how we do things around here and run through your duties. Though in all honesty there's only one thing I expect you to do."

She eyed him warily. "Which is?"

He grinned. "Whatever I say."

ON DAY 337 of The Big Lie, Grace looked at the calendar and closed her eyes. She could do it. Just four more weeks of lies and half-truths, disguises and evasions. What could be easier?

A small sound caught her attention, and looking up, Grace noticed a beautiful young woman standing in the doorway of the reception area. She carried a huge diaper bag over one arm; in the other she clutched a baby.

"May I help you?" Grace asked, shoving her glasses higher on her nose.

The young woman shot Grace a suspicious glance, then shook her head. She peered around rather frantically. When her gaze landed on Luc's door and the plaque that read *Luciano Salvatore,* she let out an exclamation of relief. Eyeing Grace with a measure of defiance, she sidled toward Luc's door.

Grace stood. This did not look too encouraging. A young woman, infant in arms, acting as though Luc's door held the answer to all her prayers... "Excuse me, but do you have an appointment?" she asked, though she could guess the answer to that one. This little entrance had "surprise visit" written all over it. Her hands closed into fists. How would Luc take to his newly discovered papahood? she wondered in despair. She already knew how *she* felt about it, the sick, sinking feeling in the pit of her stomach all too clear an indication. When had her feelings for Luc changed? she wondered. When had she begun to care?

There was no mistaking the young woman's resolve. She glanced from Grace to the door as though judging her chances of winning a footrace. As Grace came around the desk, determination glittered in the woman's huge sloe eyes and she literally threw herself at Luc's door. Yanking it open, she launched into a spate of very loud Italian and slammed the door in Grace's face.

Grace's mouth fell open.

"Miss Barnes!" Luc's roar rattled the rafters an instant later. "Get in here!"

It took her a split second to gather her wits sufficiently to obey. Then she, too, charged the door and threw it open. Mother and infant had found sanctuary in Luc's arms, and between sobs the woman poured out what appeared to be a most heartrending story. Luc fired a quick question and the woman stepped back, her Italian loud and furious. Startled from a sound sleep, the baby burst into tears, his wails competing with his mother's.

"You bellowed?" Grace asked.

He stabbed a finger at her. "Don't start. Go down the hall and drag my brother Pietro out of his office. I want him in here. Now."

She turned to leave, only to discover Pietro standing behind her. "What's all the shouting?" he asked, then took one look at the woman at Luc's side and cried, "Carina!"

The sudden realization that the child was, in all probability, Pietro's and not Luc's, grabbed Grace's full attention. Fighting to ignore an overwhelming sense of relief, she slipped farther into the room, watching this latest development with intense interest.

"Luc," Pietro said. "This is Carina Donati. Carina, my brother Luciano and his assistant, Miss Barnes."

"*Buon giorno.*" Carina acknowledged them with an abrupt nod.

"Carina and I... Well, we met at UC Berkeley," Pietro confessed. "She's a foreign-exchange student."

"Not any more," she interrupted, hugging the baby to her breast. "Now I am statistic. Unwed mother."

Pietro turned on her. "And whose fault is that?"

"Yours!" She offered him the baby. "You do not believe you are the papa?"

His hands balled into fists. "I damn well better be!"

"Children..." Luc inserted softly.

Grace crossed the room and held out her arms. "Why don't I take the baby?" she suggested, hoping to remove the poor infant from the field of battle. To her relief, Carina handed over her bundle without a single protest, and Grace retreated to the far side of the room.

"I hesitated to ask this, Carina," said Luc grimly, "but you now want...what?"

As though on cue, the tears reappeared. Pietro took one look and pulled her into his arms. "Darling, what is it? What's happened?"

"My mother in Italy, she is very sick," Carina confessed, her voice breaking. "I must go to her. But I cannot."

Pietro stared at her in bewilderment. "Why not?"

She pulled free, glaring at him. "Why not? You look at my sweet, little Tony and ask, why not? I come from a very small village. My relatives are old-fashioned. If they ever find out I have a baby with no husband, I would be disowned. So I come up with solution."

"Which is?" Luc asked.

The tears finally escaped, sliding down her cheeks. With a cry of distress, she snatched Tony from Grace and repeatedly kissed the tuft of black hair peeking out of the blanket. Then Carina thrust the tiny bundle at Pietro. "Tony is also yours," she said, choking on a sob. "You take care of our baby while I am in Italy. When my mama is better, I will return and be an unwed, deserted mother once more." Dropping the diaper bag to the ground, she pushed past Grace and fled the room.

"Wait!" Pietro called. Without further ado, he dumped the baby into Luc's arms. "You watch Tony. I'll go get Carina."

"Wait a minute! Come back here!" But it was too late. Pietro was gone. Luc stared in dismay at the baby, then glanced at Grace. A suspicious gleam appeared in his eyes. "Why, Miss Barnes," he practically purred, advancing toward her with his most charming—and determined—smile. He held out the baby. "Look what I have for you."

Grace held up her hands and backed away. "Oh, no," she protested. "This is your problem."

Luc stopped dead in his tracks, staring in astonishment. "You'd desert me in my hour of need?"

"Yes."

"You'd leave Pietro and Carina in the lurch?" he demanded in disbelief.

"Without question."

His brows drew sharply together. "You'd turn your back on a poor, helpless baby?"

She stared at him, stricken. He'd gotten her with that one. She adored children. She always had. Throughout her teen years, when anyone had needed a baby-sitter, they'd called her. When the church needed someone to supervise the nursery on Sundays, her name was the first one mentioned. And though she wasn't terribly experienced with babies, she was still an easy touch when it came to their welfare.

"That's not fair," she complained. But he had her. And if he didn't know it, he undoubtedly sensed it.

He crossed to the large built-in cabinet on the far side of the room. "They're probably downstairs by now. Let's see what's happening," he said, folding back the cabinet doors and revealing a bank of monitors inside. Switching them on, he called up a view from the security camera in the lobby and put it on the large center screen. "There they are."

"Oh, dear," Grace murmured. "They're arguing again."

They watched wide-eyed as Carina suddenly grabbed a huge porcelain vase from off a pedestal beside the front door and dumped the contents over the top of Pietro's head. Water, gladioli and bits of fern dripped from his shoulders and puddled on the floor.

"She shouldn't have done that," Luc said with a sigh. "He's not going to take it at all well."

"I wish she'd put the vase down," Grace said, shifting Tony to her shoulder.

"It's *where* she'll put it down that worries me."

No sooner had he said that, than Edward, Luc's head security guard, endeavored to wrest the vase from Carina's hands. For a few tense seconds they tussled. Jerking it free, it flew from Edward's hands and crashed against the side of Pietro's head. He went down like a ton of bricks.

Luc raced for a phone and called down to the security desk. "Call the staff doctor to help Pietro. Fast! I'll be right there."

"Luc, wait! You better check this out first," Grace called in a panic. "It doesn't look good."

They could no longer see Pietro. A huge crowd had gathered around him, blocking the view. Off to one side, security men were converging on Carina, who wept copiously. Far worse, two police officers came bursting through the front doors. Carina looked from the security men to the police, and apparently decided the law was a safer bet than the furious employees of a stricken Salvatore. She darted to their side.

"I don't know what tale of woe she's spinning, but it's making quite an impression," Luc observed in disgust. "She'll be gone before I even reach the elevators. Yep. There she goes. Out the door, into the first cab that passes by and on her way to the airport."

"What about Pietro?" Grace asked in concern.

"Wait a sec. He's up." Luc relaxed slightly. "Thank heavens."

"He seems to be all right, but he could still have a concussion. I wish the doctor was there," Grace fussed. "Oh, no. Now he's yelling at the police."

"Probably for letting Carina go."

"Why does that policewoman have her handcuffs out?

They're not going to arrest him, are they?'' she questioned in alarm. "He hasn't done anything wrong."

"Except give the police a hard time, knowing Pietro. They tend to frown on that." He watched the screen, an intent expression on his face. "Good. They're releasing him."

"Great, except where's he going?" She pointed to the screen. "Now he's leaving the building, too."

"Damn!" Luc thrust a hand through his hair. "He's going after Carina. I should have guessed he'd pull something like that."

"But what about Tony? He can't expect us..." Her eyes widened in disbelief.

He smiled grimly and nodded. "Looks like we have baby-sitting duties until Pietro catches up with Carina."

"Oh, no. No way. Not a chance."

Before he could respond, the phone rang. Luc snatched it up. "Edward? How's Pietro? Yes, yes. I know he left. Where's he headed?" He covered the mouthpiece and spoke to Grace, "I was right. He's on his way to the airport. Hang on, Edward. I'm putting you on the speakerphone." He punched a button.

"Er...Mr. Salvatore? Can you hear me? This is Edward Rumple speaking. Over."

"We hear you," Grace said quickly. "Is Pietro all right? He isn't hurt too badly?"

"Just a goose egg, Miss Barnes. Hardly any blood at all." He cleared his throat. "But there is just one little problem."

"What is it?" Luc asked.

A loud pounding sounded on the outer door. "Police. Open up, please."

"The police are on their way up," Edward said lamely.

For an instant Luc didn't move. Then in a calm, collected voice, he said, "Thank you, Edward. Keep everything under control down there and notify me the instant Pietro returns. I'll deal with the police." Hanging up the phone, he crossed to the door.

"Luc?" Grace said uncertainly.

He spared her a brief glance. "It'll be okay. Just try not to look worried and let me do the walking." At her nod, he opened the door and held out his hand. "Hello. I'm Luc Salvatore, president of Salvatore Enterprises. What can I do for you—" he checked their name tags "—Officers Cable and Hatcher?"

"We're responding to a report of an abandoned infant," said Officer Cable. She glanced at the baby Grace held. "Is that the child?"

"This baby isn't abandoned," Luc stated firmly, moving to stand between Grace and the policewoman.

"No?" Officer Hatcher, a tall, sturdy man, stepped forward. "Is he yours?"

"He's my nephew."

The two officers exchanged quick glances. "I'm afraid we'll have to see some identification," Cable requested.

Grace could tell from their attitudes that they were taking this situation very, very seriously. Luc removed his driver's license from his wallet and handed it to the policewoman. "Perhaps an explanation is in order?" he suggested with a quick smile.

Grace waited for Officer Cable's reaction to that smile. It wasn't long coming. She fumbled for his license, effected a swift recovery, then made a production of recording the information on her clipboard. A spot of color appeared high on each cheekbone. Luc didn't even notice. Grace sighed. He never did.

"I think an explanation would be very helpful," Hatcher interrupted, keenly attuned to his partner's reaction. He strode across the room, firing a quelling glance at Cable. Somewhat chagrined, she reverted to a more professional demeanor.

"I believe you met my brother Pietro Salvatore downstairs," Luc began.

"He was the one involved in the altercation with the young woman?"

"A small family squabble," Luc said dismissively. "We're a very…emotional household."

"The young woman is…?"

"His wife."

Grace's mouth fell open at the blatant lie—the first she'd every heard him utter—and a tiny gasp escaped before she could prevent it. She stared at Luc in disbelief; he didn't blink an eye. Nor did he look at her. But Officer Hatcher did. Grace quickly shut her mouth and focused her attention on the baby, but she suspected it was too little, too late. Sure enough, he approached.

"You have something to add, Miss…"

"Barnes. Grace Barnes. And yes, I do. Could…could you hand me that diaper bag? I believe we've had a little accident here," she murmured weakly.

The officer's eyes narrowed but he didn't call her a liar to her face, which came as a relief. He bent down and picked up the bag. She took it with a grateful smile and gently deposited the baby on top of Luc's desk, smack-dab in the center of his leather blotter. Serve him right if it was ruined, she decided. He shouldn't have lied to the police. She unwrapped the blanket around Tony and made a production of unsnapping the bottom of his jumper.

"To get back to the matter at hand," Officer Hatcher continued. "The young lady we questioned, her name is…?"

"Carina Donati…Salvatore," Luc replied.

"And she left to go to the airport?"

"Yes, her mother in Italy is very ill. My brother asked her to wait until they could all fly together, but she wanted to get home as soon as possible. I'm sorry you had to be involved." He shrugged. "It really wasn't necessary."

"About the baby," Officer Cable interrupted. "You've been left with the infant until your brother returns?"

"It's only for a few hours."

Grace kept her head down and removed a fresh diaper, wipes and powder from the bag. Sliding the rubber pants off Tony's plump, churning legs, she discovered to her relief that he was, indeed, wet. She unpinned the soggy diaper—and discovered...something else.

The officers conferred in low voices and she could tell they weren't comfortable with the situation. So could Luc, for he sighed. "Look. I'm a responsible man, respected in the community. I'm baby-sitting my nephew for a few hours. Why is that a problem? Would it help if I provided references?"

"You have someone who can vouch for your baby-sitting abilities?" Hatcher retorted. Clearly, he resented Cable's less-than-professional reaction to Luc and intended to make matters as difficult as possible. "You look like a busy man," he added, his gaze suspicious. "Are you sure you can provide adequate care?"

"*Cara,*" he muttered to Grace. "Let me change Tony. I need to show them."

"Not now!" she whispered frantically.

"Yes, now." He grabbed her left hand and held it out toward the police officers. "Perhaps I should have said my *fiancée* and I will be baby-sitting little Tony."

"Luc, the baby," Grace whispered. He frowned at her, and she snatched her hand from his grasp. "I have to finish changing...him."

"You're engaged?" Officer Cable asked, not hiding her disappointment. Hatcher shoved his hat to the back of his head and grinned.

Grace shot Luc a fulminating glare. "Yes," she admitted, forcing out the lie. "I am." Fortunately they didn't ask if she was engaged to Luc. Not that she was really engaged at all....

Officer Cable gave a philosophical shrug. "I guess it's a false alarm," she said to her partner.

Officer Hatcher wasn't so accommodating. "We'll be writing this up," he informed them, without question suspecting that several vital details had been omitted from their story. "Next time I come here—and I will be back—I'll be having words with the baby's parents."

"Of course," Luc agreed.

He escorted the police officers to the elevators, leaving Grace and Tony behind. The minute they were gone, Grace returned the baby to the desk and quickly and efficiently repaired the droopy diaper. Tony fussed through the entire procedure, undoubtedly annoyed at having to suffer the same fate twice in less than five minutes.

Luc appeared in the doorway. "What are you doing?" he asked.

"Changing the baby."

"Again?"

"Yes, again. I was in such a hurry the first time, I didn't get it right."

"Why—"

She turned on him. "Do you realize what would have happened if Officer Cable had come over while I was changing the baby?"

Amusement sparked in his eyes. "She would have seen how a baby gets changed?"

"She would have seen that Tony is actually Toni."

"Come again?"

'I mean…Toni isn't your nephew but your niece!" Grace snapped. She picked up the baby and carried her to the couch, nestling her safely among the cushions.

"What?"

Grace folded her arms across her chest. "Toni apparently stands for Antonia, not Antonio."

"You're kidding!" Luc grinned in amazement. "That's wonderful. She's the first female Salvatore in…in four generations. Or is it five?"

Grace struggled to control her temper. "You're missing the point. If the police had discovered that you didn't even know the sex of your brother's child, the whole game would have been up. They'd have thrown us both in jail and taken the baby into custody."

He shook his head. "I wouldn't have let them."

"You couldn't have prevented it!" She didn't remember when she'd last been so angry. "How dare you!"

He stood, leaning against the doorframe, watching her intently. "How dare I what?"

"How dare you lie to them! I mean, when you finally cut loose with a fib, it's a whopper. But did you *have* to start with the police?"

He shrugged. "It seemed…appropriate at the time. Besides, I plan to convince Pietro to do the right thing. My father will disown him if he doesn't."

"Great," she grumbled. "So why involve me in your family problems?"

He grabbed her shoulders, hauling her close. "*Our* problems," he reminded in a soft, deliberate voice. "We're engaged. You even told the police that, remember?"

She shook her head frantically. "No. I…I didn't. I just agreed that I was engaged, not that I was engaged to—"

He cut her off. "That isn't how they'll recall the conversation."

"But, it's all a lie," she protested. "Every bit of it. I'm not engaged to you. Pietro and Carina are not married. Darn it, Luc, the baby's not even a him."

She saw the storm gathering in his eyes, saw the fury and determination lock his expression into a cold, taut mask. "Let me explain something to you. I will not allow the police or anyone else to take Toni from me. I will do anything, *anything,* to protect her."

She didn't doubt him for a minute. And she could even sympathize with his feelings. The Salvatores were a close, unified family—all for one and one for all had long been their credo. And if truth be known, she did feel a certain obligation to Luc. After all, hadn't she spent the past year lying to him? She…she *owed* him a lie. But only a small short-term one. After that, she'd consider them even.

"What do you want from me?" she asked warily.

He had her and he knew it. He relaxed, the fire in his eyes dying until the gold gleamed like banked embers. His grip relaxed into a caress. "Not much. I just want you to stay with me—posing as my fiancée should the need arise—until Carina or Pietro return.''

She really, truly tried to refuse. But she couldn't. She couldn't desert Toni, no matter how mad she was at Luc. And a part of her had to admit that she liked the idea of pretending to be engaged to her handsome boss. Besides, Dom was in Italy and Will-William was non-existent. She trusted herself to resist physical temptation for a few hours, so where was the harm? ''You don't play fair,'' she complained, none too strenuously.

''No,'' he agreed. He caught her hand in his and raised it to his lips in a graceful gesture. Then he smiled, a most charming, dangerous smile. ''I play to win.''

''GRACE, WAKE UP.''

''Go away,'' she protested in a muffled voice.

''Wake up, *cara mia*. It's time to go home.''

''Home?'' That penetrated. With a groan, she sat up, then gasped in horror. ''The baby! I fell asleep—''

''Take it easy, sweetheart. Toni's fine. I slipped her out of your arms the minute you nodded off.''

She sat up, the image of Luc watching her sleep an uncomfortable one. ''What time is it?''

''Six.''

''Six! Is Pietro back?''

''No.''

''What about Carina?''

He shook his head. ''Afraid not.''

She shoved her hair out of her eyes and twitched her skirt hem down over her knees. Her disguise was rapidly falling apart. If she weren't careful, all of Dom's fine plans would soon come undone. Had Luc noticed anything unusual? She searched his face. Responding to her scrutiny, he lifted an eyebrow in question.

''Something must have happened to them,'' she said. ''It doesn't take this long to get to and from the airport. They should be back by now.''

"They had a lot to discuss." He shrugged. "Pietro knows Toni's safe with us. We'll hear from them soon."

Right on cue, the phone rang and Luc glanced over his shoulder. "My private line."

"Thank heavens," she whispered, knowing that only family used that number.

He crossed to his desk and snatched up the phone. "Pietro? Where the *hell* are you?" He listened for several minutes, then switched to Italian. Not that it mattered. From the anger in his voice, Grace knew this discussion didn't bode well for her future. "I want an update tomorrow, you understand?" he finally said. "Or I go to Father with this." He slammed down the phone.

Night had fallen and only a small desk lamp illuminated the room. Luc thrust his chair away from his desk and stood, crossing to the window behind him. San Francisco lay sprawled below, the city lights glittering through the misty rain.

"Good news?" she joked uneasily.

He wasn't amused. "Pietro missed Carina at the airport, as I'm sure you've surmised."

"When is he coming for Toni?"

"Not tonight." He turned to face her, deep shadows cutting across his face and concealing his expression. "And not tomorrow night."

"What—what does that mean?"

"It means we're in for a longer haul than I anticipated." He moved into the light and she caught her breath as she discerned the full extent of his displeasure. "Pietro was calling from a plane phone. He's followed Carina to Italy."

From across the room, the baby let out a loud wail.

Grace hurried to Toni's side and picked her up. "You said it, sweet pea," she muttered, hugging the baby. Uneasily she recalled her promise—to stay until Carina or Pietro returned for Toni. She peeked nervously at Luc. From his cold, calculating look, he hadn't forgotten, either.

She closed her eyes and shivered. Oh, Lord. What had she let herself in for?

"All right, I'll stay," she said, sighing.

In no time, they were at Luc's apartment. "You can sleep in one of my shirts," Luc said, satisfaction glittering in his eyes. "And I'll bring you a spare robe and a toothbrush. There are only two bedrooms. Do you want the baby tonight or should I take her in with me?"

"I'll care for her tonight, and you can have tomorrow," she said, her reply conceding that there would be a tomorrow night.

He nodded. "Fine. There's a bathroom that adjoins the guest bedroom. If you'd like to grab a shower, I'll watch the little stinker."

"Stinker?" A tiny smile escaped before she could prevent it. "Diapers are in the hall."

With that, she headed for the bathroom. In minutes she stood beneath a hot, relaxing deluge, rinsing away the tension of an unbelievably stressful day. Wishing she could stand there forever, she squared her shoulders, took a deep breath and reluctantly turned the shower off. Returning to the bedroom, she found a silk shirt and robe spread out on the bed.

Dressing quickly, she brushed her wet hair. She'd have to get another bottle of color rinse and soon. Already she could see the natural gold gleaming through the muddy brown dye. Another shampoo or two and this part of her disguise would be uncovered, as well. And what would Luc say then?

BEFORE SHE knew it, it was morning, and Luc was in her room, bellowing "Rise and shine!"

Grace rolled over and groaned, flinging an arm across her face to block out the blinding sunlight. "Go away," she muttered.

Luc chuckled. "I have coffee," he said in a wheedling tone.

She peeked out from beneath her elbow. "Coffee?"

"A cup for now and a whole fresh-brewed pot waiting in the kitchen."

She sat up and looked over at the crib. It was empty. "Where's Toni?"

"On a blanket in the living room shaking her fist at dust motes." He headed for the door. "We have a lot to do today, so hurry up and get dressed."

Drawing her knees to her chest, she said, "I don't have anything clean to wear."

"We'll stop by your apartment on the way to the stores. You can change and pack a few days' worth of clothes."

She eyed him suspiciously. "A few days?"

"A few days," he confirmed. "Pietro called." And with that he breezed from the room.

It took ten minutes to pull herself together. The coffee helped substantially. After locating her glasses on the living room couch and popping them on the end of her nose, she swept the carpet for her scattered hairpins and pocketed them. Reluctant to face reality—even more reluctant to hear what Pietro had to say when he'd called, she played with Toni for a while. Eventually, hunger forced her to track Luc down in the kitchen. Open confrontation seemed the best course of action.

"What do you mean a few days?" she demanded, jumping right in. "What did Pietro say?"

"He missed connecting with Carina in Italy. Her mother is being seen by a specialist in Switzerland, and Carina went there. Pietro's following."

"Did you tell him about the police? Did you tell him we haven't a clue how to take care of a baby? When's he coming back?"

"Yes. Yes. And as soon as possible." Luc ran a hand through his hair, an edge of impatience creeping into his voice. "You're upset about this, and so am I. But there isn't anything I can do about it. Not yet. So let's make the best of things."

Right. Until the police showed up. Or worse, Dom. And

then Luc's clever little scheme would come crashing down around both their ears. And so would Dom's... She tried to stay calm. Shrieking wouldn't accomplish a thing. Except make her feel a whole heck of a lot better. She took a deep breath, wavering between anger and capitulation. "What's your plan of action?" she finally asked, giving in to the inevitable. At least, with Luc, it was the inevitable.

"First we go to your apartment. Then we go shopping for Toni."

Thirty minutes later, they'd crossed the Bay Bridge out of San Francisco and reached the small apartment Grace rented on the Oakland-Berkeley line. A short walk from the electric railway, it was an easy commute to work each day and much less expensive than living in the city.

"I'll just run upstairs and pack a bag," she suggested. "Why don't you wait here with Toni."

To her dismay Luc released his seat belt, climbed out of the car and calmly unfastened the baby from her car seat. "Toni would like to see your apartment and so would I. Besides, I want to make sure you don't pack any of William's clothes."

She stared at him in confusion. "William's clothes?"

"Two sizes too large and three decades too old."

Having no choice, she led the way to her door. "Make yourself at home," she said with more than a hint of irony. "I'll go pack."

In the bedroom, she yanked a small cloth suitcase down from the shelf in her closet and began tossing in the essentials. A minute later, Luc and Toni appeared at the door.

And in Luc's hand was her third-place award for Salvatore's young-entrepreneur content.

He held it up, his eyes cool and watchful. "What's this, Grace?"

Crossing to Luc's side, Grace took the award from him and placed it on her bureau. "You know what it is."

"You're right, I do. I guess my question is, what are you doing with it?"

Returning to her packing, she carefully folded a blouse and tucked it into the suitcase. "I think that's obvious, too. I won it."

"In this past year's contest?"

"Why the questions, Luc?" she snapped. "What's the problem? Yes. I won third place in this past year's contest. As a result, I met Dom."

"And?"

"And," she finished impatiently, "he thought highly enough of me to recommend me for the job as your assistant. I thought you knew all that."

"No. I didn't."

He frowned, his gaze searching, and she glanced hastily away. But it was too late. He suspected she was hiding something, and knowing Luc he wouldn't leave it alone until he'd settled the issue to his satisfaction. She could practically see the wheels turning as he mulled over what he perceived to be a puzzle.

"Let's try this tack and see if it gets us anywhere..." he began. "*Why* did you take the job as my assistant?"

"This is ridiculous. I took the job for the same reason millions of people all over the world take jobs." Using less than her usual care, she balled up another blouse and thrust it into the suitcase. She just wanted to end this conversation and get out of here before she did something...said something...incriminating. "I needed to earn money."

"Yes, but contestants who enter the young-entrepreneur contest are interested in starting their own business, not working for someone else."

"What's your point, Luc?" There was an edge to her voice.

His eyes narrowed. "Are you? Interested in starting your own business?"

She couldn't lie. She'd told him enough of those already without making it any worse. Looking directly at him, she said, "Yes. I'm interested in *someday* starting my own business. In the meantime, working for you should be good experience."

He settled Toni in the crook of his arm and propped a shoulder against the doorjamb. "And has it been? Has working for me been good?"

She turned back to her packing. They continued to tread on dangerous ground—different ground, perhaps, but dangerous, nonetheless. "Yes. It's been good," she agreed shortly. In fact, it had been more than good. Working for Luc had been surprisingly enjoyable. She'd thrived on the challenges, appreciated the fast pace. She'd even relished their heated arguments. She frowned. She'd miss all that when she left.

"What sort of business do you plan to open?" he asked.

She glanced hesitantly at him. Would he laugh when she told him? "It'll be a toy store. One that specializes in babies. All the toys will be unique—handcrafted by local artisans, educational and safe." Her mother had always insisted on that.

He glanced down at Toni, a smile curving the corner of his mouth. "Seems we picked the perfect woman to help us, after all." He approached, his movements lithe and graceful. "Here. Take the kid."

She obeyed without thought. Not until he turned and began to rummage through her suitcase did she realize his motives for handing her the baby. "Cut that out, Luc! You have no right going through my things."

"I just want to make sure what you pack is practical." He yanked out the skirt and blouse she'd just shoved in. "Which this is not," he decided, and reached for the next garment. "Nor is this."

"Stop that! Those are eminently practical and you know it."

"Practical for the office, not for taking care of a baby." He glanced at a skirt label. "This has to be dry-cleaned. One good burp and it's history."

"Luc!" Toni's little face screwed into a frown and Grace

quickly moderated her tone to reflect sweetness and light. "Let me put it this way. You take one more item out of my suitcase, and I'll kill you." Too bad her glasses hid the glare she shot in his direction—not that he was looking anyway.

"As long as we're dispensing with the impractical, I think we'll dispense with the ugly, as well," he said, ignoring her threat. Clothes flew through the air and landed on the bed. "Ugly. Impractical. Ugly. Ugly. And very ugly. Don't you get depressed wearing this stuff?"

"No, I don't." At least, not often. Dom's promised reward offered more than adequate compensation. She scowled in impotent fury. "And what difference does it make if they're ugly? They don't belong to you."

He glanced up, a dangerous glitter in his golden eyes. "They may not belong to me, but I have to look at them. And so does Toni. I won't have you around my niece day and night, displaying such a lack of taste."

She looked about, desperate for a safe place to deposit the baby so she could stop him—physically, if necessary. "What are you doing now? Get out of there!"

"Hello. What's this?" He yanked free a mint green dress. "Ah, much better. Do you save this for when William's here...?" He lifted an eyebrow, his expression turning wicked. "Or perhaps it's to wear when William isn't around."

"William loves that dress!" she protested, then blinked. What the dickens was she saying?

"Sure he does. That's why he has you running about looking like a bag lady most of the time. That's one sick relationship you have going there."

"My relationship with Will...William is none of your concern." How she wished she could get that name past her lips without stammering. Unfortunately, nine times out of ten it wouldn't come.

"Your relationship with him isn't my concern...yet. But, give it time."

Grace stared in alarm. What did he mean? That at some

point her relationship with William would become his concern? And precisely what did he have in mind, once it did? Confronting the nonexistent William? A tightness settled in her chest. Matters grew more complicated by the minute.

Rummaging through what she privately referred to as her off-duty clothing, he stripped a pair of soft rose-colored slacks, tight black pants and several brightly patterned pull-over sweaters from their hangers and dropped them into her suitcase.

She hugged Toni to her breast. "Are you quite through?"

"No. Where are your cosmetics?" He crossed to her dresser. "Never mind. I've found them."

"I can do that," she insisted.

His response sounded suspiciously like a snort. He rifled through the bottles and tubes cluttering the tabletop with a knowledge and decisiveness that could only have come from long experience—a fact that didn't escape her. Clearly, he was familiar with women. With everything about women. But then, she'd long suspected that when it came to the fairer sex, Luc was an expert.

"Fascinating colors here," he said in disgust. "Not one of them suits you. Except... Here we go." He swept foundation, blush, eye shadow, mascara and lipstick into a cosmetic bag and tossed it into her suitcase. Then he turned and folded his arms across his chest. "What's going on, Grace?"

She shoved her glasses high up on the bridge of her nose and cuddled Toni close, as if for protection. "I don't know what you're talking about," she claimed. But they both knew she lied.

He lifted an eyebrow, his expression sardonic. "Oh, no? Two separate wardrobes. Two distinct sets of cosmetics. And you have no comment?"

"Right. I have no comment."

The dangerous light reappeared in his eyes. "You have no comment...yet."

She swallowed. There was that word again. "Yet?"

He crossed to stand directly in front of her. "Yet. It implies a temporary situation.'' He leaned down until they were almost nose to nose. ''One that *will* change in the near future. Are we clear on that?''

She took a hasty step backward. ''Crystal.''

''Fine.'' He turned to her suitcase and zipped the bag closed. ''Just so you know, I'm taking this new Grace home with me. I've been forced to hang around the other one at the office for quite long enough.'' He lifted the suitcase off the bed and eased Toni from her arms. ''Get changed and meet me down at the car. Next stop—Toy's-a-Trillion.''

Two hours…and three carts later, Grace decided to call a halt to his shopping binge. ''This is ridiculous, Luc. The baby can't use a tenth of what you're buying. It'll go to waste.''

''Don't fuss,'' Luc replied, swooping up a dozen rattles. ''Anything Carina and the baby can't use, I'll donate to charity. Relax and enjoy yourself. Spend some of my money. Better yet, spend a lot of my money. I'm having fun. Aren't you having fun?''

''Yes, but…''

''Then, not another word of argument.'' He leaned closer, his eyes dark and intent. ''I'm tired of the office Grace,'' he murmured. ''Send her home and let the other Grace come out and play. The one who wears pale green dresses that match her eyes and tight pants with soft wool sweaters. I want to get to know that Grace.''

She shook her head, suddenly afraid. She was out of her depth and knew it. All her lies were steadily unraveling and soon she'd be exposed and vulnerable. She didn't dare consider what might happen then….

To her relief, Toni chose that moment to put an end to both their conversation and the shopping spree. Finished with her nap, she began to complain bitterly and at great volume at being trapped for so long in the baby sling.

''Time for a bottle, young lady,'' Grace decreed, lifting her off Luc's chest. ''If you'll let me have the diaper bag, Luc, I'll go feed and change Toni while you give your credit card a workout.''

By the time she finished with Toni, the most important of their selections were paid for and loaded in the car, the rest to be delivered the next day. It amazed Grace what charm and money could accomplish.

Having fastened Toni into her car seat, she buckled her own seat belt and sighed. "I need to get back to work so I can rest," she joked.

"You can rest tonight. I've invited my brothers over for dinner, and you can relax—in your mint green dress—while they entertain Toni."

She glanced over at him, quelling her panic about the dress order momentarily, overcome as she was with curiosity. "Do they know about her?"

He started the engine and pulled out of the parking space. "I thought I'd surprise them. That way I can impress on them the importance of keeping this information quiet until Pietro and Carina return."

"And do your brothers always fall in with your demands?"

He inclined his head. "They tend to find it in their best interest to do things my way."

"Because you're the oldest?"

He grinned. "That, and the fact that I'm their boss. He who controls the purse strings…"

"Calls the tune?"

"The metaphor may be mixed, but the meaning's accurate enough."

Accurate, indeed. She nibbled her lip. If she were smart, she'd do well to remember who called the tune she danced to…and who controlled the future purse strings for Baby Dream Toys.

LUC NOTICED her first. To her dismay, he didn't seem the least surprised by her altered appearance. With an annoying calm, he settled Toni more comfortably on his lap. But then a slow smile of satisfaction slid across his face.

Luc's brother Rocco noticed her next, stumbling to a halt

in midsentence. His mouth opened and closed, but he couldn't seem to get any words out. At that, all conversation stopped. If the varied reactions to Toni had been amusing, the reactions to Grace's transformation were even more so. Luc's four brothers, whom she'd met over the course of the past year, scrambled to their feet, tripping over themselves as they fought their way to her side. An instant later four large, gorgeous men had her completely surrounded.

It felt wonderful.

"Grace!"

"What the hell have you done to yourself?"

"Never mind that! What the hell were you doing running around looking like you did when you could have looked like… Damn!"

Anxious to change the subject, Grace scooped Toni out of Luc's arms. "So, what do you think of your niece?" she asked the room at large.

Her question brought a slew of responses, each proud uncle attempting to outflatter the others. It was clear they adored the newest member of the family. Within minutes, she'd been snatched away from Grace, and even as they enjoyed their meal, Toni continued to be ensconced on one or the other of her uncles' laps. On the receiving end of so much adoration, she kicked her little legs and waved her hands, blinking adoringly into each handsome face.

"Flirt," Rocco announced in proud disgust. "It's a good thing you have so many uncles. You'll need them to beat off the boyfriends."

"So, when does Pietro return?" Alessandro asked.

"Soon, I hope," Luc responded. "Until he does, Grace has agreed to help me with Toni."

"You're staying here?" Marc questioned with an impudent grin.

Throwing a troubled glance Luc's way, she nodded. So much for keeping this episode from Dom. She could only hope he'd be reasonable. If she could continue to hold Luc at a distance, she didn't think there would be a problem. The only question being, could she do it? She hadn't realized how much she'd come to depend on her disguise for protection. With that blown, she'd just have to cling even tighter to the imaginary William.

"Yes," she said. "I'm using Luc's guest room until Pietro or Carina returns. Which reminds me..." She slipped from her chair and addressed Luc. "I need to call my fiancé and give him an update. Do you mind if I use the phone in your study?"

"Feel free." She couldn't read his expression, but somehow she suspected it held amusement. "Oh, and Grace..."

She glanced back over her shoulder. "Yes?"

This time she couldn't mistake his amusement. "Be sure and give him my regards."

Sitting in Luc's study, she punched in her home phone number and spoke sheer drivel to her answering machine for the next ten minutes. Luc appeared in the doorway just as she'd cradled the receiver.

"How's Will-William?" he asked.

"Anxious for Carina and Pietro to return so our lives can get back to normal," she lied with composure.

Folding his arms across his chest, he tilted his head to one side. "Have I told you how beautiful you look tonight?"

"Thank you." She practically leapt from the chair, anxious to end this conversation and put some extra bodies between them. Nice, tall, protective bodies in the form of four Salvatore brothers. "Shall we join the others?" she suggested. He didn't move and to her distress, now that she was standing, they almost touched. Perhaps leaving the safety of the chair had been a mistake.

For a long minute he stood without speaking, his thoughtful gaze narrowed on her, as if trying to analyze something that defied analysis. His attention dropped briefly to her engagement ring and a small smile touched his mouth before he released her. "By all means. Join my brothers. They're about to leave, anyway." He moved toward the phone. "I want to make a quick call. I'll join you in a minute."

"All right." She hesitated, something in his face setting off warning bells. But she couldn't figure out why.

He picked up the receiver and raised an eyebrow in question. "Anything else?" he asked.

She shook her head, and without another word went in search of Luc's brothers. She found them grouped in the living room, slipping on coats and giving Toni goodbye hugs and kisses. Grace smiled. That little girl was going to grow up being very spoiled…and very much loved.

"Time to move out," Alessandro announced, throwing open the front door and handing Grace the baby.

"Look!" Marc exclaimed. "She smiled at me."

"So what?" his twin scoffed. "She's been doing that to me all evening."

"Only because she got the two of us mixed up."

Luc suddenly appeared, bringing up the rear. "Quiet down," he ordered. "And don't forget. No one is to know Toni's here. One run-in with the police was enough. We can't risk another."

"You got it."

"Mum's the word."

"Not a problem," Alessandro assured. "Oh, hello, Mrs. Bumgartle. Were we being too noisy again?"

Grace drew a sharp breath. Luc's nosy neighbor had already asked questions about the baby, and expressed her opinion that Luc was "up to no good."

A long, sharp nose poked around the doorway opposite. "This time I'm calling the manager. He'll take care of you hooligans. See if he doesn't!"

"I'm sorry, Mrs. Bumgartle," Luc said, crossing the hall to speak to her. "My brothers were just leaving. You won't hear another sound out of them." He threw a stern glance over his shoulder. "Right, boys?"

She peered at Luc, then at his brothers, her eyes narrow with dislike. "Hooligans, the lot of you!" And with that she slammed the door.

"Whoo-hoo," Marc said with a chuckle. "I do love seeing

Mrs. Bumgartle. It reminds me there's one woman on this planet you can't charm.''

"Two women," Stef, another brother, corrected. "You're forgetting about Cynthia. Remember? The tall, gorgeous brunette? Totally immune. She could freeze Luc dead in his tracks with one look."

Rocco slapped Luc on the back. "Don't worry, big brother. Two out of millions. We won't hold it against you."

Luc grinned. "Get out of here, before I knock some heads together. I'll let you know when I hear from Pietro."

LOCKING HERSELF IN Luc's room—it was his turn with Toni tonight—did nothing to make Grace feel safe from temptation. Three hours later, and on the verge of true madness, she started to drift off to sleep. An urgent banging put paid to that. Totally disoriented, it took her several seconds to realize the pounding came not from outside her bedroom but from outside the apartment. Grabbing her robe, she thrust her arms into it as she dashed for the door. For endless moments she fumbled with the lock and by the time she'd reached the hallway, Luc raced just ahead of her. Wearing the pajama bottoms she'd left out for him, he opened the front door, running a hand through his hair.

"What—" he began.

To Grace's horror, she saw a pair of policemen standing there, Mrs. Bumgartle right behind them, a self-righteous expression on her face.

"Arrest him," Mrs. Bumgartle demanded, pointing an accusing finger at Luc. "Arrest them both! Those... those...those babynappers!"

For a long moment, no one moved. Then Luc asked, "What's the problem, Officer?"

"Mr. Salvatore? I'm Officer Hatcher. We met two days ago at your office."

"I remember," Luc replied evenly. "Is there a problem?"

"Babynapper!" Mrs. Bumgartle proclaimed from behind the policeman's broad shoulders. "He told me the baby was his niece—that she was his brother's child. But all his brothers visited tonight and she wasn't theirs. And he—'' she pointed a finger at Luc with dramatic emphasis ''—warned them that they couldn't afford to have the police called in again.''

Officer Hatcher glanced from Luc to a clearly nervous Grace. ''Perhaps I better come in and straighten this out. Carl,'' he addressed his partner, ''escort Mrs. Bumgartle to her apartment and take a statement.''

''There's nothing to straighten out,'' Luc insisted, leading the way to the living room. ''I explained before that we were baby-sitting my niece and that's precisely what we're doing.''

Hatcher pulled a notepad out of his pocket and flipped through the pages. ''According to my notes, you said you were baby-sitting for a few hours. It's now been almost two days. Would you care to explain the discrepancy?''

Luc glanced briefly at Grace, then said, ''I believe I mentioned that my sister-in-law's mother is ill. My brother and his wife were going to fly to Italy with the baby, but decided at the last minute to leave Toni with us.'' He caught Grace's hand in his and pulled her close. ''Is that a problem?''

Officer Hatcher began adding to his notes. ''You have something from the parents stating this?''

''No,'' Luc admitted. ''I didn't realize that would be necessary.''

The policeman's gaze sharpened. ''A medical release form? A birth certificate? Anything?''

Luc shook his head. ''They should be back soon.''

Hatcher glanced at his notes again and froze. ''How old is your niece, Mr. Salvatore? What's her birthdate?''

Grace started, staring up at Luc in a panic. His arm tightened around her, crushing her to his side. ''She's three months,'' Luc said stiffly. ''I'm...I'm not sure of the exact date of her birth.''

''And when did her sex change from male to female?''

Hatcher asked with unmistakable sarcasm. He had them and he knew it.

Luc swore beneath his breath.

"You didn't know she was a girl, did you?" The patrolman's mouth twisted in a parody of a smile. "Is she even your niece?"

"I didn't know she was a girl until we changed her diaper," Luc was forced to conceded. "Carina called her Toni, and since Salvatores have a history of producing boys, I assumed..." He shrugged, then stated forcefully, "But she *is* my niece."

Officer Hatcher checked his notes again. "The baby's name is Antonia Donati...Salvatore? Or was that a lie, too?"

Luc closed his eyes, releasing a long, drawn-out sigh. "Carina and my brother aren't married. Yet. I expect that to change very soon."

"Let me get this straight." The officer's words fell, cold and hard as chipped ice. "You said the parents left the baby in your care and would be back in a few hours. That was a lie. You said the child was your nephew. That was a lie. And you said the baby's parents were married. Another lie. You don't have any legal authority to care for this baby whatsoever, do you?"

Luc's fist clenched at his sides. "Look. Carina, the baby's mother, left Toni with my brother because of a family emergency. That much is true. And she needed someone to care for Toni during her absence. That is also the truth. Since my brother Pietro is the baby's father, he was the natural choice. The only problem was, Pietro didn't know about Toni until Carina arrived at my office."

Understanding dawned. "Which explains the argument in the lobby."

"Yes. My brother went after Carina to try and stop her. Thanks to your intervention, he wasn't in time. When Pietro does catch up with her, they'll marry and return for Toni. Until then, my fiancée and I are taking care of the baby. She's perfectly safe and in good hands."

"That's not for me to decide."

Luc stiffened. "What the hell does that mean?"

Hatcher eyed him sternly. "I mean that what happens to the baby is up to social services, not me. Legally, she's been abandoned."

"No, she hasn't!" Luc bit out. "The mother left her child with the father."

"Mr. Salvatore, I don't intend to argue with you about this. I'm taking the baby into custody. If you resist, I'll arrest you."

Before Luc could respond, Grace asked, "What will happen to Toni?"

Hatcher explained while writing. "The law requires we have her transported by ambulance to the local hospital. She'll be examined there and kept overnight at the child-protection center. In the morning they'll put her in a temporary foster home while an emergency-response worker investigates the case." He spoke coolly and dispassionately.

"How do we get her back?" Grace questioned.

He hesitated, glancing up. For the first time, his guard relaxed slightly. "To be honest, I'm not sure you can. The best chance you have is to get in touch with the legal guardian—presumably the mother—and obtain a signed custody statement and a medical-permission slip. A copy of the birth certificate wouldn't hurt, either."

Grace gazed at Luc. "Can we do that?" she whispered.

He gave a brief nod. "Pietro can fax it to us."

"Even then, it's questionable whether the authorities will release her to you. Though—" Hatcher hesitated, eyeing Grace "—a *permanent* female presence in the home could possibly tip the scales in your favor." He snapped his notepad closed and pocketed it. "Take me to the baby."

There was nothing they could do after that. Luc went into the spare bedroom and packed a diaper bag with several days' worth of clothes, diapers and baby paraphernalia. Fighting back tears, Grace carefully bundled up Toni for the trip into the frigid night air. The entire time, Officer Hatcher stood in the doorway, watching their every move.

"Here's my business card," Luc said. "My home phone number's on the back. I'll expect the emergency-response worker's call first thing in the morning." It wasn't a request.

Hatcher inclined his head. "I suggest you get those papers together and fast. You haven't a prayer otherwise."

And with that he left, Toni gently cradled in his arms.

The minute the door closed behind him, Luc slammed his fist against the wall, knocking a hole in the plaster. Grace came up behind, not sure approaching him at this time was the wisest course of action. "It's all right," she murmured. "We'll get her back."

He whirled to face her, his eyes dark with a passionate intensity. "You and I," he informed her in a hard, determined voice, "are now officially married."

"You *can't* be serious," she exclaimed, taking a quick step back.

His hands dropped to her shoulders, holding her in place. "I'm dead serious. Hatcher said having a permanent female presence in the house might tip the scales in our favor, and that's just what I intend to have."

"But what about Will...William?"

"What about him?" he demanded.

There was a recklessness about Luc that worried her, and her gaze slid nervously from his. Perhaps this wasn't the best time to mention her supposed fiancé. "I'll...discuss it with him. But do we have to claim we're married?" she asked. "The police think we're engaged. What happens if they compare notes?"

"Then we'll show them our marriage certificate."

She stared at Luc in shock. *"What?"*

"Tomorrow we apply for a license and have all the required testing done, just in case a temporary marriage is necessary."

"No! I won't do it."

He approached, towering over her, his face set in hard,

determined lines. "Oh, yes, you will. I don't care what it takes. I'll give you whatever you want, but you will do this. If not for me, for Toni."

She closed her eyes, knowing she should turn him down flat. A strident voice of logic told her there wasn't a single valid reason for helping him, and every reason in the world for refusing. If she was smart, she'd listen to that voice. If she was smart...

"All right," she whispered. "I'll do it."

And then he kissed her, a kiss of such passion and heat that it was more than enough to still even the voice of logic.

PIETRO CALLED at the crack of dawn—from Italy—and Luc ordered him to fax the documents they needed.

"Get dressed," Luc ordered Grace briskly when he hung up. "If we're going to get Toni home tonight, we've got a list of chores a mile long to accomplish beforehand."

First on his list turned out to be moving as many of her belongings as possible to his apartment. In no time, they'd practically stripped her place bare and filled up his car with personal possessions.

Jingling the car keys in his pocket, he stood by her front door. "Ready?" he asked, obviously impatient to get to the second item on his list—the marriage license.

"I'll be right out," she said, suddenly remembering her answering machine. Who knew when she'd return to her apartment. She'd better check messages before she left. She didn't doubt there'd be at least one from her father.

To her dismay, there were three. Each one urged her to call home, that he had a surprise for her. Well, this surprise would have to wait until her situation returned to normal. Next on the tape was her ridiculous conversation with the fictitious William. Shooting a nervous glance over her shoulder, she fast-forwarded through the nonsensical spiel. To her horror, right after her monologue came a message from Luc.

"Well, well..." he practically purred into the tape. "How very interesting."

She stared at the machine in confusion. What...? Then she remembered the call he'd made in the study—right on the heels of her own. He must have pushed the redial button and discovered that far from calling William, she'd phoned her own apartment.

She shut her eyes. So he knew there was no William. And now he knew she knew he knew...

The next few hours passed in a mad dash. After setting the wheels in motion for a quickie wedding should the need arise, Luc purchased a wedding band for Grace, overriding her heated objections with callous determination.

"I don't have time to argue with you about this," he informed her impatiently, shoving the ring over her knuckle. "You've pretended to be engaged for the past eleven months—who knows why. Now you're pretending to be married. What's the difference?"

She glared at him. "Give me a minute and I'll tell you."

"We don't have a minute. The emergency-response worker assigned to our case is meeting us at the apartment at noon. That doesn't give us much time to get everything in place."

Realizing her arguments were fruitless in the face of such overwhelming resolve, she gave up and returned with Luc to his apartment. At the stroke of twelve she positioned the last of her personal possessions, and as if in response, the doorbell rang. Joining Luc at the door, they welcomed the social worker together.

Ms. Cartwright proved to be a very pleasant, no-nonsense careerwoman in her late thirties, and it took Luc precisely three minutes to totally charm her.

Luc introduced Grace as his wife and explained that they would take turns caring for Toni until his brother and his "wife" returned.

"Wife?" Ms. Cartwright frowned. "I understood that Ms. Donati was a single parent. In fact, I'm a little concerned that you first told the police that your brother and Ms. Donati were married, then later admitted that wasn't true."

A variety of emotions chased across Luc's face... frustration, anger and finally resignation. "To be honest, Ms. Cartwright, I would have said just about anything to keep Toni with her family," he confessed in a low voice. "I know it's a terrible admission, but my brother had entrusted Toni to my care and I didn't want to let him down."

"I understand your feelings, but I must insist on absolute honesty from now on. Lying to the police, or to us for that matter, is a grave offense. If we uncover any further... discrepancies, you will not be permitted to care for your niece now or any time in the future. Are we clear on this?"

"We're clear," Luc said grimly.

Ms. Cartwright sighed. "I still have to do some routine investigation of your situation. It would help if you'd provide references, both financial and personal."

"Done. Will that take care of it?"

"Not quite. *If* you can get a letter of consent from the mother, a copy of the baby's birth certificate and a medical-permission slip in my hands by the end of the day, then I'll recommend that Toni be returned to you."

"Returned tonight?"

She smiled. "I'll do my best."

A few minutes later, Ms. Cartwright left and Luc grabbed Grace, wrapping his arms about her waist and twirling her around until the room spun in a dizzy arc. "We did it!" he announced jubilantly, setting her back on her feet. "Didn't I tell you everything would work out?"

"Yes, you did," Grace murmured, clutching his shoulders.

But she wasn't quite as confident. If she didn't get out of this situation soon, she'd lose everything...Baby Dream Toys, for one. But far worse, her heart.

IT WAS as if the very thought of losing everything made it happen. She was barely awake the next morning when Luc propelled her and Toni into his closet.

"Stay there," he ordered. "Don't move and don't make any noise."

"Luc!" She thrust the door open and poked her head out. *What is going on?*

"In case you weren't aware of it, when you open your mouth and speak, you make noise. You've got to be *quiet!*" Kissing her swiftly, Luc pushed her toward the back of the huge closet. "My dad's here. Now keep it down." He closed the door.

Fortunately, Luc was as adept at charming his father as he was at charming women. He surreptitiously checked his watch as he escorted Dom to the door a half hour later. "It's great having you home, Dad. Thanks for dropping by."

"It is very good to be home. I decided to return early so I could have the whole family over for Thanksgiving dinner." He paused in the entranceway. "Would this be convenient?"

"Terrific. Just terrific." Luc opened the door.

A young woman dressed in a business suit stood there, poised to knock. "Oh, my goodness," she exclaimed. "You startled me." Recovering swiftly, she held out her hand. "Hello. I'm Miss Carstairs," she announced. "I'm your—"

"My masseuse!" Luc greeted her loudly. Grabbing her hand, he yanked her into the apartment. "At last!"

"No! I—"

Dom chuckled and wagged his finger at Luc. "One of these days, my boy…"

Luc wrapped an arm around the shocked social worker. "Talk to you later, Dad, and welcome home." He slammed the door closed.

Miss Carstairs wriggled from his hold, stumbling back against the door. "Oh, my," she murmured, red-faced and breathless. She tucked a stray curl back into the tight knot on top of her head. "I am *not* the masseuse!"

Luc lifted an eyebrow. "You're not?"

"No! I'm Miss Carstairs, from social services. Are you Mrs. Salvatore?"

"In the flesh. Pleased to meet you." He offered his hand. She stared at his outstretched fingers as if they had fangs and a rattle. "I'm…I'm your case manager." She peered up at him suspiciously. "Are you sure you're Luc Salvatore? Mr. Luc Salvatore, whose wife is Mrs. Grace Salvatore?"

"That's right. Listen, I'm sorry but Grace and Toni aren't in." Dropping his hands to her shoulders, he peeled her off the door, opened it and glanced up and down the hallway. Dom was nowhere in sight. "How about coming back tomorrow?" Planting his hand in the small of her back, he propelled her into the hall.

A loud baby bellow resounded through the apartment and Miss Carstairs's eyebrows flew up. "Your wife and Antonia are out? And what, may I ask, is that crying? It certainly sounds like a baby to me."

Before he could stop her, she charged back into the apartment, leaving him no choice but to give chase. Following the sound of a very cranky Toni, she hustled into his bedroom and hesitated in front of the closet. Shooting him a look of disbelief, she threw open the closet door.

Luc inhaled sharply, positive he'd never seen a more appealing sight in his life. Grace sat there on the floor, Toni clutched to her breast. Wispy golden curls framed her sleep-flushed face. She blinked up at them, her light green eyes soft and drowsy. Clearly, she'd just woken up.

"You make your wife and niece live in a closet?" Miss Carstairs demanded, turning on him.

Luc released a gusty sigh. "My father doesn't know about Toni. For that matter, he doesn't know that Grace and I are married. We…eloped while he was still in Italy. And until I tell him…"

"Your wife and niece will be kept hidden away in the closet?" the social worker suggested dryly.

"We'll use the bathroom next time," Grace offered. "Would that be all right?"

"Perhaps it would be best if you told him the truth," Miss Carstairs said in no uncertain terms. "I suppose that also explains the rather…unusual greeting at the door."

A hint of amusement lightened Luc's expression. "I'm

sorry. I didn't want to introduce you to my father. He'd already assumed the worst as far as your presence was concerned, and I just went along with it. I apologize, if I offended you.''

Color spotted Miss Carstairs's cheeks and Grace could tell that the infamous Salvatore charm was working its magic once more. ''This is all highly irregular,'' the young woman muttered.

''How about if we start over,'' Luc suggested. ''Come on into the kitchen and have a cup of coffee, and then we'll show you around and answer any questions you might have. Coffee, Grace?''

''Sounds great,'' she agreed.

''And a bottle for Toni, I think.''

Once again Luc would talk his way out of a sticky situation, Grace mused. How she wished she had his gift. Little did she know that such a gift would have certainly come in handy over the next few days....

LIFTING THE BABY out of the crib the next morning, Grace headed for the kitchen, when a peremptory knock sounded at the door. Later, she realized she should have peered through the spy hole first. But at the time, she didn't think twice. She opened the door.

Dom Salvatore stood there.

He looked appalled, and for an instant she thought he'd burst into tears. Then he slowly followed her into the apartment. ''All my plans...ruined,'' he moaned.

''It's not so bad,'' she attempted to reassure him, wondering desperately which story to tell. Did she mention Pietro and Carina? Did she claim Toni as her own? Lord, how she wished Luc was here to help. He had already left for work.

To her relief, Toni came to the rescue. Reacting to the heightened emotions, her face screwed into a frown and she began to cry. ''Oh, dear,'' Grace said, ''I think we'd better get busy with that bottle.''

''Please wait.'' For a long minute Dom stared at Toni,

uncertainty clouding his face. Grace could see his quandary, his delight at the possibility of a grandchild warring with his outrage at the circumstances behind that grandchild's conception. Then his hands inched out and he took the wailing baby into his arms. He jiggled Toni gently and when she stopped crying, he beamed. ''And who have we here?''

''This is your granddaughter, Antonia,'' Grace said simply.

A look of wonder dawned on his face. ''A granddaughter,'' he murmured in astonishment. ''But…this is marvelous. How old is she?''

Grace's gaze slipped away from his. ''Three months.''

He gaped at Grace. ''Three…'' He burst into volatile Italian, stabbing the air with his free hand. She didn't understand a single word he spoke, but she knew exactly what he said. In order for her to have given birth to Toni, she would have had to tumble into Luc's bed her first day on the job. At long last, he drew breath. *''Three months!''* he exclaimed.

What possible explanation could she give that would appease him? ''The disguise didn't work,'' she said, her face burning with humiliation.

''Not even for a single day?''

''Not really. Luc's not an easy man to fool.''

Dom clicked his tongue. ''But a girl with such an impeccable background. Could you not resist him?''

''He's hard to resist,'' she confessed.

''But still…'' He seemed to be searching for a reasonable explanation. ''I thought starting your own business was important to you. I thought that, if nothing else, such an agreement would keep you from my son's arms.'' He shook his head and released a deep, heartfelt sigh. ''You must love Luciano very much, to give up your dream.''

To her dismay, tears welled in her eyes. ''Starting Baby Dream Toys meant more to me than anything. I wanted to keep our agreement. I really did. Please believe I tried. I wore the disguise and pretended to be engaged. But, Luc… He…

I...'' Her throat closed over and helplessly, she bowed her head.

"I am sorry, my dear. I did not mean to upset you." He stroked Toni's head with a gentle hand. Then, he looked up, pinning her with a reluctant, though stern gaze. "I must tell you I am very disappointed in you both. It is my deepest hope that you and Luc have taken proper responsibility for your unthinking actions. As much as this grandchild means to me, as much as my son means to me, I would throw you out of the family if I thought you had not." He paused, waiting for her response.

Grace swallowed, realizing she was treading on very shaky ground. "You'd throw us out of the family if we hadn't... what?" she asked hesitantly.

"Married, of course! You are wed, yes?"

A footstep sounded behind her. And then, "Of course, we're married, Dad," Luc announced from the doorway.

Grace spun around, her eyes widening in horror. Without any question, he'd overheard every word of their conversation. And he was *furious*.

"What are you doing here, Dad?" He spoke in a deceptively mild voice. "I thought we agreed to meet at the office."

"So we did," Dom agreed, not seeming to notice anything amiss. He set the bottle on the table and lifted Toni to his shoulder, patting her back. "It occurred to me we might drive into work together." He fixed his calm, dark gaze on Luc. "You forgot to tell me something, yes?"

Luc hesitated, then asked, "If I had told you, what would you have done?"

"I would have come home," came the prompt response.

"There's your answer. The doctors wanted you to retire. You know you wouldn't have, if you'd returned early from Italy."

"Bah! Doctors. What do they know? I am strong as a horse."

"A sixty-five-year-old horse with a heart condition."

Dom stirred uncomfortably. "I wish to talk about Grace and this situation we now find ourselves in, not about my health. You uncovered the truth about her, I am right?"

Luc leaned back against the counter and sipped his coffee. For a split second his gaze locked with hers. She froze, held in place by the icy fury she read there. "Uncovered the truth about her disguise and the fake engagement? Yes. I uncovered that much." But not about his father's bribe. Grace caught the omission. Not about his starting her up in business.

And Luc's expression warned he wouldn't easily forgive that exclusion.

Betraying his nervousness, Dom ran a hand along his jaw. "You…ah…you are not upset with me?"

"Should I be?"

Dom stiffened. "Is this why you did not tell me about Antonia? You were angered that we deceived you?"

Luc's expression softened. "*No, Papa.* I wouldn't do that. I've explained why I didn't notify you. You needed to get away from Salvatore Enterprises. This past year has allowed you time to recuperate and me time to take control of the business."

"Then, it was good I hired Grace. She has helped you focus on your work."

Grace winced, waiting for Luc's tenuous control of his temper finally to snap. "You didn't need to involve someone else," Luc bit out, slamming his coffee mug to the counter. "You should have trusted me to take care of the work situation without interfering."

"Perhaps." Dom shrugged, not in the least intimidated by his son's wrath. "But I wished to ensure you would have a full year to concentrate on work and not be subjected to…irresistible temptations." He glanced at Grace and smiled apologetically. "This will not be a problem anymore, eh? Once a Salvatore falls in love and marries, it is for life. The eyes, they become blind to every other woman."

It was all Grace could do not to weep. How she wanted

that to be true. She had come to love Luc, whereas he simply needed her; for him, she was merely a means to an end. He was attracted to her, sure, but that attraction would surely fizzle when their enforced togetherness ended....

"Would you excuse us?" she murmured, scooping Toni into her arms. "I think it's time we got dressed."

Twenty minutes later Grace returned with Toni, in time to bid Dom farewell. She stood next to Luc and smiled calmly, striving to appear the perfect wife. The minute his father disappeared down the hallway, Luc turned on her.

"Every damned word out of your mouth has been a lie, hasn't it?" he snarled, kicking the door shut. It bounced back ajar, but he ignored it, stalking after her.

"Not every word." She backed toward the living room, clutching Toni to her breast like a shield. Realizing she couldn't continue to hide behind a baby, she spread a blanket on the floor and set Toni on it. Then she turned to face Luc. "Besides," she said, refusing to be intimidated by his fury. "What about all *your* lies?"

"I lied to protect the baby," he was quick to defend. "They were necessary lies."

She lifted her chin. "They're still lies. As far as protecting the baby... Haven't I done everything possible to help you since Toni arrived? Haven't I lied to the police and to the social-service people, in order to cover for Pietro and Carina? And for what? For you! What more do you want from me? I even lied to your father. And that cost me the chance to start my own business."

Luc thrust his hands into his trouser pockets, a muscle leaping in his jaw. "Explain it to me. The deal you had with Dad."

"You already know most of it."

He paced in front of her. "I sure as hell didn't know you were in cahoots with my father."

"That's the only fact you didn't have. You knew about the disguise, the fake engagement..."

He nailed her with a disbelieving look. "And my *father* put you up to it?"

Reluctantly, she nodded. "He seemed to think it was the only way he could retire. All your employees kept falling in love with you and making a mess of the office situation. He thought I'd be different."

"Why?"

She shrugged. "He thought I'd be more levelheaded, that with the disguise and the engagement ring, you'd keep your distance—and because of his offer, I'd keep mine."

"Ah, yes. The offer." A cynical note colored his words. "A business of your own, wasn't it?"

"Yes," she confirmed. "When we met during the young-entrepreneur's contest, Dom realized I was desperate to open my own store and offered a deal. If I'd work for you for one year—keep our relationship strictly professional, no personal involvement—he'd finance Baby Dream Toys."

"Desperate?" He seized on the word, his eyes narrowing. "Why were you so desperate to start your own business?"

The question hung between them. "Because of my mother," she said at last.

He stilled, watching her closely. "Your mother?"

Grace bowed her head. "We were going to start the business together. We dreamed about it, planned it. She used to make the most beautiful stuffed animals. She'd call them her 'baby dreams.' That's where the name for the store came from."

"What happened, *cara?*" he asked gently.

"She died right before the contest." Grace's voice broke and she buried her hands in her face. "I wanted to open the store so much, to name it in her honor. It was wrong to deceive you, I know that. But at the time…all I could think of…" She shook her head, fighting for control.

"Why didn't you tell me?" he demanded. "When all the other deceptions were uncovered, why didn't you come clean? Didn't you think I'd understand?"

She crumpled his handkerchief in her fist. "You had all

these wonderful, generous excuses for why I'd deceived you. But they weren't true. I knew when you found out my motivation was greed, you'd hate me. I'm sorry,'' she said, choking on the words.

He groaned, the sound low and rough. "*Cara*, don't. Don't cry. Of course I don't hate you." Crossing to her side, he swept her into his arms. Gently, he pushed her hair from her face and forced her to look at him. "Dad was right about one thing. If it hadn't been for that damned engagement ring, I wouldn't have been able to keep my hands off you."

He kissed her with an urgency she couldn't mistake, sweeping her into a firestorm of desperate need. She didn't resist. The thought never entered her mind. She loved Luc and she wanted him....

"*Grace!*" An appalled masculine voice spoke from the doorway to the living room.

"Oh, criminey!"

Luc glanced down at her, then over his shoulder at the man and woman hovering just inside the living room. "Who the hell are you?" he demanded. "And what are you doing in my apartment?"

"Dear Lord!" The man continued to stare in shock. "I'm...I'm Reverend—"

"I'm Miss Caruthers with child protective services," the woman interrupted, pushing past the reverend and stepping boldly forward. She brandished her clipboard like a sword. "I'm your case manager."

"No. You're not," Luc contradicted. "Miss Carstairs is our case manager."

"Not anymore. I've taken over. Her report was so strange—closets and elopements and so forth—"

"You want to tell me how you got in here?" Luc demanded.

"The door was open," the reverend replied in an apologetic voice. "Would you mind telling me what elopement this woman is talking about? And what baby?"

Grace grabbed Luc's arm, as if to physically restrain him. "Don't say it..." she whimpered—to no avail.

"My elopement," Luc announced. "And Grace's elopement."

"You're *married?*" the reverend gasped. "Oh, good heavens."

"Yes, we're married," Luc confirmed.

"No, no!" Grace denied. "You don't understand. Just give me a minute to explain!"

Miss Caruthers began scribbling madly and Toni, fed up with being neglected, began to cry. Grace gave serious consideration to crying, as well.

The minister's gaze seemed drawn to Toni like a magnet. The baby stopped crying and stared, as if even she realized something important was going on. "You have a *baby?*" he whispered in disbelief.

"No!" Grace shouted.

"Maybe!" Luc shouted louder. "It depends on who you are."

"*Grace!*" the minister exclaimed, clearly shocked.

She shut her eyes. "I'm...I'm sorry." Peeking at Luc, she said, "Did I ever mention that my father is a Methodist minister?"

"No," he replied dryly. "I don't believe you did. Let me guess. This is him, right?"

"Bingo."

"I should warn you that if you aren't married, there will be dire repercussions," Miss Caruthers announced. "Now are you or are you not married?"

Luc sighed, then forced a smile to his lips. "Now, Miss Caruthers," he began.

The social worker stumbled backward. "Get away from me, you...you...devil! We'll see what Mrs. Cuthbert has to say about all this. She's my superior. And I guarantee she won't be pleased!" Spinning around, she scurried form the room. A minute later, the front door slammed.

With deep dread, Grace glanced at her father. "I bet you're wondering what's going on," she said with a hesitant smile.

"I think what's going on here is painfully obvious," Reverend Barnes said, with more than a touch of irony. "But introductions are in order first, don't you think?" He looked pointedly at Luc, who stepped forward.

"Luc Salvatore, Reverend Barnes," he said, holding out his hand. "It's a pleasure to meet you."

"Under other circumstances, I might agree with you," the minister replied, shaking hands.

"I'm sorry about that," Luc said, though his gaze remained direct and unrepentant.

"You're Grace's employer, aren't you?"

"Yes, she's been with me for almost a year."

"And is she also your wife?"

Luc shook his head. "No. Not yet."

"You're certain? There seemed to be some doubt a few minutes ago."

"I'm positive."

"We're not married, Dad," Grace informed him quietly, though Luc's use of the word "yet" had thrown her. He couldn't possibly mean what she thought he meant by that, could he?

Her father glanced at her, a concerned frown lining his brow. "Considering what was going on here a few minutes ago, I'm not sure whether to be relieved or dismayed. What about the baby? Whose is it?"

"Toni is my niece," Luc said. "Grace is staying with me to help with baby-sitting duties. And for the record, our relationship has been regrettably innocent, save for a few kisses."

"Thank heavens," Reverend Barnes murmured, his relief palpable.

Before Grace could manage to insert a single word, Luc added, "You should also know that we applied for a marriage license last week."

Grace closed her eyes and groaned.

Reverend Barnes glanced from one to the other. "You're engaged?"

Grace glared at Luc, who merely smiled.

"Yes," she muttered, "I agreed to marry him."

Her father's eyes narrowed. "I'm beginning to realize there's a whole lot about this situation that I don't know," he said. "Nor am I sure I want to know. In fact, I'm positive I don't want to know. I'd like to make a suggestion if I may..." Reverend Barnes announced in a determined voice.

"You want me to make an honest woman out of her, is that it?" Luc guessed.

"Yes, I do. Assuming you love my daughter." He clasped his hands together, the gesture betraying a certain level of nervousness. "Well, do you?"

After a brief hesitation, Luc nodded. "Yes, I love her."

Satisfied, Reverend Barnes relaxed and turned to Grace, his gaze less severe. "I know you're ready, willing and able to marry this man. You wouldn't have allowed...er...matters to progress so far today if you weren't in love with him. Am I right?"

"Yes, Dad," she whispered. Luc may have been lying for her father's sake—and for Toni's sake—but in her case it was true, and she was prepared to marry him, whatever the consequences.

"Very well, we'll begin." He settled his bifocals on the end of his nose. "Dearly beloved—"

Just then, Dom hustled into the room. "Luc, I forgot to tell you—" He stopped cold. "What is going on?" he demanded. He regarded Luc and Grace with a hurt expression. "Why did you tell me you were married when you were not?"

Luc sighed. "You know why."

Dom nodded grimly. "Because I would have thrown you out of the family if I had known you had a baby with Grace without benefit of a wedding ring. I still might."

"*What?*" Reverend Barnes stared at them in shock. His

gaze slid to Toni, kicking and gurgling on the blanket. "She's...she's your baby, Grace?"

"No!" She covered her face with her hands. "Dad, could you finish the ceremony? Please? I promise I'll explain everything then."

"I think you'd better explain everything now."

A loud, determined banging resounded through the apartment, and Grace ran to the door. Luc threw his hands into the air. "That's it. Who the hell's left to barge in here? Wait a minute. What about the police? They haven't shown up yet. In fact, they're the only ones who haven't."

"I came in their place," a tall, stunning brunette announced from the doorway. "Cynthia Cuthbert, social services." She smiled at the horrified gathering, her gaze shifting slowly to Luc and Grace. "Hello, Luc. It's been a long time."

If the identity of their latest visitor came as a surprise, Luc didn't show it. "Not long enough," he said dryly. "Hello, Cynthia."

Cynthia, thought Grace. The one woman Luc's brothers had said he couldn't charm.

The social worker glided across the room. "You must be Grace," she said, offering her hand. She lifted an eyebrow. "Am I interrupting something?"

"You know damned well you are!" Luc spoke up.

"If this little event has been staged for Antonia's benefit, I'm afraid you're too late. The jig is up." She planted her hands on her hips and fixed Luc with an annoyed glare. "You lied, Luc. You told the department the two of you were already married. Ms. Cartwright warned you of the consequences if you told any more lies, and you ignored her warning."

"Um...excuse me," Reverend Barnes interrupted. "I'm very confused. Exactly whose baby is this, and why are you trying to take her away?"

"This I would like to know, too," Dom chimed in, folding his arms across his chest.

"She's *my* daughter," a voice spoke from behind them. "And no one's going to take her away. Not if I have anything to say about it."

Everyone turned. "Pietro!" Grace exclaimed in delight. "You're back."

"Back..." He held out Carina's hand. A diamond-encrusted wedding band decorated her third finger. "And married. Everyone, my wife, Carina Donati...Salvatore."

"Antonia is Pietro's?" Dom questioned in confusion. "*Per dio!* Am I told nothing anymore?"

Spying her daughter, Carina wrenched her hand free of Pietro's and darted across the room, snatching the baby up from the blanket. "Toni!" she cried, bursting into noisy sobs.

It took close to an hour to straighten everything out. To Grace's secret amusement, Pietro proved to be the one capable of charming the uncharmable Cynthia. By the time she left, he'd managed to straighten out most of their problems and had set up an appointment to settle any final questions.

Grace stood quietly by her father, grateful for the supportive arm he'd wrapped around her. She watched the happy reunion with a calm facade she hoped concealed her inner turmoil. *Luc didn't need to marry her anymore.* If she left now, she could do so with some dignity. A few minutes longer and she'd break down. She glanced up at her father. "I guess there's no more reason for the wedding," she told him quietly.

He covered her hand with his. "I'm sorry, Grace."

She blinked back tears. Obviously, he understood far more than she'd realized. Was her love for Luc so apparent? "Let's go, Dad."

"You're not going anywhere." Luc moved to stand in front of her, blocking her escape.

"Luc, don't," she pleaded. "Toni is safe now. You don't have to sacrifice yourself. There's no point."

"You're right. There is no point. Except this." He took her hand in his. "I want to marry you, *cara mia.*"

Tears shimmered in her eyes. "I love you, Luc."

"Bellissima mia," he murmured. "Haven't I told you how much I love you? You're the only woman I see anymore. You've made me blind to all others. Awake or asleep, I see only your face, hear only your voice. The air I breathe is filled with your scent." He held out his hand. "Will you marry me?"

"Try and stop me," she said with a huge smile, and slipped her fingers in his.

Luc turned to Reverend Barnes. "From the top, Reverend. And this time...don't skip a single word."

And he didn't.

ONE-NIGHT WIFE

Day Leclaire

"Anna. Anna, wake up."

The voice was stark, demanding. She attempted to shake her head. Pain—immediate and cute—stopped her and she held very, very still. "Chris…" She managed to gasp the word, though she didn't quite know why she said it.

He bent over her, so close he eclipsed all else. "Who's Chris?" he asked sharply.

She couldn't answer. The throbbing grew worse, the pain in her head driving out every other thought. Her hand fluttered weakly upward to investigate. But he stopped her, catching her fingers in his and squeezing gently.

"Don't," he warned. "You've injured your head. It's bandaged. But you're all right now. You're safe."

"Who are you?" The question exhausted her and her lids drifted closed.

"It's Sebastian. Your husband."

She fought to gather strength enough to protest, but it was impossible. With a sigh, she gave up the battle, the words dying on her lips…*I don't have a husband!*

WHEN SHE REGAINED consciousness, the pain had subsided and she felt much stronger. A paper rustled, catching her attention, and she turned her head toward the sound. Sebastian sat in a chair at her side, engrossed in a copy of *The Wall Street Journal.*

She studied him curiously. Thick black hair curled about a toughly hewn face—a face well accustomed to the sun and salt air. A nearly invisible scar slashed a silvery path from the corner of his right eye to the top of his lip, marring otherwise perfect features.

She frowned. No. Not marring. The scar lent character,

offered enticing fantasies of pirates and buccaneers and danger.

One thing she knew for certain. She'd never seen this man before in her life.

At that moment, Sebastian slowly lowered the paper, and she found herself gazing into eyes the precise color of a stormy winter sky.

"Anna," he said in a deep, cool voice. "It's good to see you awake. How do you feel?"

Her brow crinkled. He'd called her Anna. Which meant even if she didn't know *him,* he knew *her.* But, Anna? The name felt as alien to her as he did.

"Anna? Are you all right?"

"No, I'm not all right." A torrent of questions pressed for release. Who are you? Why don't I know anything, remember anything? Where am I?" she questioned tautly.

"In a hospital in south Florida. You were injured in a car accident two days ago. You have a concussion. A stitch or two under that bandage. Bruises, scrapes." A muscle jerked in his jaw. "It's a miracle you weren't killed."

"I should know you, shouldn't I?" she said.

"Are you saying you don't?"

"No, I don't." She gathered every ounce of fortitude she possessed, and admitted, "I…I don't even know who I am."

"I'm your husband. Sebastian," he informed her, folding his arms across his chest. "And you're Anna Kane…my wife."

"No! No, that's not possible. I'm not married." She held out her left hand. "See? No rings. Not even a mark."

He made a small sound of annoyance. "I don't know what game you're playing, but you're deluding yourself if you think I'll play along."

"It's not a game," she protested.

"You can't escape the repercussions with this little act." He ran a hand through his hair, irritation edging his words. "Damn it, Anna. What were you thinking? Why did you leave like that? And who the *hell* is Chris?"

She winced at the sudden, stabbing pain in her head. "I don't know any Chris."

His skepticism was unmistakable. "When they first brought you here, you called to him. You must know who he is."

"Well, I don't," she repeated.

"I would have bet my life you'd never resort to deception," he murmured. "But then...the past two days have taught me a lot."

"Please," she said, raising a hand to her brow. The pressure built, her headache returning with a vengeance. "I can't answer your questions. I don't *know* the answers."

"Anna, look at me," he ordered softly. "We can work this out. Just tell me what the problem is."

She stared at him in confusion. "I'm telling you the truth. I don't know you. Why don't you believe me?" The throbbing intensified and she closed her eyes, too exhausted to argue further.

"You're in pain again," he said, standing to leave. "I'll get the doctor."

Almost immediately he returned with the doctor and a nurse.

"This will help you sleep, Mrs. Kane," the doctor informed her, removing a syringe from the tray. "With a few days' rest, I suspect your memory will return. In the meantime, we'll run a few tests, just to be positive nothing's been overlooked." A needle pricked her arm. Instantly she felt an odd floating sensation and her mind began to drift.

"Bring in a specialist," she heard Sebastian order, his voice muffled, as though coming from a long distance. "A neurologist. Money's no object. I want the best."

"Of course, Mr. Kane."

"What about visitors?" the nurse questioned. "There's a gentleman who's been asking to see her."

"Who?" Sebastian demanded. "What's his name?"

"Why...he didn't say."

"No one is permitted in this room without my express

authorization,'' Sebastian stated implacably. ''In the morning I'll make arrangements to move my wife to a private clinic.''

The room began to roll like a ship on a stormy sea. She could still see Sebastian, but he'd changed. His hair brushed his shoulders in thick, tight curls, a red scarf banding his forehead. A thin, linen shirt fell open to his waist, revealing a broad, muscular chest furred with crisp, dark hair. And in his hand he held a pirate's cutlass.

''No,'' she whispered. ''It's not possible.''

In response, Sebastian took a step toward her, his expression full of determination. With a moan, she closed her eyes, allowing the darkness to consume her.

THE NEXT THREE DAYS passed in quick succession, and though she improved physically, her memory didn't return. Sebastian installed her in a small, private clinic, claiming it would enable her to receive the best possible medical care, but she couldn't help wondering if there weren't another reason for the move—like the stranger who had attempted to visit her in the hospital.

It was a disturbing notion.

What little she managed to see of this new facility astonished her with its sheer opulence. She might have been in the most exclusive of hotels instead of a medical facility.

Her days consisted of tests and more tests, her nights filled with boredom. On her fourth day at the clinic Sebastian came into her suite and said, ''It's time we had a talk.''

His announcement didn't surprise her. She'd anticipated the need for this conversation for days now. Sebastian had remained amazingly quiet since her accident, limiting their discussions to the mundane. Waiting, it seemed…for her memory to return? For the doctor to find a physical cause for her amnesia? Or had he deliberately chosen to avoid the subject of their past—and their future—for reasons of his own?

''We could go into the sitting area,'' she suggested.

''There's a central courtyard that offers more privacy.

We'll go there. But first I'll need to get a wheelchair for you.''

She turned to face him. "A wheelchair?" she protested. "Is that really necessary? I feel fine."

"The administration insists on it for safety reasons. I'll be back in a few minutes."

He left her then and she went into the bathroom to brush her hair. Now that the moment had come, she wasn't certain she wanted to hear what he had to say. She couldn't escape the instinctive sense that something was out of kilter. That feeling of "wrongness" had returned full force.

She heard movement in the bedroom, and assuming Sebastian had returned, started to open the bathroom door. Two staff workers were busy making her bed, talking quietly. Anna froze as she realized just what they were discussing.

"Are you sure? He hired a private investigator?" one questioned skeptically. "Why would he do that?"

"Probably because he doesn't believe she has amnesia any more than the doctors do. And I get the feeling there was something very odd about that accident of hers."

"Well, he obviously doesn't trust her. Why else would he have standing orders that she isn't to leave the room unattended? I think it's to make sure she doesn't run off."

"That would explain why she isn't allowed any visitors. Maybe she has a secret lover he's trying to keep her from."

The other laughed, moving toward the door. And with that, they were gone.

Dear Lord, what was going on? Anna covered her mouth with her hand, all her earlier doubts returning with a vengeance. *Calm down!* she ordered sternly. There was some mystery surrounding her accident, that much was clear, as well as concern about the stranger who'd attempted to contact her in the hospital. All she had to do was ask Sebastian. Ask him flat out about their past…about the accident.

"Anna?" Sebastian called, pushing a wheelchair into the room. "Are you ready?"

She took a deep breath. "Yes, I'm ready."

Sebastian wheeled her to a large arboretum and parked the chair by the entrance. "Let's walk."

They wandered down various pathways where little nooks with benches were set among the brilliant flowering plants and bushes.

"What's wrong?" he asked, breaking the silence between them.

"You mean…aside from the fact that I have amnesia and the man who claims to be my husband is a complete stranger to me?"

"Perhaps we could find some way to refresh your memory," he murmured. "Something the doctors might not have considered."

She pulled back, suspecting she knew what he had in mind. "I don't think so," she said. "We're here to talk, remember?"

"And we will." He eased her into his arms, slipping her into the cradle of his hips. "But first things first."

Without giving her time to draw breath, let alone argue, he lowered his head and brushed her mouth with his. It was a fleeting caress, nothing that should have stirred the fierce, primitive reaction that swept through her.

She broke free of his hold and turned away. "You aren't going to resolve my doubts by seducing me. Can't you understand? I have no way of knowing whether or not we're really married."

"You have my word."

"Perhaps that's not enough," she said quietly, the conversation she'd overheard underscoring her reservations.

His fingers brushed her lips before tracing the long, graceful curve of her neck. "If it's all a fabrication, then why does your body react to mine with such heat? I can feel your pulse pounding beneath my hand. Your body remembers me, even if you don't."

"That isn't desire," she claimed, struggling to rationalize her response. "I'm angry, not excited."

A faint laugh escaped him. "You're fooling yourself, if that's what you believe."

She took a deep breath. "You say we're married, but for some reason it feels...wrong."

A muscle jerked in his cheek. "You are my wife, and by heaven, it's time you remembered that much, at least." He slid his hands down her spine and brought her close. "Perhaps this will help recover your memory."

She knew what he intended, could read it in the resolute lines marking his expression. "Sebastian, please! This isn't necessary."

His mouth firmed. "I think it's very necessary."

His lips stole over hers with a sensuality that caught her completely off guard, lingering, teasing. With a soft moan of surrender, her head fell back and her lips parted beneath the persuasive pressure of his. He took instant advantage, kissing her with a depth and passion that stripped her of all defenses. It was as though he intended to stamp her with his possession so thoroughly, she'd never again forget she'd known his embrace.

"Do you still have doubts about who I am?" he muttered against her mouth. "Does your response tell you nothing?"

"Sebastian... Please, don't do this to me. Not now. Not like this. Not when I'm so confused."

"You will remember me, Anna," he told her with unmistakable tenderness. "I swear by all I hold dear, I'll find a way to get through to you."

"Why are you pushing this?"

"I want my wife back, the Anna I knew before."

Her hands clenched at her sides. "I don't know who or what that Anna is!"

"Don't you?"

So there it was. The first open expression of his disbelief. She'd begun to suspect he doubted her. Here, finally, was the proof. "You don't believe I have amnesia, do you?"

He hesitated. "The possibility that you're faking has crossed my mind."

"Why in the world would I fake something like that? It's ridiculous. Unless… There's something you haven't told me, isn't there? What is it? Was our marriage unhappy?"

"Interesting that you'd leap to that particular conclusion. Why is that, I wonder?"

She clasped her hands together, almost pleading with him. "If you believe I'm faking, there has to be a reason. So, tell me. Was I unhappy with you?"

But he wouldn't relent. His hands closed about her upper arms and he drew her close. "Judge for yourself. You know how it felt to be in my arms. You trembled when I kissed you, came alive beneath my hands. Can you honestly suspect you were dissatisfied as my wife?"

"I don't know." His hands tightened, warning that he wouldn't let her get away with such a vague response. She sighed. "All right, no. I probably wasn't dissatisfied. At least not that way. But you still haven't answered my question. Was I unhappy? Was I planning to leave you?"

"Leave me? Now, why would you think that?"

"Because there must be something," she insisted in frustration. "Some reason to explain—"

"You're chasing shadows."

"Am I?" She searched his face. "Then why did you check me out of the hospital and bring me to this clinic? Explain why I'm not allowed to leave my room unescorted. And tell me why you hired a detective to investigate the crash."

"Where did you hear that?" he demanded.

"Is it true?"

He released her and moved away with lazy grace, a coolness frosting his voice. "Yes. It's true."

"You checked me out of the hospital because some man tried to get in to see me. Who was he?"

Sebastian shrugged. "I don't know. A reporter, I suppose. But I wasn't going to take any chances. I'm a wealthy man. And like it or not, you have to pay the price of that wealth, just as I do. Which means taking advantage of the security this clinic affords and tolerating the occasional escort if I feel the situation warrants it.''

"And this situation warrants it?"

"Until you regain your memory…yes."

"Assuming I've actually lost my memory," she reminded dryly. "And the detective?"

"I hired him as a precaution. He'll investigate the crash to make sure nothing is overlooked."

It made perfect sense. She wanted to believe him, to give herself into his care without hesitation or reserve. The attraction between them couldn't be denied. But something held her back. And until she discovered the reason for her misgivings she'd proceed with caution.

She lifted a skeptical eyebrow.

"Then tell me, Sebastian. If we truly loved each other, how could I forget you?" she asked, bringing into the open the issue that had been bothering her most of all. "How is that possible?"

He turned sharply. "Perhaps," he stated with cold finality, "you never loved me. Perhaps you found me easy to forget. Whatever the reason, we will get to the truth, you can count on it."

She fought to speak past the thickness blocking her throat. "And how will we do that?"

"By going home, of course."

Home. The word should have brought a sense of reassurance. It didn't. "Home? Where is that?"

"In the Caribbean. To be precise, it's on a small island called *Rochefort*…Strong Rock."

"When do we leave?"

"Tomorrow. The doctors advise against flying, so we'll go by boat. It shouldn't take more than a week…"

With an urgency born of a sudden, inexplicable apprehension, she scrambled for an alternative. "Can't…can't we stay here?"

"There's no point in remaining in Florida. The doctors advised that the best chance you have of regaining your memory is at home. And that's where I'm taking you—willing or not.''

She caught her breath, recalling the strange hallucination she'd had while in the hospital. Sebastian on the deck of a ship, the wind lifting the unruly mane of thick black curls, his cutlass half raised, as though ready for action.

She knew an odd sense of helplessness. Like that buccaneer of old, he'd swept into her life and planned to steal her away. She had no rights, no choice. She was his booty, his plunder, and he intended to take what he wanted.

She drew herself up. ''You're taking me, willing or not?'' she repeated. ''I think you've been living in the Caribbean too long. That sounds like the threat of a pirate.''

To her surprise, he grinned, his teeth a flash of white in a bronzed face. ''A pirate?'' he repeated, his dark eyebrow winging upward. ''You've given yourself away with that one, my love.''

She stiffened. ''What do you mean?''

''I mean, you're right. I *am* a pirate...'' His smile faded. ''As you damned well know.''

TO ANNA'S DISMAY, Sebastian left with those words still ringing in her ears. She scarcely heard the arrangements he made to pick her up the next morning. All her focus remained on his statement: ''I *am* a pirate... As you damned well know.''

What did he mean by that? Was it possible...could he be a *real* pirate? She shook her head. No. The very thought was ludicrous.

Throughout the long, endless night, she considered her options, and realized she had only one. For the time being, she'd have to follow where Sebastian led, be his wife in name—and in name only—until her memory returned and she discovered the truth. The truth about her past, her marriage...but especially the truth about her husband.

All too soon morning arrived, and with the coming of the

dawn, came Sebastian. He strode into the room, a force as powerful and elemental as nature itself.

"Shall we go?" His hand curved around her arm, and he lead her to his car, a sleek black Range Rover. He opened the door for her and helped her climb in.

"Fasten your seat belt," he requested, and started the engine.

She complied, shooting him a troubled look. "Wasn't I wearing one when...?" She couldn't finish the question, flinching from the mere suggestion.

"Yes, you were." He turned the key, the Range Rover coming to life with a muted roar. "According to the rescue crew, it saved your life."

"Was I driving?"

"You were alone in the car when you were found."

"Tell me what happened."

"It was raining. The roads were slick. The car took a curve at too high a speed and didn't make it. End of story."

But it wasn't. She couldn't shake the overwhelming impression that he kept some vital detail from her.

"Where were you?"

"At a nearby hotel. We'd come to Florida on business."

That caught her by surprise. "What sort of business?"

"I design small private aircraft. The police arrived at the hotel to inform me of the accident."

Her brows drew together in confusion. "They knew how to get in touch with you? You're that well-known?"

"Yes."

No hesitation, no equivocation. Just a flat, cool confirmation. No wonder he'd been so impatient with her doubts about their marriage. Rich, famous... If he were that renowned, what in the world had he seen in her?

The questions poured out, fast and furious. "How did we meet?"

"You worked for me."

"And we fell in love. Just like that?"

"I'd say that about sums it up."

"Did we know each other for long before we married?"

"About six months."

She turned to study him. "That's hardly any time at all," she observed.

"Now that's one of the few things you've said that I agree with." A wry smile touched his mouth. "Put your head back Anna, close your eyes and relax. We still have an hour's drive ahead of us."

"But, I have more questions."

"And I'll answer them. But give it a rest for now."

As much as she hated to admit it, he offered sound advice. She stifled a yawn. She was tired. Very tired. A restless night worrying about returning "home" combined with several days' worth of stress caught up with her and sleep finally claimed her.

She dreamt....

She rode in a car, arguing heatedly with someone. But she couldn't hear the words, nor see whom she spoke to. When she looked back out the windshield, the total darkness disoriented her. And then the sky lit up and she realized too late that the road ahead turned.

"Look out!" she shrieked, coming bolt upright.

The Range Rover swerved violently, then skidded to a halt on the shoulder of the road. "What the *hell* is the matter with you?" Sebastian bit out. "Why did you scream like that?"

"I'm sorry! I didn't mean to." Anna covered her face, her hands trembling uncontrollably.

With a soft curse, he thrust open his door and exited, circling the vehicle to the passenger side. In a matter of seconds he had her free of her seat and wrapped in his arms. He held her for several long minutes, letting her cry it out.

His knuckle slipped beneath her chin and he tilted her face upward, gazing down at her in concern. "What happened?"

"I'm not sure. I was dreaming. I think I remembered the accident," she said, struggling to summon the disjointed images. "I think I was angry, but I'm not certain why. I remember looking out of the windshield and everything was pitch black. Then the sky lit up and I saw that the road ahead curved and...and..." She shook her head, unable to continue.

To her relief, he didn't press. He pulled her close, holding her within the hard, protective strength of his arms. "It's okay, Anna. Let it go," he murmured.

She offered a shaky smile. "Perhaps my memory is returning."

"Looks like it." He glanced at the Range Rover. "Can you handle getting back in the car?"

Her laugh sounded watery. "Without falling to pieces, you mean? I think so."

Determined to erase all traces of tears, she reached in the back for her tote, removing the bag of cosmetics.

To her relief, they arrived at a pretty little harbor just as she capped her lipstick. Sebastian parked and, grabbing her tote from the back, guided her along the quay.

"Through here," Sebastian said, unlocking a gate that lead onto a private dock.

She stopped dead, indicated the sleek powerboat secured to the cleats a few feet away. "We're going to your island in that? Looks like fun, but sleeping may be a problem."

An odd smile touched his mouth. "No. We're going in *that.*"

She looked where he pointed and froze, her brows pulling together. *That* was a huge boat anchored offshore. No. More like a ship. The *QE III*, perhaps? "You own it?" she questioned in disbelief.

"Yes."

She shook her head. "No. No way."

"What's wrong now?"

How could she explain. How could she possibly put into words what she felt? She didn't belong to this world. She knew it with an instinctive certainty. Nothing about this situation was the least bit familiar or comfortable.

"I know there's something very wrong with our relationship. And it has to do with that night, doesn't it? You're so desperate to get me on that boat and to your island because you'll have me on your home turf, beneath your control.''

"Anna, you have to trust me. I swear on everything I hold dear, I'd never do anything to hurt you."

"Then why won't you tell me the truth?" she cried.

"The truth is something we'll have to discover together. "Don't fight me over this. You'll only wear yourself out resisting the inevitable."

"Resisting the inevitable? You mean resist being abducted by a pirate," she shot back.

"Abducted?" He had the audacity to laugh. "Does it appeal to the romantic in you? Shall I indulge your fantasies?"

"No!"

Before she could ward him off, he swept her into his arms. With a dangerous smile, he leapt with catlike grace into the boat, depositing her stunned and breathless into the passenger seat. Her heart raced, her body felt hot and aroused.

He stood above her, tall and indomitable, more in his element than she'd ever seen him. "You play this game very well, Anna. But you won't win. You'll slip up. And when you do, I'll have the truth from you."

She stirred nervously. "Why does that sound like a threat?"

"Because it is," he stated with a directness that stunned her. "But until then, there's one final detail to take care of." He thrust his hand into his pocket and pulled out a small jeweler's box. "Your wedding rings."

Anna stared at the bands tucked into the folds of white velvet, the blood draining from her face. The diamonds caught the sunlight, shooting off sparks of multicolored fire. Time froze and in her mind's eye, she saw those very same rings. Only the light catching in the diamonds was different—harsher, whiter, striking off them as they tumbled over and over through the air. She dragged her gaze from the mesmerizing sparkle, struggling to free herself from the painful flash of memory. "Where...where did those come from?" she whispered.

"I gave them to you. On our wedding day." His eyes narrowed. "Do you remember them? Do they mean something to you?"

She held up a hand. "Please. Keep them. I'll...I'll wear them when I get to your island."

"Oh, no, my sweet." He caught her hand in his. Removing the rings from the box, he slipped them onto her finger. They fit perfectly. "They stay there, do you understand?"

"Why?" she cried, pulling free of his hold. "What difference can it possibly make? Either we're married or we're not. This doesn't change a thing."

"In the hospital, you said we couldn't be married because you wore no rings, because there wasn't a mark on your finger to indicate you'd ever worn them. Well, the rings are now on your hand. And, by heaven, there will be a mark on your finger by the time you reach *Rochefort*."

She lifted her chin. "And if there isn't?"

"There will be," he said, refusing to back down. "I hope we understand each other."

THE NEXT FOUR DAYS blended one into another, the intense sun and incredible blue ocean a constant delight. Anna fell in love with the boat, finding the subtle blend of old and new of immense appeal. To her surprise, Sebastian kept his distance, focusing on paperwork and rarely leaving his private quarters.

It should have been perfect.

For some reason, it wasn't.

With each day that passed her apprehension increased as she waited to see if *this* would be the day he came to her.

"Excuse me, Mrs. Kane."

A crewman approached, and she waited anxiously to hear what he had to tell her. She'd soon discovered the only time they disturbed her was if they had a message form Sebastian. "Yes, Josie. What is it?"

The crewman touched his cap with a thumb and forefinger. "Mr. Kane wanted you to know that we're approaching

Rochefort. A speedboat will be here within the hour to take you to the island.''

"Thank you." She stood at the rail and stared in equal parts wonder and alarm at the dark rocky island they rapidly approached. It thrust out of the sea, an odd mist clinging to the upper peaks and along the convoluted folds of the landscape. As they motored closer the lushness of the forest became more apparent, the mountainside seeming to rise straight up out of the heaving ocean, without beach or break. It looked hard and secluded and untamed.

Like Sebastian.

SEBASTIAN WAS WAITING for her in the speedboat. "Do you think you can climb down the ladder?" he called up to her with a wicked grin. "I'll catch you if you fall."

She hesitated, then nodded, waiting for a crewman to assist her. It seemed an impossibly long way, but she climbed down, rung by rung until he fastened strong hands about her waist.

She tumbled into his arms, clinging to him as though he were her sole lifeline.

He searched her face, his gaze probing. "I expected you to look rested."

"It's hard to relax when everything is so uncertain."

"Your memory...?"

Unbidden, tears drenched her eyes and she swiftly turned her head, cursing herself for her momentary weakness. "It's still a blank."

He didn't comment, simply nodded. "In that case, have a seat, and I'll give you the grand tour."

"I'd like that." She fumbled in her skirt pocket for a pair of sunglasses to hide behind, suspecting it was too little, too late. Sebastian had already seen far more than she cared to reveal.

Turning the wheel, he opened the throttle wide, the speedboat slicing through the waves as it moved away from the yacht. He pointed toward a low section of the island and a cluster of small houses and buildings. "Only a couple of hundred people make their homes on *Rochefort*. Most live in the town that surrounds the harbor.

The boat began to skirt the harbor and she glanced at him in confusion. "Don't we land at the village?"

He shook his head, the wind tossing back his thick black hair, intensifying his roguish appearance. "You'll see."

They circled the island, and when they were on the opposite side from the village, Sebastian headed in toward a sheer rocky cliff. "Hang on!" he shouted above the crash of the waves as he ripped the engine wide open and jetted them through an almost invisible break in the face of the mountainside.

Before her lay the most beautiful scalloped lagoon she'd ever seen. The water was clear and a shade of blue that defied description.

"It's...it's unbelievable. How did you find it?"

He shot her a humorous glance. "I didn't. My ancestors settled the island. They found that a back door off the island came in handy."

She was tempted to ask what he meant, but something in his expression gave her pause.

He eased the boat toward a short wooden pier, docking with the speed of long practice. After securing the lines, they crossed to a shed that housed a rather battered Jeep.

"It's a long climb to the house," he explained in response to her surprised reaction.

The Jeep had no doors or roof, only a hinged windscreen attached to the hood. She settled into the bucket seat and fastened her seat belt, eyeing the rough dirt road ahead with a frown. It wasn't much of a road, more a path, and it seemed to vanish into the dense undergrowth within feet of the forest's edge. "What about driving during inclement weather? Isn't it too hazardous?" she asked in concern.

He rested his forearms on the steering wheel. "Much too hazardous," he agreed. "Just promise me you'll stay off the mountainside when the weather turns rough."

That would be an easy promise to keep. The mere thought of skidding down that treacherous road during a raging storm left her trembling in dread. "You have my word," she said.

It took twenty minutes to gain the top of the mountain. Once there, Anna stared in wonder at the fortress built quite literally into the rock. "Dear heaven, Sebastian. Is this where you live?"

A teasing smile swept across his mouth. "No, my love. This is where *we* live."

She let the correction pass, awed by the sprawling grandeur of the estate. Curved stone walls were draped with deep rose-colored bougainvillea. Ahead of them lay the front entrance—a massive arching portal with double iron rings instead of doorknobs.

"It's huge!" she exclaimed. "When was it built?"

"In the early 1700s."

Sebastian ushered her to the front entrance. Inside, the masonry walls provided a natural insulation, the entranceway cool and dim. The flooring was stone, worn smooth from centuries of foot traffic. Arched doorways led off in all directions. She glanced around in amazement, before focusing on a life-size portrait that dominated one wall.

She gasped, taking a swift, instinctive step backward, and bumping into Sebastian. He steadied her, gripping her shoulders with heavy hands and cradling her against the protective warmth of his body.

"What is it? What's wrong?"

"The portrait," she whispered, shocked. It was Sebastian. A Sebastian from centuries gone by. *A Sebastian she had seen in a drug-induced hallucination.* "It's you!"

He chuckled. "Not quite. It's my ancestor, Nicholas Kane."

She stared at the portrait in disbelief. "He's... He's a..."

"A pirate." Sebastian sounded amused. "Yes, I know."

So many minor details finally made sense. The hallucination at the hospital, Sebastian's comment about being a pirate, the need for a "back door" off the island. *Rochefort* had been settled by privateers led, no doubt, by Nicholas Kane. She found the knowledge unsettling.

But there was another fact that she found far more unsettling...

There could be no more lingering doubts about her marriage. She'd been here before. The portrait, alone, made that fact indisputable. No matter how unsettling she found it, Sebastian was unquestionably her husband. "That's what you meant when you said you were a pirate," she whispered.

At that moment, a woman appeared beneath an archway, giving them a broad smile of greeting. "Welcome home, Miss Anna! It is good to have you back where you belong," she said, her words accented with a rolling calypso lilt.

"Anna, this is Dominique," Sebastian introduced them. "Our housekeeper."

Anna stepped forward and offered her hand. "You'll have to excuse me for not remembering. I'm afraid my memory is a little muddled from the accident."

"Mr. Sebastian, he told me. Don't you worry none, mom. A few days of rest and some of Dominique's cooking and you'll be right as rain."

"Has the luggage arrived?" Sebastian asked.

"Not yet. Josie called from the boat. They be along sooner rather than later. They want to make harbor before the storm."

Anna couldn't prevent a shiver of apprehension. "Will it be bad?"

Dominique smiled reassuringly. "Don't you worry none, mom," she said again. "We batten down, no troubles."

"Can you manage an early dinner?" Sebastian asked. "I'll show Anna to her room."

Dominique inclined her head. "Something special, I think, to welcome Miss Anna home." With a flashing smile, she disappeared into the far recesses of the house, her sandals a soft whisper on the uneven flagstones.

Anna followed Sebastian through the house. She walked into the bedroom he indicated and stopped dead.

"Oh, no. Not a chance," she exclaimed, taking a hasty step backward. "I'm not sleeping here. This is your room."

"Our room," he corrected, planting himself in front of the doorway and effectively blocking her retreat. "We've shared this room before. We'll share it now."

"You can't realistically expect me to sleep with you. It's unreasonable."

"One night in that bed and you won't find it unreasonable ever again."

She refused to back down, anger giving her the courage to defy him. "So you're demanding your conjugal rights, regardless of what I want?"

"If you choose to put it that way... Yes. Though it is what you want, no matter how much you deny it. You give yourself away every time I touch you. Shall I prove it to you?"

"No! Don't bother." She wouldn't attempt to debate his statement. How could she? He spoke the truth. "What if I refuse to cooperate?"

"Why fight me on this? We're married, Anna," he reminded her impatiently. "Or have you forgotten that minor detail?"

She offered a cool smile. "As a matter of fact, I have forgotten. And no amount of seduction is going to help me remember. Making love to you would be paramount to making love to a stranger."

He didn't relent. "I'm not a stranger."

"You are to me! Doesn't it matter that I have no memory of you? No memory that I married you...loved you."

She could feel the anger that swept through him, his tension clear in the tight line of his jaw and fierce light in his eyes. "Then what do you propose?" he demanded.

"Perhaps we could start over," she suggested tentatively. "We could get to know each other the way we did before, fall in love all over again. Perhaps it would even help me regain my memory."

"We could try it your way. For the time being, anyway. I

assume you'll want separate rooms, but you realize I won't wait forever.''

"I do realize that."

"We'll continue to play this game your way...for now. But one of these days you're going to have to face the past. And when that day arrives, the time for games will be over."

AT DINNER that night Anna was surprised when Sebastian bypassed the formal dining room, and led the way to a screened terrace overlooking the garden. Flowers skirted the area in dense profusion and a table set for two held center stage.

"It's lovely," Anna murmured.

He lifted an eyebrow. "You did say you'd like to recreate our time together, didn't you?"

"We've dined like this before?"

"Many times." Sebastian poured wine into her glass and offered it to her. "Relax and enjoy the evening, my love," he urged gently. "Let nature take its course. A few days of leisure will do us both some good."

She took a sip of wine, delighting in the light, dry flavor. A gentle breeze stirred the air and the flames of the candles flickered. For an instant the silvery scar curling across Sebastian's cheek stood out in stark relief.

She didn't mind his scar, in fact she found it rather appealing. She touched her temple self-consciously. The same couldn't be said of hers. Did it bother him? Did he find her less attractive because of it?

He noticed her action and a small frown pulled at his brows. "It'll fade in time. You should be proud of it. It marks you as a survivor."

"It doesn't bother me. Well... Not much." She glanced at his cheek. "How were you injured?"

"In a plane accident."

She gasped and her arm jerked reflexively, knocking over her wineglass. Sebastian caught the fragile crystal before it hit the floor. Mopping up the wine, he repositioned the glass toward the center of the table.

He lifted a questioning eyebrow. "Are you okay?"

She stared at him mutely, unable to explain the severity of her reaction to herself, let alone to him. Finally she found her voice. "I'm sorry," she whispered, choking on the words. "You caught me off guard. What happened? How did you crash?"

He refilled her glass. "I was sixteen and trying out a new plane. The engine malfunctioned."

The muscles in her stomach clenched, and her heart raced as though she'd run a mile. She held out her hands. "Look at me," she said with a breathless laugh. "I'm shaking. Silly, isn't it?"

His gaze grew tender. "It's all right, Anna. It happened a long time ago. And it worked out for the best in the long run. The accident determined my future. I decided that I wanted to design and build planes. Only mine would be flawless, tested with scrupulous care."

"And it's worked out?"

He inclined his head. "Until a year ago when there was a fatal accident involving my last design," he explained reluctantly. "It's prompted a lawsuit. After months of tests, the authorities cleared me of any responsibility. But Samuel, the man who's suing me, isn't satisfied. It was his parents who were killed and he refuses to concede the possibility of pilot error. He wants the engineering data and test pilot reports for the plane. But that information is valuable, and I'm not about to let it out of my possession."

Dominique appeared in the doorway, pushing a cart. "What is this?" she demanded, frowning at them. "You talk business when romance is in the air? That don't do nobody no good."

Anna smiled. "You're right. No more business talk."

Dominique placed several platters on the table.

"It looks delicious," Anna informed her warmly. "Thank you."

Dominique beamed in delight. "You eat now. Enjoy," she said, and left them to their own devices.

Anna scooped out a sampling of crab. It practically melted on her tongue. "This is wonderful!"

"Now have some pineapple with it."

Sebastian held out a sliver and, after a momentary hesitation, she allowed him to feed it to her. His thumb brushed her lower lip, then he leaned forward and captured her mouth in a swift, light kiss.

She pulled back, staring at him wide-eyed. "You promised."

"Yes, I promised to reenact our time here. And that's what I'm doing."

"And this reenactment includes kissing me?" she demanded.

"Of course." A slow smile crept across his mouth and his eyes were alight with secrets.

"Eat," he prompted.

"You don't make it easy," she murmured.

"That wasn't my intention. Here." He cut a slice of a creamy cheese covered in grape seeds. "It's called *grappe.* Try this while we discuss our plans for tomorrow."

He kept the conversation light and relaxing from then on. By the end of the meal Anna found she'd finished the crab, several servings of the *grappe,* and part of a custard flavored with soursop, a fruit grown by the villagers. It was late by the time the last dish was removed.

"You should turn in," Sebastian said at last. "We've a busy day tomorrow. I'll walk you to your room."

"Good night, Sebastian," Anna said when they reached her room.

"There's a storm moving in," he reminded her. "Are you going to be all right?"

"Of course," she lied. "Storms don't bother me." She opened the door and slipped across the threshold.

He stood in the hallway, unmoving, and it was then that she realized just how serious a threat he posed. Did he sus-

pect how tempted she was to invite him in, to lose herself in
the strength of his arms, the passion of his kisses, to surrender
everything?

He smiled then, a smile of blatant seduction, his unwav-
ering gaze a wicked enticement.

And she realized that he didn't just suspect how close
she'd come to surrender…he knew.

THE STORM HIT on the stroke of midnight, carrying nightmares within its roaring winds.

Anna's door crashed open, rocking on its hinges.

"*Bastian!*" Her cry was one of terror and panic.

He was beside her in an instant, sweeping her into his
arms. "I'm here, sweetheart. I'm here."

"I keep seeing it," she said, crying uncontrollably. "The
accident. It keeps replaying over and over. I can't get it out
of my head. Please! Make it go away. Make it stop!"

His arms tightened. "Listen to me, Anna. The accident's
in the past. It can't hurt you anymore. You're safe now. I'm
with you and you're safe."

He reached out and turned on the bedside lamp. Light
bathed them in a warm, reassuring glow. He held her for a
long time while she wept. Gradually she gained control, the
tears coming to a slow end.

"I'm sorry," she whispered, wiping her cheeks.

"It's the storm, isn't it?" he asked. "It's brought back
memories of the accident."

Before she could answer, he stood, lifting her high in his
arms. "What are you doing?" she demanded in alarm.
"Where are you taking me?"

She knew precisely where he planned to go. "No!" She
fought for release, but he didn't even break stride. "You
promised!"

"I promised to give you time. Well, guess what?" His
face was dark and stern and totally unrelenting. "Your time's
up."

"But… You agreed I could have my own room."

A great boom of thunder reverberated through the house. Anna shuddered, the fight leached from her. She buried her face in Sebastian's shoulder. Dear heaven, but the storm frightened her, dredging up a hidden terror she couldn't bring herself to face.

Sebastian pushed open the door to his room and crossed to the bed, easing her onto the mattress.

He knelt on the bed beside her. "Lie down, Anna."

She shook her head frantically. "No! Please, Basti—" Her breath caught in her throat and she stared up at him, wide-eyed.

Thunder boomed again, and with a smothered cry of alarm, she covered her ears. He had her in his arms before the echo even died away.

"It's all right, sweetheart," he murmured. "I'm here." Repositioning the pillows, he lay back, tucking her close. "Try and sleep. I won't let anything happen to you."

"I can't," she protested. "Not with the storm."

But her eyes drifted closed even as she spoke. And for the first time in weeks she slept. Truly slept, safe and secure within Sebastian's arms, knowing that he would protect her.

ANNA WOKE to an empty bed.

Afraid that Sebastian might walk in at any minute, she slipped from the mattress and hurried back to her own room. She found a maid there busily removing garments from the closet and dresser.

The girl turned with a wide, beaming smile. "'Mornin', Mrs. Kane."

"What are you doing?"

"I be movin' your t'ings to the other room," the girl replied, stacking a pile of blouses on the bed.

Anna stiffened. "What other room?"

"To Mr. Kane's room, mom." She shrugged. "He say better I do it sooner than later."

Anna kept a firm hand on her temper. How dare he? How

dare he go behind her back, like a thief in the night, and have her things removed? Well, two could play that game.

Grabbing a pair of jeans, a cotton blouse and undergarments from the pile on the bed, she hurried to get dressed.

She eventually located Sebastian in the dining room. At her appearance, he poured her a cup of coffee.

"I told Dominique not to bother serving breakfast," he announced without preamble. "There's a café in the village that offers a selection of pastries. You always had a fondness for their cinnamon rolls. After we finish our coffee, I'd like to drive there. I also thought you might enjoy walking through the markets afterward."

"Fine." She accepted the coffee. "Though right now I'm more interested in discussing why you had Ruby move my things to your room."

He lifted an eyebrow. "You have a problem with that?"

Her cup clattered in the saucer. "Of course I have a problem with it! You agreed to separate rooms until I recovered my memory."

"After last night, that went by the wayside." He took a long swallow of coffee, asking pointedly, "How did you sleep?"

A flush burned her cheeks. She'd slept with all the depth and abandonment of an infant. She'd woken once during the night, only to discover herself wrapped in his arms. She'd been half lying on him, her head cradled securely against his shoulder, her hand buried in the thick thatch of hair spanning his chest.

She met Sebastian's eyes. "I slept well enough," she admitted cautiously. "But—"

"Then that ends the discussion. You stay in my bed, with me."

She lifted an eyebrow. "And you'll let me sleep?" she asked pointedly.

He gave her a dry smile. "Yes. I'll let you sleep." He finished his coffee and stood. "Are you ready to go?"

Short of starting an argument she would undoubtedly lose,

there didn't seem to be anything she could do about it. Draining the last of her coffee, she followed him to the Jeep.

They arrived at the village and the next several hours were sheer delight.

Once she and Sebastian had finished eating at the café, they wandered down to the harbor.

Eventually they ended up on the main street, the teeming walkway lined with baskets of produce, fish, lobsters and crab. Further along the street, artists displayed their crafts— paintings, shell and bamboo jewelry and grass rugs. As she walked, children raced up to her, festooning her with necklaces and bracelets they'd made.

"Don't refuse," Sebastian murmured in an aside, when she attempted to protest. "It's their way of welcoming your return."

Anna noticed that a coin found its way into every tiny hand as Sebastian thanked each child personally.

They passed the rest of the day in leisurely exploration of all the village had to offer. The sun was waning in the sky when Sebastian finally suggested they leave.

He started the Jeep with a roar, and headed up the mountain. He pulled onto a narrow turnout and switched off the engine.

Reaching into the glove compartment, he pulled out a flashlight and tucked it into his pocket. "Come on. We walk from here," he said, and lead the way up a rocky path.

It didn't take long to realize that he was headed for the very top of the mountain. Up a final incline, Anna was amazed to see that a passage was cut right through the peak. The hollowed section was tall enough that Sebastian didn't have to duck, and wide enough for the two of them to stand side by side.

"This is Eternity's Keyhole," Sebastian informed her. "As far as we're aware, it's a natural formation." He gestured for her to join him inside the passage. "Now watch."

She stood in front of him, framed by the stone keyhole, staring out at a flame-dipped sun as it slowly plunged into the blue Caribbean waters. "It's so beautiful," she said, scarcely daring to breathe.

"Now turn around."

She swiveled, staring out at the opposite side of the island into a dark, ebony sea. A moment later a splash of white shot across the blackness of the ocean. And then the moon tipped over the horizon, turning the water to molten silver.

Sebastian stood behind her, holding her tight within his arms, her spine pressed against the rigid muscles of his chest and abdomen.

"I envy you all this," she confessed. "This island, this sense of history and belonging. I have no memories, no connections."

"You have me. And I can tell you what I know of your background. You grew up in Florida. Your father died when you were young. Your mother was a nurse. You collected stray cats and your favorite was a ragged-ear tiger named Creeper."

Anna smiled. "Tell me more about how we met."

"I was working in Florida when I hired you. I needed an assistant, someone to run my errands, and do my bidding. There were plenty of applicants to choose from. But I took one look at you...and I knew. You were the one I had to hire. It was a mistake, one glimpse of those great golden eyes of yours warned me you'd be nothing but trouble. But I hired you anyway."

She bowed her head. "And was I trouble?"

His laugh was short and self-derisive. "What do you think? You've turned my life upside down from the minute you stepped into it. Anyway... After I hired you we worked together for six months. The first five were out of Florida. And then I brought you here."

"What happened next? Did we fall in love?"

He was silent for a long moment and she didn't think he'd reply. Then, in a raw, brutal voice, he informed her, "I seduced you."

She swiveled in his arms, searching his expression in the

ghostly light of the moon. "You say you seduced me. But we married, didn't we? And if we married, we must have loved each other...right?"

He shut his eyes. "You're asking me something I can't answer."

"Why?"

He reached for her, his hands sinking deep into her hair. "Because on our wedding night, you slipped from our bed, stripped the rings from your fingers and tossed them onto the sheets..." He tilted her head and stared straight into her eyes. "And then, my sweet wife, you left me."

Tears welled up in Anna's eyes. "No," she whispered, shaking her head. "I wouldn't have done that to you. I couldn't have. Not on our wedding night."

"It happened," he stated gravely. "It happened just as I said."

She licked her lips, searching frantically for an explanation. "Why? At least tell me why I left you."

Anger blazed in his eyes. "How the *hell* should I know? You never bothered to say. You walked out of the door and out of my life without a single word of explanation. I didn't even know you'd gone until the police arrived at the hotel a half hour later to tell me there'd been an accident."

The puzzle pieces began to fall into place. She closed her eyes, a horrible numbness gripping her. "Why didn't you tell me this sooner?"

Deep lines slashed across his cheeks. "You'd never have come to *Rochefort* if you'd known," he explained roughly. "And I couldn't risk that. I wanted you here, with me, where we could uncover the problem together."

"You mean here under your control," she retorted with a bitter edge.

He gripped her arms, forcing her to listen...to believe. "All I ever wanted was to find out why you left. You never said. And it's been eating at me ever since. Put yourself in my place. What the hell should I have done?"

A sudden, shocking thought struck her. "That's why you

hired a private detective and insisted on escorts if I left my room,'' she whispered, horrified. "To make sure I didn't run.''

His hands tightened on her arms. "Damn it, Anna! Don't look at me like that. I was desperate. I didn't know what else to do.''

"It didn't occur to you to tell me the truth?''

"It occurred to me,'' he retorted harshly. "But having your wife run out on your wedding night without a single word didn't inspire a lot of confidence in frank dealings or honesty.''

She frowned. "If I left you on our wedding night, perhaps that explains why I was so certain you weren't my husband...and why there weren't any marks from the wedding rings. If we'd only just been married that day and then I left...'' She shrugged. "Perhaps I didn't consider myself truly married.''

"Don't kid yourself, Anna. We were married. And the marriage duly consummated.''

Color flared in her cheeks. "I didn't mean to suggest—''

He lifted an eyebrow. "Didn't you? You were my wife, even if it was only for a night.'' He released her, his gaze locking with hers. "Shall I prove it to you?''

Her eyes widened in alarm. "No! That's not necessary. Sebastian—''

Before she realized what he intended, he flicked open the buttons of her blouse. "You have a mole...here.'' He grazed the underside of her left breast, pinpointing the exact location through the scrap of peach silk. "And another on the inside of your right thigh.''

"Please,'' she whispered. "Don't do this.''

"Don't do what? Don't remind you of how it was?''

She fumbled with the shirt buttons, her hair sweeping forward to cover her burning face.

"That's merely physical,'' she objected, not allowing him to see how deeply affected she was by his touch. "What about the feelings? I asked you before... Did we love each other? Well?'' She looked up at him, pleading for reassurance. "Did we?''

"Love?'' He regarded her with a bleakness that nearly broke her heart. "I don't think I believe in that emotion anymore. I don't trust it. I'm not certain I ever did.''

Her gasp was almost inaudible. She blinked rapidly, backing away from him, fighting to keep the anguish from her voice. "I can't live without love,'' she told him fiercely, wrapping her arms about her waist. "I won't live without it. If that's how you truly feel, you have to let me go.''

He shook his head. "Not until I know the truth,'' he said, rejecting her plea with icy resolution.

"Until you remember why you left me, you stay here.''

"Regardless of what I want?''

His smile broadened. "You want to stay. You want to know what happened every bit as much as I do.''

She shook her head. "No!''

"Liar. You requested that we reenact our past and that's precisely what we're going to do. And maybe, just maybe, we can recover what we lost.''

"That's impossible,'' she insisted shortly.

"Is it? Then prove it to me. Prove to me that what we had is gone forever.'' His hand closed on her hair, brushing it back from the long sweep of her throat. "Show me that you no longer care.''

He lowered his head, nuzzling her neck and shoulder. She groaned, fighting the sensations that burst to life, fighting to conceal the devastation he wrought. He straightened, gazing down at her, and she knew then that resisting him would prove futile.

He knew it, too. "Don't look so tragic. The islanders claim that when the sun and the moon lock together within Eternity's Keyhole, your dearest wish will be granted. What's your dearest wish, Anna? Make it now, while I hold you in my arms and take your mouth with mine.''

And then he kissed her, teasing her lips apart and slipping inside. She shifted in protest, but all that accomplished was to bring her closer, fit her more securely within his grasp. She could feel him, every burning inch of him from knee to shoulder, pressing against her. It was like a spark falling onto dry tinder.

The flames caught.

Little by little a restlessness sprang to life deep in her loins, growing to an ache, a sharp craving. She loved him. Dear heaven, how she loved him.

And in that moment, held in the sweetest of embraces, all she could wish for was his love in return.

THE NEXT TEN DAYS passed beneath an uneasy truce. To Anna's relief, the nightmares were held at bay, she suspected, by her continued presence in Sebastian's bed. To her surprise, he kept his word. Not once did he try and force a more intimate relationship. Instead he seemed determined to tempt her beyond endurance, teasing her with all the sensual pleasures he swore they'd enjoyed in the past.

"That's it, Sebastian!" she protested, leaping to her feet and brushing the sand from her knees. "I did not run around without clothes, like some modern-day Eve. Don't try and tell me I did, because I don't believe you."

He lifted onto an elbow, his eyes gleaming with laughter. "I'm just trying to help you remember."

She planted her hands on her hips. "You're just trying to help me out of my bathing suit, you mean."

His grin faded, replaced by a hot, intense stare. "That, too," he conceded.

"Well, it's not going to work." It wouldn't…unless he kept looking at her like that. She turned her back on him and moved down the beach a few paces, glancing over her shoulder. "Come up with another plan."

He stood, gathering up their towels. "Another plan, huh? Okay. How about a swim?"

"Sure. Should I get the snorkels and fins?"

"You won't need them for where we're going," he replied rather mysteriously. "Come on."

He held out his hand and left the beach for the shelter of the forest. A narrow, overgrown path led up the hill, past lichen-covered rocks and between broad expanses of thick ferns.

"Not much farther," Sebastian called over his shoulder.

She could hear the rush of water now and realized they were approaching the river that fed into the lagoon. A heavily laden frangipani blocked her way. She pushed past and a cluster of the richly scented blossoms showered down on her, rose-colored petals catching in her hair and blanketing her shoulders. She lifted a hand to brush them away and stopped dead, staring in amazement at the glade.

He'd brought her to Eden.

And for the first time, a haunting feeling of *déjà vu* struck her.

A huge pool occupied most of the rock-strewn glade, fed by a dazzling waterfall. Plants graced the glade, their vivid flowers adorning this hidden pocket of paradise.

She glanced at Sebastian, suddenly aware that he'd been watching her reaction, enjoying her amazement and delight. "It's...it's incredible."

"I thought you'd like it."

"Did I...before?"

"This was a very special place for us," he told her quietly. "Don't you feel it?"

Her lips parted and she closed her eyes. Yes! She could feel it, sense it, almost reach out and touch it. The glade came alive with dreamy wisps of memories. A laugh, a passionate glance, a warm, stroking touch, a driving passion. And then, in a brief, explosive flash, an image burst through the blackness like a piercing ray of white light.

"Do you remember something?" Sebastian questioned sharply.

"We were together," she admitted in a low voice. "In a small hollow behind the waterfall."

He grew still, searching her face with razor-sharp intensity.

"There is a hollow there. What else do you remember, sweetheart?" he questioned gently.

"The niche was covered with a downy moss, soft and velvety to the touch."

"A natural bed," Sebastian said, slipping her into his arms. "A bed we shared."

"Yes." Her response was barely more than a whisper. "The waterfall was a solid sheet beside us, nature's curtain, concealing us from the rest of the world."

"I took you in my arms…" he prompted in a husky voice. "And then what happened?"

Tears spilled to her cheeks. "You made love to me for the first time."

"Yes. I made you mine. Here. In this place. And afterward?"

She struggled to remember, to push the memory further. But nothing came to her. All she had was that one brief glimpse, a peek at a scene from her past that was so breathtakingly beautiful she found it impossible to believe she could ever have forgotten it.

Her shoulders sagged. "I'm sorry. I don't know what happened next," she confessed.

Without warning, he swept her high in the air, carrying her toward the pool. She wrapped her arms around his neck, relishing the feel of his warm, taut skin beneath her hands, appreciating the play of lean muscle and sinew as he moved in long, easy strides. At the water's edge, he lowered her to her feet, his arms locked about her waist. She tilted back her head and gazed up at him for an endless moment.

"What are you thinking?" he questioned tenderly.

A hint of color warmed her cheeks. "I was thinking about how much I'll treasure these moments I've spent with you," she confessed in a low voice. "That if I never recall another second of my past, I'll have this instant to hold on to, this image to call to mind when nothing else is left."

His expression softened. "I can't give you back the past,"

he murmured. "But I can give you some new memories. Will that do?"

She didn't hesitate. Her hands slipped into his thick, black hair and she lifted on tiptoe to kiss him. It was as though a captivating magic filled the glade, the mystic charm of time and place charging the atmosphere. In her mind's eye she saw again that moment in the hollow.

Sebastian had reared above her, the mark of passion full on his face, his bronzed skin slick and glistening. And she'd arched to meet him, moving with an instinct as old as time. The sensations she'd experienced were unlike anything she'd known before...hot, heavy, driving. She'd called out his name, "Bastian!" And the cry had bounced off their rocky nook and blended with the roar of the waterfall.

She shivered, the past merging with the present.

Sebastian lifted his head and stared down at her. "You will remember," he told her quietly, as though aware of the turbulent path her thoughts had taken. "It will come back to you. And then we'll know what really happened." With that he pulled her into the pool, submerging them in the cool, swirling waters.

And she found herself praying she'd never, ever remember. Because she had the uneasy suspicion that to remember would bring their marriage to a bitter end.

ANNA KNOTTED the wrap-around skirt at her hip and glanced at Sebastian. He lay stretched on a rock, his face relaxed in sleep. He looked rested, peaceful...and unbelievably tough. Silently, she left him, picking her way across the rocks, following the terraced steps down toward the lagoon—just to see how far she could go. To her delight, she reached the beach with ease.

She followed the miniature delta to where it emptied into the sea, glancing at the hard metallic-blue sky in concern. An oppressive sultriness weighted the air and she wondered if it meant they were in for another storm.

The roar of an engine interrupted her thoughts and she

looked up, astonished to see a boat shoot through the rocky opening to the lagoon. She shaded her eyes. A man with reddish-brown hair piloted the craft and, spotting her, he cut the engine and jumped to his feet, the boat rocking wildly beneath him.

"Chris!" he shouted, waving his arm in an urgent signal. "Chris, it's me. Come on! Swim out here."

She took a step into deeper water, staring at him in confusion, aware of a frightening sense of familiarity. "Benjamin?" she whispered, then tested the name, calling out, "Benjamin?"

"Yes! It's me. Hurry, before he comes!"

She stood, vacillating, totally bewildered. He knew her. This…Benjamin…knew her. And apparently, she knew him, as well. Why else would his name come to her with such ease? But…he'd called her Chris, which didn't make a bit of sense. She took another step toward the boat, intent on questioning him, the waves lapping at her thighs.

Footsteps pounded across the sand behind her. With a huge splash, Sebastian sprinted to her side, his hand closing on her wrist in a viselike grip. For a long minute the two men faced off, glaring at each other across the turquoise waters.

There was no question as to who would win this battle for dominion, for possession. The power emanating from the man at her side was absolute. A vehement curse drifted across the water and the speedboat roared to life. Swinging in a tight arc, Benjamin gunned the engine and sped from the lagoon.

Sebastian turned on her. Wrapping an arm around her waist, he hauled her from the water. "Who the hell is that man?" he panted, dumping her to the sand.

She'd never seen him so furious, so out of control. "I don't know!"

"You're lying to me!" He grabbed her by the shoulders, his hands biting into her tender flesh. "I heard you. You said his name. You called him Benjamin."

"I'm not lying!" How could she explain it to him, when

she couldn't even explain it to herself? "I don't know him. The name flashed into my mind. But that's all I remember. You have to believe me!"

He thrust her away, as though not trusting himself to touch her any longer. "I don't believe you, Anna. It's all been one, huge lie, hasn't it? You never lost your memory."

She blinked back tears, too proud to allow them to fall. "I did...I have!"

"It was all some sort of con job, wasn't it? And this Benjamin is somehow involved."

"No!" Her breath came in great, heaving sobs. "I don't know him. Bastian, please!" she said again. "You have to believe me."

He shook his head. "Not anymore, Anna. Not anymore." Suddenly he froze, his eyes narrowing. "Or...is it Anna? He called you Chris."

"I don't understand. That's not my name." She gazed up at him in apprehension. "Is it?"

He tilted his head to one side. "No, but it is the name you first uttered—in the hospital after the accident. You called out the name, Chris." He frowned, his brow furrowed in concentration.

To her relief, his intense fury had died, but this frigid remoteness was far worse.

"Come on, *wife*. It's time to find out what the hell is going on."

He turned and strode across the sand toward the Jeep. Anna hastened to climb in as Sebastian started the engine. But instead of charging up the mountain as she'd expected him to do, he flipped on the CB radio and spoke into the mike, barking orders in fastpaced island lingo. He received an immediate response.

"Who did you call? What did you say?" she questioned hesitantly.

"I called the village and told them that we had an intruder—an intruder I want brought in for questioning."

"You can do that?"

He shot her a cool, arrogant look. "It's my island. I can do anything I damn well please."

"And if they succeed in bringing him in?" she asked, dread balling in her stomach. "What then?"

"Then I'll ask him if he's the man who stole you away on our wedding night. I'll ask him if he was the one who drove you off the road and came within a hair of killing you. I'll ask him if he's the bastard who left you there, injured and alone and unconscious, while he escaped from the wreck and disappeared like a thief in the night." He slammed the Jeep into gear, his expression a savage mask. "And if he is, I'm going to take him apart piece by piece."

LOUD VOICES emanated from the study and Anna pushed open the door, stepping inside.

"Come on in, Anna," Sebastian said, not taking his eyes from their "guest." The man sported a black eye. Clearly, he hadn't come of his own free will. "Let me introduce you. Anna Kane, this is Benjamin Samuel. He claims the two of you are old friends."

Her eyes widened. "Samuel?" she repeated, instantly making the connection. "The Samuel who's suing you?"

"The very same."

"Chris, for heaven's sake," Benjamin interrupted furiously. "Tell that bastard how you really feel about him and let's get the hell out of here!"

She shook her head, moving closer to Sebastian. "I'm not going anywhere with you. And how do you know me?" she demanded. "Why are you calling me Chris?"

Bewilderment clouded his eyes. "What are you talking about? Chris is your name. Chris Bishop. And we're..." He glanced uneasily at Sebastian. "We're...old friends."

"I don't remember you," she stated coolly.

He stared, dumbfounded. "How could you not remember? We've known each other for years."

"The accident left her with amnesia," Sebastian explained. "You do remember the accident, don't you? The accident you ran from while your...*friend*...nearly bled to death.''

Benjamin backed away, holding up his hand. ''I went for help. I did! I walked for miles, but I lost my way.''

Anna covered her mouth with her hand and turned instinctively toward Sebastian, needing his strength, his comfort. He didn't hesitate, but took her into his arms. The questions came rapid-fire after that.

''What was she doing in the car?'' Sebastian demanded.

''She'd decided marrying you was a mistake and called, begging me to come and get her before you discovered the truth about us.''

Sebastian's eyes narrowed. ''And what truth is that?''

''That she was helping me win my lawsuit.''

''You say you're friends. Were you intimate?''

''That's none of your business,'' Benjamin said with an indignation that didn't quite ring true.

''As her husband, it's very much my business. *Were you intimate?*''

Benjamin hesitated, appearing to debate whether or not he'd answer. ''Yes!'' he finally said, throwing Anna an apologetic look.

Anna refused to remain silent any longer. ''And why was I leaving my husband?''

Benjamin glanced at her, then away. ''You were working for me on the sly. And you were leaving him because you were afraid he'd find out about it.''

She stiffened. ''I worked for you! Like a...a spy?''

''Yeah,'' he admitted. ''I needed someone on the inside to help me gather information for my lawsuit. I offered you money to apply for the job as his assistant.''

Anna stared at him, appalled. ''And I...I *agreed* to this? To spy for you for money?''

Benjamin shrugged awkwardly.

''What was she supposed to get for you?'' Sebastian continued the interrogation.

"I wanted the engineering data for the Seawolf," Benjamin answered. "And the test pilots' reports."

Sebastian's eyes narrowed. "Then why did she marry me?" he demanded.

"Maybe she thought she could make even more money married to you than she could helping me."

Anna gasped, stunned by the viciousness of the remark. Sebastian didn't care for it, either. His hand closed into a retaliatory fist, but a knock interrupted him.

Dominique's burly husband entered. "The room's ready," he announced. "You done with him?" He jerked his head in Samuel's direction.

"Yes, Joseph. We're quite finished." Sebastian turned to Benjamin. "Joseph is going to show you to your room for the evening."

"Wait a minute!" Benjamin protested. "You can't hold me here against my will!"

Sebastian released a short, harsh laugh. "Yes, I can. But that's not why you're staying. There's a storm moving in and it's not safe to leave right now. First thing in the morning, I'll arrange for you to be transported off the island."

The explanation seemed to mollify him. "And Chris?"

"That's none of your concern."

"But—" Joseph dropped a heavy arm on Benjamin's shoulder, propelling him toward the door.

Sebastian glanced at Anna, an enigmatic expression darkening his eyes. "So... It would seem I married a spy."

"I'm sorry, Sebastian. I know you have no reason to trust me, but I sincerely regret whatever part I played in this whole business."

"Then you believe him?"

"I don't want to believe it. But without proof to the contrary..."

"Don't worry about the proof. Tomorrow I hear from the detective I hired after your accident. He'll be able to confirm...or deny Benjamin's story."

"And when he does?"

"Then I'll know how much trouble my wife has gotten herself into."

THE STORM BROKE as Anna was slipping into Sebastian's bed. He wrapped her in his arms and pulled her close.

It felt like she'd come home.

"I shouldn't be here," she murmured, daring to slip her hand into the thick hair covering his chest.

"Because Benjamin claimed you and he were lovers?"

She bit down on her lip and nodded, finding his frankness difficult to match.

"There's something I haven't told you," Sebastian said, cupping her cheek and stroking the curved sweep of her jaw. "Something you should know. When I made love to you in the hollow behind the waterfall, you were a virgin."

"Do you mean that?" she whispered, tears of gratitude leaping to her eyes. "You're not just saying that?"

"It's the truth. And after we made love, I proposed to you. Benjamin can't know you very well if he thought you were prone to affairs. So the question remains...who the hell is he to you?"

"I don't want to think about it," she told him tautly. "I don't want to think about *him*."

His voice deepened. "Then what do you want to think about?"

"I want to remember how we were together. Before the accident, I mean. I want you to make love to me for the first time...again," she pleaded. "Make me your wife, even if it's just for this one night."

He didn't need a second bidding. Sebastian stripped his shorts in one easy move. Lightning flared and she could see the extent of his desire. She trembled and his brows drew together in concern.

"Don't be afraid," he told her gently. "I won't hurt you."

Slowly, with infinite care, he lowered his head and captured her mouth. He cupped her bottom, drawing her close, allowing her to grow accustomed to the feel of him, to the undeniably masculine shape of his body.

She let him touch her where he willed, opening herself to him without hesitation or restraint.

What came next was so perfect, so shattering, so intensely elemental that it rivaled the ferocity of the storm beating at their windows. It caught her totally unaware. She wasn't prepared for the force of her desire, for the tempest of sensation that broke over her as he took her, showed her all she'd dared to forget.

Afterward, she lay gasping, fighting for breath, and a frightening realization broke over her. One night wasn't enough. She wanted more.

She wanted the experience to go on and on for the rest of her life. Exhaustion gripped her, and sensing it, Sebastian gathered her close.

She snuggled, safe in his arms, the final shattering moments of their passion still rippling through her. Slowly, she drifted off to sleep. And she began to dream…to remember.

SHE DREAMT….

Lightning flashed across the midnight sky, igniting the hotel bedroom with a momentary brilliance. Anna turned her head and glanced at Sebastian. He slept deeply.

Snatching up her purse, she reached for the doorknob and froze. One final, terrible obligation remained. She tugged the precious wedding rings from her finger and pressed them to her lips before tossing them gently toward her pillow. A flash of lightning blazed, catching on the rings as they tumbled over and over through the air. She struggled to hold the tears at bay.

She was late. She had to go.

A car was waiting in front of the hotel. She stepped from the curb and took a final wistful look back.

"Did you get it?" Benjamin demanded as they roared away from the hotel.

She shook her head. "No."

"What do you mean, no?" he shouted, skidding into a turn.

"Benjamin, be careful," she urged. "Slow down."

He ignored her, fury tightening his mouth. "You were our only hope. How could you do this? Did you really think I'd drop my suit just because you're stupid enough to fall for the guy?"

"Yes! Or I'd have left him months ago. He's innocent, Benjamin. You're going to have to face the fact that it was a tragic accident."

He pounded on the steering wheel. "I warned you what would happen if you didn't get the information. I'll tell him who you really were. I'll tell him you're my stepsister."

"It doesn't matter anymore. I've left him. And I sent a letter explaining everything." Tears spilled down her cheeks. "You have nothing left to hold over me, nothing left to blackmail me with. It's over."

He swore violently. "What the hell are we supposed to do now?"

"Give up."

"Never," Benjamin snarled, stomping on the accelerator in his fury. "I'll never give up until that man pays for murdering our parents. Until he's broken, in jail and destitute, the bast—"

And ear-splitting crack of thunder swallowed the last of his words and lightning streaked wildly across the sky revealing a blind curve just ahead. Anna screamed, knowing Benjamin would never make the turn.

For a brief instant the car soared through the air. Crashing to the ground, the doors popped, throwing Benjamin clear before flipping, tumbling over and over and over, like wedding rings tossed onto a bed. The sickening shriek of ripping metal deafened her, then the pain came, sharp and intense. "Bastian!" she screamed. And at long last, blessed darkness engulfed her.

ANNA SAT UP with a gasp. She remembered. She remembered
it all.

Anna turned, about to wake Sebastian and tell him she'd
remembered everything, until she realized just what that
would entail. She hesitated. She needed to think first, consider what she'd say. Silently, she slipped from the bed and
dressed.

She crept to the kitchen to make coffee, but paused outside
Sebastian's study, drawn by the furtive rustle of papers. She
pushed open the door. Benjamin sat behind Sebastian's desk,
riffling through the drawers.

"What are you doing? Are you insane?" she said with a
gasp.

His head jerked up and he glared at her. "If you know
what's good for you, you'll get the hell out of here."

"Benjamin, please. You have to end this vendetta. Our
parents wouldn't have wanted this, not if it destroys you in
the process."

He released a short, cynical laugh. "So you were faking
the amnesia."

"I wasn't faking. Everything came back to me last night
during the storm."

"How convenient. You now remember. So what are you
going to do about it?"

"I'm going to tell Sebastian the truth."

"And how do you suppose he'll respond? Forgive you for
deceiving him? The truth is, you did take that job in order
to spy for me—"

"But not for money! I did it because I sincerely believed
the Seawolf was at fault for the crash."

"It was!"

"I saw the files, Benjamin. I read all the reports. There's
nothing wrong with the plane."

"You know how to access the information?"

"Yes, but—"

He shoved back the chair and stood. "Where does Kane
keep his files?" he demanded.

"Not here. The computers are at the airstrip." Tears filled her eyes. "Please, Benjamin. It's not your fault. You flew that plane the best you knew how. I don't blame you for the accident, I swear I don't."

It was the wrong thing to say. His expression hardened and he grabbed her arm. "Come on," he said. "We're leaving."

"I'm not going anywhere with you," she protested, twisting in his grasp.

His hold tightened. "There's a Jeep parked out back. We'll take that."

"I won't come," she told him, digging in her heels. "You can't make me."

He turned on her, yanking her close. "I'll use force if I must. I don't want to, but I'm out of options here."

"Then please—let me drive."

A bitter smile twisted his mouth. "I guess I can't blame you for that." He gestured toward the driver's side of the Jeep. "Be my guest."

Sliding behind the wheel, she started the engine and released the clutch, heading toward the village. The road was slippery, too slippery for safety.

Dawn arrived just as they started down the hill toward the airstrip. It was then that she realized they were being followed, and she knew that it had to be Sebastian.

She forced her attention back to the road. For now, she had to concentrate on her driving. She rounded a sharp curve and bounced through a torrent of water, horrified when she saw the ground collapsing just after they passed. Sebastian! He'd never be able to stop in time! She slammed on the brakes.

"What the hell are you doing?" Benjamin shouted.

There was no time to explain. Leaping from the Jeep, she dashed back up the road, hoping to warn Sebastian before he got to the curve. But she knew, with a horrifying certainty, that she would be too late. His car rounded the corner and his Jeep skidded violently, plummeting over the side of the hill.

"Bastian!" she shrieked.

She ran to the edge of the landslide, sobbing. Sebastian sat slumped over the steering wheel, unmoving.

Benjamin appeared at her side, took one look and grabbed her arm. "Come on. Hurry."

He took the driver's seat, starting the engine just as she jumped in. It took mere minutes to reach the accident.

To her horror, Sebastian's face was covered in blood. "Head wound," Benjamin announced tersely. "He needs medical attention right away."

"But there's no doctor on the island," she told him. "If there's a serious accident Sebastian always flies them to the hospital in San Juan."

Benjamin froze. "In his plane? A Seawolf?"

She clutched her hands together. "Yes. Can you do it? Can you fly it?" It was a lot to ask, an almost unthinkable request to make, but there wasn't anyone else available.

For an endless moment he stared at Sebastian, then he turned and looked at her, a terrible expression filling his eyes. "I'll do it. I'll take him to the hospital...in exchange for the computer files."

"No! You can't mean that! Benjamin, for God's sake, you can't bargain for a man's life."

"Do you want my help, or don't you?"

She didn't have any choice and they both knew it. "I'll hate you for this for the rest of my life."

"Then hate me," he said callously. "But if you want to save him, you'd better make up your mind. Do you agree or not?"

She looked at her stepbrother and gave a tight-lipped nod. "I agree," she whispered. "May heaven help me. I agree."

FROM THE MOMENT she climbed aboard, to the instant they touched down, Anna never once took her eyes off her husband.

An ambulance waited for them at the airport. And when at long last they wheeled Sebastian into the emergency room, she turned on Benjamin, blocking his access.

"You have what you wanted," she told him with cold bitterness. "Now take your files and go."

"Chris—"

"It's not Christianna anymore," she cut in sharply. "I changed my name at your request when I went to work for Sebastian. Remember? It's just plain Anna now."

He nodded awkwardly. "Okay...Anna. Please, try and understand why I'm doing this."

She drew away. "Oh, I understand. I understand that nothing matters to you anymore except finding a scapegoat. You can't live with the fact that you flew the plane that killed our parents. Well, those computer files aren't going to give you any peace. Go away, Benjamin. I don't want you here." And with that, she turned on her heel and left him.

The wait for the doctor's report was interminable. When the doctor appeared in the doorway, she leapt to her feet. "How...how is he?" she asked.

"He'll be fine, Mrs. Kane. It looked much nastier than it was."

She could have wept in relief. "May I see him?"

"Of course, though I should warn you he's been sedated."

A nurse led the way down a long corridor and finally pushed open a door. "Ten minutes, Mrs. Kane. There'll be plenty of time to visit tomorrow."

"Bastian?" she called softly. Tears gathered in Anna's eyes. "Oh, my love, what have I done to you?"

She drew closer, knowing that if she didn't say the words now, she might never speak them. "I betrayed you, Sebastian," she forced out the confession. "I did work for Benjamin because...because he's my brother and he asked for my help. And there's something worse. I...I gave him the computer files."

She waited for a response, for him to give some indication

that he heard. He didn't move. Tenderly, she swept the hair from his brow.

"I love you, Sebastian," she whispered. "I should have said it last night. And if all I ever had was a single night as your wife, it would have been worth it. One night as your wife is worth a lifetime in the arms of any other man."

There was nothing left to be said. She closed her eyes and held him, hoping to give him a small piece of her strength, willing him to recover…to come back to her.

A few minutes later, the nurse poked her head in the door. "I'm sorry, Mrs. Kane. It's time."

Anna gazed down at Sebastian. "I have to go now, but I'll be back," she told him. "I promise. I'm not running away this time."

JOSEPH MET ANNA at the hospital early the next morning. "I'm sorry, Mrs. Kane. Mr. Sebastian has left."

She stared, stunned. "Left? Where did he go? Who authorized it?"

Joseph shrugged. "Mr. Sebastian, he need no authority but his own. But he did make arrangements for your transportation to Florida."

She shook her head. "No! I have to speak to him. I have to explain…."

"No, mom. You have to go to Florida."

She opened her mouth to argue again, then closed it, her shoulders sagging in defeat. What was the point? She didn't know where Sebastian had gone, how to get in touch with him. And clearly, Joseph wasn't going to help her.

"Very well. I'll go to Florida. But you can tell Sebastian for me that this isn't over. Not by a long shot."

Joseph grinned. "Yes, mom. I tell him dat for you."

The next day and a half inched by. She ran the gambit of emotions between hope and despondency. By the time she reached Florida, despondency had won.

A car met her in Florida. "I have orders to deliver you to the *Island Oasis,*" the driver informed her.

She stared in shock. "No. There must be some mistake. "That's—"" That's where they'd spent their honeymoon night. He couldn't be so cruel. He couldn't! "And if I refuse to go with you?"

The driver shifted uncomfortably. "If you refuse, I'm to tell you that Mr. Kane will have you and a Mr. Benjamin Samuel arrested for theft."

Again she'd been left with no other option. Nodding, she stepped into the limo.

Once at the hotel, a porter escorted her to the same room as the last time—the Honeymoon Suite. He opened the door then quietly slipped away.

Anna walked in and there stood Sebastian, looking impossibly remote, dressed in a business suit and tie. A stark white bandage covered a corner of his brow, drawing her gaze. "Are you all right?" she asked hesitantly.

"Just one more scar to complement all the others," he said in a grave voice.

"I'm sorry," she said awkwardly. "I tried to warn you."

"I know. Thank you for that." He led the way into the living room, tossing a pair of envelopes onto the brocade sofa. He nodded toward the envelopes. "Those are for you. One's a letter from your stepbrother. A letter of apology, I should imagine."

Her gaze flashed to his. "You know Benjamin's my brother?"

He lifted an eyebrow. "You told me in the hospital, remember?"

"Well…yes," she said, disconcerted. "But I didn't realize you'd heard me."

He met her eyes with stunning directness. "I heard every word you said."

"Then why didn't you say anything at the time?"

His mouth twisted. "If you recall, I wasn't in any position to comment. Later that night, Benjamin stopped by."

She could barely take it in. "Benjamin came to the hospital? What did he tell you?"

"The truth, for a change."

"He told you everything?" she asked in wonder. "Of his own free will?"

"Yes," Sebastian confirmed. "He had no intention of dropping the suit. Instead he planned on blackmailing you. Something along the lines of—give him the information or he'd reveal everything, perhaps?"

She nodded. "He called on our wedding night while you were in the shower. But I couldn't do what he asked. I couldn't betray you, no matter what the cost. I lied, told him that I had the information and would meet him in front of the hotel. I knew the only way to end his incessant plotting would be to leave you. Permanently."

He approached. "Which brings us to the night we made love. Your memory returned that night, didn't it?"

"Yes," she whispered. "I think making love to you is what brought it back."

His eyes darkened. "Why didn't you tell me?"

"Because I was afraid you'd assume the worst. It looked rather damning, especially considering where Benjamin and I were headed the next morning."

"To the airstrip. To examine the computer files."

"Only we didn't get there," she stated bleakly.

"Because I came after you and took a tumble off the mountainside. At which point…you made a deal with Benjamin. My life in exchange for the computer files."

She bowed her head. "It was one more betrayal. I didn't think you could possibly forgive me."

Disbelief gathered in his eyes. "Not forgive you? For saving my life?" He snagged one of the envelopes from the couch. "Last time you chose to disappear, rather than betray me. Which brings us to our second bit of mail." He held it out.

"The letter I sent you the night of our wedding. But…" She looked at him in confusion. "It's not opened."

"It would seem my new assistant isn't quite as efficient as my old one. She saw no urgency in getting this to me. It explains everything, doesn't it? Your identity, why you left, says goodbye.''

She nodded, too overwhelmed to speak.

"Tear it up."

"I...I don't understand."

"Get rid of it." His expression grew tender. "Have you any idea why I brought you here?"

Mutely, she shook her head, the tears finally escaping.

"You thought it was to punish you, didn't you?" He pulled her into his arms, wiping the tears from her cheeks. "It wasn't a punishment. I brought you here because this is where we left off. This is where our marriage was put on hold. And this is where it resumes. We never finished our honeymoon. Now we will."

She gazed up at him. "Do you mean that?"

"I mean it."

"I love you, Bastian."

He cupped her face. "And I love you. I'll love you to the end of my days...and beyond. Despite what you said in that hospital, one night as my wife isn't enough. Not for me. Not by a long shot."

"Then let's make it two," she suggested, lifting her face, her love gleaming in her eyes, filling her voice.

He didn't need any further prompting. He took her mouth, sweeping her into a special world of warmth and light and passion...and opening the door to the rest of their lives.

A SECRET VALENTINE

Dixie Browning

against her, his eyes lazy-lidded as he took

Closing her mind to the sheer physical magnificence of the

The trucks—cobalt blue and clearly marked with the QD emblem of the engineering firm, were already in the school yard, and Grace's lips tightened as she saw Terri flirting with the construction workers. She wondered, not for the first time, if it had been a mistake to go for a teaching position instead of an office job. In an office she wouldn't have been called on to deal with discipline problems.

Grace took a deep breath and adjusted the imaginary ramrod along her spine as she opened the door to her classroom and let the students in. "Good morning, girls."

"Good morning, Miss Spencer," came the obedient response—so why did it always sound like "Miss Spinster" to her ears?

Grace closed her mind to the competing attraction just outside the window and began her lesson on the intricacies of word processing.

"Carly, watch for the prompt," Grace said with frayed patience. "It will tell you what you've done wrong, and all you have to do is look in your manual and find out how to correct it."

"Why do I have to learn all this junk when I'm planning on being an engineer?"

Grace reminded the red-faced eighteen-year-old, "Last month you were planning to be a paralegal."

"That was *before*," Carly replied, and Grace didn't have to ask, before what? Before that uncouth giant came two weeks ago to litter the landscape with his monstrous machines and his tightly jeaned, bearded, hard-hatted crew!

At three-fifteen she saw her last class file out and snatched up her briefcase. It was Friday, thank the Lord, and for two whole days and three glorious nights she intended to forget she had ever heard of any piece of office equipment more sophisticated than a pencil!

Well…not so glorious, at that. She had promised Elliot she would go to dinner and a movie with him. She couldn't drum up much excitement. More's the pity, she admitted to herself as she swung along toward the charming, if somewhat shabby, house where she lived with an assortment of inherited cats and houseplants.

She checked the mailbox automatically, not allowing herself to admit disappointment when there was no letter from All Seasons Greetings.

Stripping out the pins that held her hair in a tightly confined knot, she padded out to the kitchen.

The kitchen was impossible, the bathroom even more so. Great-Uncle Henry had known better than to complain to the rental agent. He had patiently bailed out the back part of the house every time it rained rather than risk having his rent raised.

After finishing some sharp cheese and polishing off an apple, she braided her long brown hair into one thick plait.

The house had belonged to her great-aunt and -uncle, or at least they had rented it for so long that they considered it theirs. Grace had first seen it when she had been delegated to attend the funeral of her great-aunt Aldonia. Grace had readily accepted the mission, looking on it as a vacation of sorts. She had been working hard for too long, as well as going to night school for the past three years, and her relationship with her family still held a certain amount of tension.

Grace's rebellion had been the cause of the rift. Her father, Colonel Bergen Spencer, USMC retired, had more or less drummed her out of the family. Jilly, her younger sister, had rallied around during the financial nightmare, but Jill, bless her, could offer little but love and uncritical support.

Living in the same small New England town, although in her own cheap apartment, Grace had gradually reinstated herself with her family until she was once more able to join them for the occasional Sunday dinner and family birthday parties.

By the time the telegram from Brunswick, Georgia, had come, she was near exhaustion from years of work and night school, but she had found herself immediately warming to Uncle Henry. Grace had put off going home again and again. She felt more relaxed in the shabby old house with Uncle Henry than she had in years—than she *ever* had at home.

They had fallen into a pleasant rut that had lasted until Henry had died, eleven months after his wife. Grace applied for a teaching position at a local junior college. Now, after her first two months of teaching, she felt reasonably certain that she had settled.

Her daily bread was assured—and the butter would be provided by All Seasons Greeting Cards, Inc., as it had been for the past six years.

If anything good could be said to have come from her disastrous affair with Don, it was that. Someone had mentioned that she ought to try sending her ideas to a greeting card company after seeing the cleverly illustrated rhyming notices she had placed around The Apple Barrel. All Seasons had liked her things enough to use her as a continuing contributor on a freelance basis. The pay wasn't great, but the satisfaction kept her soul intact through the bad times.

After grabbing a sweater, Grace let herself out and headed for one of her favorite places of inspiration. She tucked her portfolio and India ink pen under her arm as she followed the narrow, winding road to a small clearing she had come to think of as her sanctuary. The late-November warmth had gone with the setting sun. New developments were encroaching on both sides, with paved streets and all the usual city-type facilities, but her own few acres had been left untouched, thank goodness.

She had not gone more than a hundred feet along the road when she heard the sound of an approaching vehicle. Grace stepped off into a clump of saw palmettos.

The tranquil atmosphere was shattered by the sight of a familiar cobalt-blue pickup. Suddenly all the daily frustrations of competing with QD's construction workers for her students' attention boiled up in her again. Grace hurled a stone to the ground. It bounced away, lost in the cloud of dust thrown up by the truck.

The engine noise ceased and the sound of a rock striking metal rang out like a shot in the hushed atmosphere.

Oh, blast! How was she to know the rock would ricochet? It was precisely the childish sort of behavior that had gotten her in trouble with her father years ago.

She stepped back onto the road and walked slowly toward the stationary pickup truck, cutting a wary glance toward the high, blue cab. There was no mistaking the arrogant angle of that head, the breadth of those shoulders. It was the one the girls called the Incredible Hunk. She heard the opening and slamming of the door.

"Girl!"

Girl? Grace refused to dignify the impertinent summons with recognition. She veered off onto an almost invisible animal track.

The large figure moved from the cab and crossed the few yards into the underbrush to confront her. Bracing herself, she lifted her chin. "I—I didn't mean to hit your truck."

The man was as big as a fortress. The eyebrows alone—thick, black as tar and arched over obsidian eyes, would have set him apart, even without the mustache. That was thick, well trimmed and salted with gray.

When he spoke, his voice was a curiously gentle rumble, "My truck?"

Some of the painful rigidity drained from her backbone. "You mean I didn't hurt your truck? Then why did you come after me?"

Hooking big, well-shaped thumbs into his wide leather belt, he allowed his grin to fade. "To apologize for the dust bath, for one thing, and to warn you that you're near invisible at this time of day on a dusty road. I'd have slowed down if I'd seen you.''

Grace mumbled something about not having expected any traffic and managed to tear her eyes away from the man's face. So this was what the girls were panting after!

He swung away then with a casual salute, and Grace watched him drive off with relief.

IT RAINED the first three days of the following week, precluding any outside work by the QD crew. To Grace's immense satisfaction several of her morning students applied themselves with surprising diligence, with only a few longing glances at the unpopulated construction site.

On Thursday the blue and orange trucks arrived just before eleven. A day and a half to go before the reprieve.

At times she had to remind herself of the reasons why she was now a levelheaded career woman rather than the dreamer she had once been. She had started out as an art major—leaning toward the commercial end of the spectrum as a compromise to her father. The colonel did not look kindly on anything that smacked of frivolity.

And then, in her second year, she had met Don, a bearded potter who had dreams of setting up a small business that dealt in handmade musical instruments, natural foods and high-quality crafts, including his own distinctive pots, all in a coffeehouse atmosphere.

Grace was ripe for a close relationship. When Jill was born, all yellow ringlets and big, sky-blue eyes, the colonel seemed to forget he even had another daughter. Grace no longer crept through the house, afraid her father would appear suddenly around a corner to demand that she recite the eleventh line of multiplication tables or threaten her with shoulder braces if she didn't straighten up.

She had been content to drift through her high-school years, daydreaming, drawing and writing bad poetry. There had been occasional dates, but her father catechized her high school friends so severely before he allowed them to take her out that few of them returned for a second drilling. No sparks had been struck. None, that was, until Don Franklin had noticed her.

Don had easily persuaded her that he wanted nothing so much as to set them both up in a cozy little business. They could live together, love together, for the rest of their natural days.

She had all but dropped out of school, pouring all her energies into their joint project. When she had told her family she was considering moving into Don's apartment in the back of the shabby old house they had rented for the store they had named The Apple Barrel, it had been the last straw. She had been told that she was no longer her father's daughter.

Don took to spending whole weekends away from the store and had stopped talking about a lovely homemade wedding in the spring, with fiddles and flutes. By the time the bills started pouring in, he had disappeared altogether, leaving her with only the consignment goods and a mountain of debt and legal entanglements.

In the subsequent years she had worked hard to pay back her debts and then to put herself through business school.

On Friday she was late getting away. Elliot would be coming at six. With luck she'd just make it. Elliot, who lived with his mother and a widowed sister in an eminently respectable part of town, liked to dine at six on the nose, and they usually made the seven o'clock movie feature. That way he was home before his womenfolk could begin to worry. For all his almost-too-perfect features and his manly pipe and tweeds, he didn't make her heart beat one whit faster, and that was precisely why she continued to date him.

The potatoes were underdone, and to make it worse Elliot rather ostentatiously ignored it, except for an oblique comment. "You shouldn't walk when you have a schedule to keep, Grace. Especially with a bag of groceries and a briefcase to carry."

Grace frowned as something tugged at the edges of her mind. "My briefcase!" She jumped up from the table and raced into the front room. Her briefcase was not on the plant-filled table where she always slung it when she came in. Nor was it on her bed or anywhere else.

"What's wrong?" Elliot glanced surreptitiously at his watch, reminding her that they were off schedule.

"I forgot my briefcase, darn it! And it's Friday."

"If it's important we could run by and pick it up," he offered grudgingly, and Grace shook herself out of her mood and smiled at him. Her briefcase carried almost a month's accumulation of new work, all ready to be transcribed and mailed off to Mr. Harris, and all her drawings, including a rather intricate design of palmetto whorls and one of flower faces she had been working on in her spare time.

"I can do without them until Monday." Elliot didn't know about her sideline. She had told no one of the foolishly romantic little verses and the whimsical drawings she had been selling for several years. "Let's put the dishes in to soak and I'll do them after I get home tonight."

ON MONDAY she raced to school to find her briefcase. It was not where she thought she had left it, but she located it on the table beside the copying machine and breathed a sigh of relief.

QD and company were out in full force today. She tried to ignore the swarming men and the whispering, distracted girls and plowed on with her lecture on interfacing terminals. Boring. She caught herself in a sigh and her glance slipped sideways through the wall of glass.

Suddenly it seemed that everywhere she went, she was confronted by that immense, curly-headed creature with the outrageously fresh grin. Crossing the campus to the parking lot, she saw him standing beside one of the blue QD trucks. "Afternoon, Pigtails."

She killed a crazy impulse to reach up and assure herself that her neat chignon was still intact.

"You look like you've had a tough day." His soft Georgia drawl flowed over her like warm molasses. "Did you know your eyes are the exact color of lapis lazuli?"

Feeling oddly as if she were walking down an up escalator, she stared at him for several long moments before she remembered to scowl.

He reached out one hand and touched her neat, business-like chignon. "If you used a wrench, you could probably tighten up another half turn on this thing." Before she could react, he sauntered off, a casual "See you" tossed over his massive shoulder.

She stood there blinking after him. He was too big, too tough, too uncouth, too—too *everything!* She closed her mind quickly to the small voice that whispered he was also too attractive. Dangerously so.

A COLD FRONT dropped down into East Georgia unexpectedly on Friday. The phone was ringing when she let herself into her home.

To her delight, it was the president of All Seasons Greeting Cards, Inc., congratulating her. The entry Mr. Harris had selected for the annual competition had been one of Grace' valentine designs, both artwork and verse, and it had won first place!

"You've made my day, Mr. Harris—my whole week. In fact, my whole year!" Elated, she rattled on until Claude Harris pleaded another call.

She dialed swiftly, then listened to the distant *burr, burr* picturing the austere blue, gray and white foyer of her parents' house. The colonel answered, his voice a testy growl.

"Daddy, it's me—Grace."

He interrupted her. "Your mother's with her board members. Some silly new female cause she's got herself mixe up with. She'll call you later, and now, if there's nothing else, I'm late.''

She slowly placed the phone in its cradle, dismissing the momentary blight her father's lack of interest had created. She turned to one of the cats, who was contentedly curling her claws in and out of a crewel-embroidered pillow. ''Have you heard the big news, Miss Maudie? One of my designs won a top national contest and I'm to be awarded the phenomenal sum of one hundred and twenty-five smackeroos, not to mention one genuine rayon satin rosette.''

*

A DISMAL gray rain was drumming down on the metal roof when Grace woke up on Saturday morning. She decided to hurry and get her bath before the water rose any higher. The bathroom always sunk first. Somewhere along the line the owner had tacked on a rudimentary bathroom by closing in a corner of what had been a back porch, but the house was at least sixty years old and it had been slowly sinking into the ground all those years.

Half a mile or so in either direction fancy new homes were going up, and Grace feared for her small, private domain. Even in its genteel shabbiness, the little frame house had a warmth that she had never found in any of her previous homes. Not the military housing on the various bases, nor the big square two-story house her father had bought after he retired, nor the two sparsely furnished rooms she had lived in while she worked to put herself through business school.

Still, something was going to have to be done or the back part of the house was going to float off down the Back River one of these fine days. Without waiting to eat breakfast, she dialed the agent who handled the property and outlined her situation.

''You understand, Miss Spencer, that the property you rent

for next to nothing should have been condemned years ago.
Sooner or later the whole area will be cleared for develop
ment.''

"Well, meanwhile, Mr. Ogleby, I'm in danger of washing
away.''

"Yes, well, all right, Miss Spencer, I'll see if the owner
wants to bother with fixing it up.''

She made herself some breakfast and took it into the back
living room. Curling her feet under her on the sofa, she
snapped open her briefcase and took out the sheaf of original
verses that had accumulated over the past year. She submitted
word-processed editions to accompany her carefully rendered
illustrations, but she retained the original verses, initialed
with the tiny ''GBS,'' and the field drawings.

They were supposed to be in order, but they weren't. Just
when had she been so careless?

The delicate, old-fashioned drawing she had done for the
prize-winning valentine had pink roses, tiny wild irises and
forget-me-nots that formed a heart shape that had been edged
with paper lace. She quoted the verse from memory:

"Rose pink are your lips, my love,
Iris blue, your eyes.
Forget-me-not, for in your hands
My happiness yet lies.''

Feeling the beginnings of a burst of creative energy, she
uncapped her fountain pen.

By noon the rain had slackened and a watery, lemon
colored sun timidly fingered the trailing clouds. She heard
vehicle drive into the yard and cut the engine.

The whole house registered the heavy footsteps crossing
the front porch, and by the time the screened door rattled
under a summoning fist, Grace was already there, a feeling
of numbed certainty creeping over her.

"What are you doing here?'' She held the door open

cautious six inches as she peered through at the man outside. The hard hat was missing and instead he held a battered Stetson in his hand as he leaned with one arm against the side of her house.

"I've come to fix your plumbing, Miss Spencer," he told her. The way those appreciative eyes moved over her made her uncomfortably conscious of the fact that her newly shampooed hair was still unconfined, and the knit shirt and faded jeans clung far too faithfully to her body.

"It's certainly not a bulldozer job, and how did you know my name, anyway? Who are you, anyway, Mr....."

"Donovan, Miss Spencer, and in case you wondered, Ogleby sent me."

Just for an instant there was a gleam of something that struck her oddly in those dark, enigmatic eyes, and then it was gone.

"All right, Mr. Donovan. The problem is easy enough to recognize if you'll just go on around to the back. I'll be inside if you should need anything. Oh, one thing," she added. "Send your bill to the rental agency, if you don't mind. I promise you, if Mr. Ogleby can't collect from the owner, I'll be glad to pay your going rate." She closed the door firmly and leaned back against it, blowing a strand of brown hair off her forehead.

Pacing from room to room, she cleaned up everything in sight in an effort to work off some of her restlessness.

The phone rang as she was tugging on her rubber boots, and she answered it to hear Elliot confirming their date. "Elliot, I'd really like to go to that new place over on Lanier Island. I've heard they have a band on Saturday nights, and I haven't danced in years!" She could picture his expression as his brain clicked out the probable cost of such an evening. "Elliot? Why don't we make it my treat?"

The sound of a clearing throat came over the line. "That won't be necessary, Grace. If you'd like to go there, of course

I'll take you—that is, if I can get reservations this late,'' he added.

Elliot asked little enough of her on their weekly dates— just a sympathetic ear for his indignation over the practical jokes his math students played on him, and an occasional murmur as he recited his mother's opinions on just about everything. Even his good-night kiss asked nothing of her— which was all on the plus side, wasn't it?

She pulled on a bulky wool sweater, collected her portfolio and stepped out the back door. Donovan had stripped off his shirt, and with each movement of those brawny arms as he deepened the canal that led away from her house, his powerful muscles gleamed in the pale sunlight.

He leaned on his shovel and wiped a hand across his wet brow. Even in early December it could be hot when you were shoveling wet dirt.

"Would you like something to drink?" Compunction made her inquire.

"I'd really enjoy a cup of hot coffee." His eyes were softly wistful. With a sigh she nodded and turned to go back into the kitchen. "I'll just step in here and clean up a bit," he said from behind her. The bathroom and kitchen doors were only a few feet apart across a tiny vestibule that was all that was left of the back porch.

She had a subliminal vision of his large tanned hands touching her personal belongings, and it brought a distinctly hollow feeling to her middle.

The kettle was at a boil when he appeared in the kitchen, almost filling the opening. Taking a deep, steadying breath, Grace reached for two small mugs.

"When's the last time you had your chimney inspected?"

Thrown off base by the unexpected question, Grace stared at him blankly. "My—why…I suppose Uncle Henry had it done."

"I'll send someone out next week," he said in his soft baritone drawl.

"Look, I'm sure you mean well, Mr. Donovan."

"Call me Quinn."

"Mr. Donovan," she stressed determinedly, "but if I need a handyman, I'm sure Mr. Ogleby can find—"

"Clark Ogleby couldn't find his glasses if they were on top of his head." He leaned back and smiled sweetly at her. "There's a new supper club that's opened up over on Lanier Island. How'd you like to try it out tonight?"

"I've heard about it." She watched his eyes warm with anticipation and then continued, almost reluctantly, "My date is taking me there tonight."

Fleeting expressions of disappointment crossed his face, but then the familiar 220-volt smile flashed on again. "Right. I thank you kindly for the coffee, ma'am. I think you were on your way somewhere." His smile was just as wide, just as attractive, but there was a subtle difference—a hardness behind it that made Grace suddenly realize that for all his easygoing manners, here was a man who'd be dangerous to cross.

She watched him duck out through the back door.

ELLIOT WAS precisely on time, as usual, and Grace greeted him at the door. He looked thoroughly taken aback.

"Grace? Am I too early? You haven't fixed your hair."

"I thought I'd just leave it down for a change, but if it bothers you...?"

"No—I— No, that is...I'll help you with your wrap."

The supper club was crowded. She caught a glimpse of them both in a mirror as they made their way to the table and was startled. She hardly recognized the slender girl in the short, swirling dress and the flowing, leaf-brown hair. To her amusement, Elliot was still slightly disapproving of her metamorphosis. After all, what would Mother think?

She ordered from the right-hand side of the menu, selecting the least expensive entrée, and sipped her modestly priced white wine.

Grace spied a broad back and a familiar set of shoulders while on the dance floor with Elliot. There was no mistaking the crop of dark curls, nor could she miss the slender, silver-tipped fingers that were reaching around his shoulder to tease the strip of tanned skin that showed between the black curls and the pristine shirt.

She was dismayed to realize that her heart was beating far too rapidly. More dismaying still, she wasn't all that shocked to see him there. It was almost as if she had been expecting him.

For the next half hour she concentrated her attention on her broiled flounder, red rice and salad. Elliot talked between courses, reminding her of his mother's invitation to Sunday dinner.

"She likes you, you know."

She saw Elliot's gaze go beyond her and up—and up and up. Grace turned. Struggling against the spell of that suspiciously benign smile, Grace made sketchy introductions. "Elliot, Mr. Donovan. Mr. Donovan, Elliot Rand." Let them sort it out between them if they wanted more.

Donovan extended his hand. "Bland—glad to meet you. I won't keep y'all, but I wanted to apologize to Pigtails here for leaving such a mess in her bathroom." He turned his guileless gaze on Grace. "Next time I'll bring my own towels, honey. You folks have a good time. See you."

He was gone. Grace stared after him, her mouth slightly agape, and watched while an auburn-haired girl with a hard sort of prettiness welcomed him back to their table. It was several moments before she turned back to Elliot, and then her eyes widened. Elliot, jealous? No. Elliot, of course, would go right home and relate the whole incident to his mother. Grace could hear her now: "She's not our kind of people, Elliot, dear. After all, a woman who lives *alone,* and in *that* neighborhood…"

She gathered up her purse and tucked her hair back behind

her ears. "I'm afraid I can't make Sunday dinner—thank your mother for me, though, will you?"

"Perhaps another time," Elliot said stiffly, escorting her out to the car. Both of them knew there would probably not be another time, and Grace was amazed at the feeling of lightness she felt.

DECEMBER fluctuated from tropical balminess to shivering chilliness to the impenetrable fogs that could drift in so swiftly over the hundreds of square miles of marshland.

Holiday fever had set in at school. The discipline problem threatened to get altogether out of hand. It had been Terri— she was certain of that—who had left the X-rated book in her top drawer, and the whole room had rocked with laughter while Grace had burned, then blanched, then burned again. How would her father have handled insubordination, disrespect—ridicule?

Carly Johns had actually looked embarrassed at some of Terri's more outrageous jokes at Grace's expense. Perhaps the girls would settle down after Christmas.

Saturday dawned with a promise of mildness. As she sipped coffee she glanced through the bills, and it occurred to her that she had heard nothing from either Ogleby or Donovan about the ditching that had been done in her backyard to channel off rainwater.

She ripped a page from her lined tablet and jotted a note to Mr. Ogleby to the effect that the work was satisfactory and as she hadn't heard from him, she assumed the owner had agreed to pay for the improvement. She signed her name, Grace B. Spencer, with a flourish. There had been a time when she would have taken the absence of a bill as proof that she didn't owe anything, but not anymore.

The slight breeze that rustled through the reeds was a whispered enticement as Grace stood in the opened back door. Amazing how the ever-changing sea of reeds and rushes that bordered practically all of Georgia's coastline had become so dear to her.

She left to saunter along the narrow, winding road that separated the woods from the marshes and rounded the last curve before reaching her destination—and her jaw fell in stunned disbelief. She let fly an oath she had once heard a Marine sergeant use and glared at the line of red flags that led her affronted eye directly to the hatefully familiar blue truck. "QD!" she exclaimed, consigning the whole outfit to perdition. And then her mind connected the man, Donovan, with the words. *QD. Quinn Donovan. Quinn Donovan Engineering.*

"Oh, rats!"

She felt something cold and wet nudge her back, and she jumped and whirled around to confront a sleek brown dog. Grace started to laugh, and the dog tilted its head inquiringly and nosed into her paper bag of crackers and liver pâté.

"Be my guest," Grace offered and unwrapped the lunch.

The dog devoured the works, circled twice and curled up with her nose close to the torn paper bag.

Grace dropped onto her knees and elbows and studied a flat rosette of curly leaves she found growing under the tall dried grass.

"I don't know about the view from where you are, honey, but from here it's spectacular."

She twisted around. Quinn Donovan had no business being so light on his feet! "Do you make a habit of sneaking up and spying on people? And why didn't you tell me who you were!"

He retorted, "Do you make a habit of kidnapping a man's dog and holding her captive when he's doing his best to train her?" He lifted one of those wicked eyebrows and she stared at him, completely losing the train of conversation. Then he turned to the pup. "Mollie, you old scoundrel, have you been moochin' again?" He tugged the dog's ears affectionately and shook his head in mock despair. "My neighbors can't have a barbecue without telling me ahead of time so I can lock this thieving hound up.''

Grace laughed. When he told her that he had a standing policy of feeding all of Mollie's victims, she was shamefully easy to persuade. "Gives me a perfect opportunity to show off my hand with Brunswick Stew," he said.

THEY HIKED along the winding trail to the truck, and Quinn told her that the red flags were staking out a hidden creek. "We're studying the feasibility of draining this place."

Grace closed her mind to the impact development would have on her domain.

They turned off a narrow blacktop onto a shelled driveway that wound through tall, straight pines and enormous live oaks, dripping with graybeards of moss. Both the site and the partially finished house bespoke a surprisingly cultivated taste, as well as the means to support it.

Inside Quinn invited her to make herself at home. The large, open space seemed to combine living, sleeping and dining facilities.

Grace crossed the dark, softly gleaming pine floor and found herself in a compact bathroom. A sweat-stained khaki shirt hung from a hook and without thinking, she reached out and touched it. Hurriedly she splashed her hands and face and left the intimate room.

"Won't be long now," Quinn called out. He emerged with a handful of silver to find her studying one of the paintings on the wall. "Like it? Edward, my youngest brother, did them. These were some of his earlier works, before he started making all the juried shows. I can't afford him now."

The conversation followed easily from her question about his other brothers and sisters, and she discovered that Quinn was the oldest of seven. He told her readily enough that all but Edward were married and caught up with families, careers or both.

The ambrosial Brunswick Stew had been served hot from

the oven. He grinned across the satin surface of a sturdy
walnut table. The wine sent a glow of warmth stealing up
over her face. He was remarkably good company.

Quinn reached out to touch the tip of her nose. It burned
like fire. "You have an impertinent nose, Grace Spencer.
With your dreamer's eyes, it makes an intriguing combina-
tion. Did you honestly think you could disguise them by
dressing like a prison matron and screwing your hair up into
a hard knot?"

His hand fell to her shoulder and lingered there. The few
inches between them disappeared.

"Grace," he whispered, just before she felt the soft brush
of his mustache and then the shattering touch of his mouth.
It was a devastating act of possession. The solid warmth of
his hard body was impressed on her every cell.

When his lips lifted, she managed to maneuver one hand
between them and push. She shook her head frantically. "I
think I'd better get out of here," she blurted.

The slow smile spread over his face, but some of the
warmth was missing, as if he were already losing interest in
her. "No problem. I've got an appointment in town anyway."

She reached for her sweater and portfolio. "I'm ready
when you are," she told him.

Not until he pulled up in front of her house and cut the
engine did it occur to Grace that she still didn't know any
more about Quinn Donovan than the fact that he was one of
seven children, and that was hardly relevant.

Adopting her most effective schoolmarm tone, she said,
"Thank you for the meal, Quinn. I won't ask you in, since
you have an appointment."

He nodded perfunctorily. His usual smile was noticeably
absent, and there was a look about his shuttered eyes that
Grace interpreted as ennui.

She let herself in the front door as the long, low sports car
snarled away. It was almost six, late for a regular business

appointment, and anyway, who kept business appointments on a Saturday evening? He was probably headed to see his hard-edged lady friend.

The feelings that were beginning to assail her now bore no resemblance to those she had felt for Don so long ago. She had been a girl then—heedless, impressionable and terribly vulnerable. Now she was a woman—heedless, impressionable and, she feared, more vulnerable than ever.

*

"GRACE, DEAR, if you'd only told us, I'm sure we could have made other arrangements," her mother apologized, and Grace murmured something to the effect that it wasn't important, that she had several options for the Christmas holidays. Her mother latched on to the mutual face-saver with obvious relief. "Oh, aren't you the lucky one?"

Not even to herself would she admit to being hurt by her parents' lack of welcome—other guests, not enough bedrooms to go around, were pretty weak excuses to her way of thinking. A militant sparkle in her eyes, Grace hung up.

Before she could unclamp her fingers from the phone, someone banged peremptorily on the door and she shook off her dismay and hurried through to answer the summons.

"What are you doing here?"

Quinn braced himself against the brash green clapboard siding and beamed at her. "Good morning to you, too, honey."

It had been over a week since she had seen him, and the spell of his potent masculine magnetism returned full force now. She stood back helplessly as he opened the screen door and came inside.

"What do you want?" she blurted.

"Invite me into your parlor for a cup of coffee and maybe I'll tell you what I want." He was grinning—fatuously,

Grace decided, and she blew impatiently at a strand of hair as she moved aside.

The astounding nerve of the man, she bristled five minutes later. He invited himself in for coffee and then had the nerve to criticize just because she had left the morning's brew on the woodstove to stay warm! His tautly muscled body was perfectly relaxed on her sofa. He had talked with infuriating blandness about the weather, the economic impact of the closing of a large local plant and the recent decline in the shrimp harvest. Eyeing his half-empty mug meaningfully, Grace waited for him to come to the point of his visit.

"When do you break for the holidays?" he asked, and she told him she'd be free as of Thursday. He continued, "You're going home to the frozen North?"

"No."

He lifted one of those darkly mocking eyebrows. "I was going to invite you to spend Christmas with me," he said to her utter astonishment.

"Why on earth would you do that?"

He shrugged. "Guess it just occurred to me that you might enjoy it."

As she stared at him in amazement a dull flush rose over his hard-hewn features, and Grace found herself scrambling madly to regain her balance at the erratic swing of her emotions. Just when she thought she had him figured out...!

"Well, thank you, Quinn, but of course, it's out of the question." Darn! She sounded so prim—so mealymouthed. To cover her confusion, she stood and reached abruptly for his mug. One of his hands closed around her wrist like a warm, solicitous manacle, and she tugged impatiently. "Quinn, don't be childish!"

But there was nothing at all childish about the touch of his iron-hard hand. He tugged her off balance so that she fell into his lap. And then his mouth came down to shut off her indignant protest.

Reaching up to push him away, she felt the muscular swell

of his pectorals. Inside her something fluttered fiercely. "Quinn. Quinn, please."

"Yes, Grace." He sighed softly.

That wasn't what she meant! This was insane! She struggled against the honeyed sweetness of her own inertia to escape the tender prison of his arms. He laughed down at her. A chilly doubt crept into her overheated consciousness. Was she wrong? No. There was an element of self-satisfaction, of...of *conspiracy* in that smile, almost as if they shared an amusing secret.

"Quinn?" she whispered uncertainly and scrambled away. He reached for her, but she escaped, her wary eyes never once leaving his face.

"What is it, Grace?" Some of the sureness seeped from his ebony eyes.

"You're absolutely insane! I politely reached for your cup and you grabbed me! And after barging in here uninvited in the first place!"

"Oh, honey, I was invited," he said, his voice softly ominous. "I'm a little too old to be playing games, but if that's the way you want it, then I guess I can go along with it."

"Playing games! Just because a—a bunch of schoolgirls think you're—you're—just don't make the mistake of believing every woman you meet is going to fall for all that—"

"All right, honey, I get the message—the real message, this time." That hateful grin mocked her. "Just what do you think? Did you expect me to swap sugary little verses with you?" The hard glitter of his eyes never left her while he stretched to ram his shirttail into his pants. "So if you've had your thrill-of-the-month, I'll be shoving off."

Before she could summon her wits to reply, he was gone.

FEBRUARY was not far off, and The Valentine would be hitting the market any day now. Mr. Harris reported that her sales were slowly increasing.

The second day back at school Donovan waylaid her before she could get across the parking lot.

"Morning, Grace."

She was astounded to see the familiar broad grin on his
face, just as if he had never tried to seduce her.

She was about to wind up their meeting quickly when they
were interrupted by Carly Johns.

"Hi, Miss Spencer." Carly had been absent the first day
back at school, and Grace turned to her now with something
of relief. "Carly, you weren't ill yesterday, were you?"

"Oh, no, ma'am. We went to Disney World after Christmas and we didn't get in until last night." Her eyes, soft as
melted chocolate, kept drifting toward Donovan, and Grace
had no choice but to introduce them. This she did, keeping
it brief, but Quinn was not to be dismissed.

"Johns, huh? Charley Johns's little girl?" When Carly
nodded, he added, "I'll bet he has to sweep the boys off the
doormat when he comes home from work every day."

It was unforgivable, Grace decided, when she saw the effect of his outrageous flattery on the impressionable girl. Her
derisive glance told him as much, and he bathed them both
in the indiscriminate warmth of his wide grin. "Well, if you
two lovely ladies will excuse me, I have an appointment with
a county official who's dead set on hog-tyin' me with red
tape."

"We'll try to bear up, Donovan," Grace retorted dryly.

"You do that, Spencer." She watched the unholy gleam
rise up in his eyes to mock her. Beside her, Carly heaved a
sigh of dramatic proportions. Grace happened to catch
Carly's eye. To her surprise the younger girl's smile held the
first note of real communication they had shared. It would
have to be over Donovan! Still, it was a beginning.

"Oh, wow," Carly breathed reverently as they followed
the narrow concrete walk. "Is he really for real, or not?"

"If he's not, then the sooner his batteries run down, the

safer we'll all be," Grace admitted, holding the door for the student to enter.

Before they turned toward the classroom, Carly hesitated and Grace looked at her questioningly.

"Look, Miss Spencer—some of the girls—well, we thought it would be a neat trick to—" She broke off, her face flooding with color, and Grace glanced past her to see several of her students hurrying toward the room. "I'll tell you later," Carly mumbled and fled inside.

Whatever confidence Carly was about to share with her had to wait. Elliot came by at lunchtime and lingered, just as if he'd never snipped off their friendship.

DONOVAN turned up on her doorstep one Saturday morning in mid-January with unsettling news.

"It occurred to me, Grace, that with the price of a house well out of most folks' reach, it's downright wasteful to neglect one that could be put into first-class shape with a little elbow grease."

Closing her eyes in a wordless prayer, Grace spun away and strode into her kitchen. Up to standards, indeed! It would take more than a lick of paint and a few snide remarks to bring this old house up to even minimum standards, and anyway, she wasn't at all sure she wanted it improved.

"Little darlin'?" he called solicitously.

"Donovan, if you call me little darling, or...or honey, or Pigtails one more time, I'm going to clobber you!" she seethed. "I'd sooner live in a dugout canoe than have to put up with your overbearing, condescending, *corn-pone charm!*"

He applauded softly. "Your vocabulary's coming right along, little—Grace," he amended. "Keep it up and I might wind up sending you a bouquet of roses and daisies." He grinned at her, his eyes lazy-lidded and deceptively slumberous.

Closing her mind to the sheer physical magnificence of the

man, Grace took a deep, steadying breath. "You're cute, Donovan—just too cute for words," she snapped. The kitchen door, as usual, hung halfway open and she gave it a shove that sent it clattering against the wall.

"We'll fix that first," he promised her.

She began to run water in the sink. "I'll get these done before I leave."

"Where are you going?" he asked with perfect equanimity.

Agitating the suds into snowy mounds, she applied herself to her chore. "I don't think that's any business of yours."

The silence stretched the boundaries of comfort to the breaking point before Quinn said, "You call the shots, honey—I just try to accommodate you. Before you go, though, how about helping me with this door. It'll just take a minute to tighten up the hinges, and then I can get started on the back porch."

She finished the dishes, leaving them to drain, and presented herself to Quinn, who was doing something with a folding rule and a plumb bob. "All you have to do is lean against it while I replace these old screws." He positioned her where he wanted her.

He was so close that she could feel his breath against the side of her averted face. "Why can't you just prop the door closed with a chair?" she asked plaintively.

"Because, my lapis-eyed darlin', a chair's not nearly as exciting as a carpenter's helper."

When she tried to duck under his elbow, he blocked her with his body, pressing her heavily against the door. The proud thrust of his nose stroked the tip of hers, and his mustache brushed over her lips, her cheeks. When she could no longer bear her own distraught nerves, she moved that necessary fraction of an inch to find his mouth with hers. It was a sweet, mutual coercion that melted the last vestige of her resistance. In mere seconds tension had spread through his hard-muscled body, igniting a similar response in hers. His mouth lifted.

"Ahhh, Grace, honey, no more games—please." He lifted her face to his. "Your eyes, Grace, are as black as mine now. You can't deny the truth any more than I can."

His words, spoken in a hoarse whisper, so nearly echoed her own thoughts that Grace closed her eyes in relief. No, she couldn't deny it—didn't want to deny the power that surged between them like an arcing high-tension line. It was far stronger than reason.

Her lips parted for his invasion, and when the phone shrilled in the next room she blinked slowly, unable to understand for a moment what was happening. A shred of sanity fingered its way in through overwrought emotions.

"I'll take it off the hook," Quinn grated.

"No, I—that is, I'd better get it." Reacting instinctively, she slid away and grabbed up the phone.

"Give me Quinn," a terse feminine voice demanded, and Grace stared stupidly at the instrument.

"What is it? Grace? Who is it?" he demanded. His voice sounded as if it had not been used in a long time.

"It's for you—a woman," she said dully. She laid the phone carefully on the table, snatched up her purse and her portfolio and ran out the door.

After a while she found an uninhabited stretch of marsh-front. Deliberately shutting out the haunting beauty of the mysterious marshes, she tried to concentrate on composing a verse for a Christmas card, but all that would come to mind were inane jingles about hearts and flowers.

Daisies have a secret;
Roses have one, too.
Listen with your heart, my dear,
They'll tell you I love you.

Good Lord, what had made her remember that one? It had

been one of her first attempts at doing valentines—she had all but forgotten it. She'd just have to force herself to forget valentines and think fall—think Thanksgiving, think Halloween!

Halloween. All she could come up with was an image of wicked, dark eyes topped with Mephistophelian brows. In spite of herself, she smiled. How would Quinn like to see his face adorning a series of scary cards?

*

ON WEDNESDAY she had arranged a class trip. The law firm that had agreed to receive a small group had its offices in a complex that also housed several medical practices. While the law firm's receptionist was describing the possibilities of working as a legal secretary, an office manager was conducting the other group through the Medical Arts Center.

Grace, with half an hour to herself, arranged to meet the two groups at a nearby fast-food place and pushed through the heavy glass doors, squinting against the low-angled morning sun. Barely had the doors swung behind her than she felt an arm slide around her back. Quinn grinned down at her.

"Playing Mother Goose this morning?"

"Playing Mother...? Oh, I see what you mean." She answered his flashing smile with a reluctant one of her own.

"Have coffee with me," he commanded genially.

"I really don't have time."

"What were you planning to do while your little ducklings are being initiated into the mysteries of the real world?"

Stung by his derisive dismissal of her girls, she said, "My little ducklings, as you call them, are what make the so-called real world go around! I doubt very much that QD Engineering would function as smoothly without its office staff!"

"Margaret." And at her mystified look, he said, "My office staff—Margaret Phillers. Which reminds me, I'm having a get-together Friday evening, in the part of my house that's finished. I'd like for you and that friend of yours—forget his name, but the one with the nose designed to be looked down—to come.''

"Elliot," she said before she could stop herself.

"You didn't have any trouble recognizing him from the description, did you?" His hand wrapped around her own. "About seven-thirty, all right? See you!" He spun away, leaving a mesmerized Grace staring after him.

AT FIRST Elliot refused even to consider the invitation. Then, when he realized Grace was going, either with or without him, he capitulated, telling her that for old times' sake he couldn't allow her to go to Donovan's house unescorted.

That Friday night Quinn threw open the door for them, gesturing expansively for them to come join the others. He slipped an arm around Grace's shoulders, but a woman in a long, sleeveless shift of navy blue inserted herself between them. The same woman who had been with him at the supper club a month or so ago.

Grace's initial opinion of a rather hard prettiness was reinforced on closer inspection. Even as Quinn was introducing her and Elliot to Margaret Phillers, Grace was aware of one swift impression. Margaret Phillers was head over heels in love with her boss. She was unprepared for the swift shaft of pain that shot through her as she watched Margaret Phillers slant a confiding little smile up at Quinn. Then several people introduced themselves, and the evening began to gather momentum.

"Hi, you're Grace and I'm Edward, and I'm told you're something of an artist yourself."

She turned to confront a broad grin that was a younger, slightly lower-voltage version of Quinn's. While the party milled around them, Edward regaled her with the course of his career as an artist and inquired into Grace's own endeavors along that line.

"I doodle," she admitted, "and am lucky enough to have found a market for some of my doodlings."

They were joined by another couple, and presently someone put on some music.

Quinn came up behind her. All night long she had managed to stay on opposite sides of the room from him. Margaret Phillers was sending hands-off signals to every female in range, with special emphasis on Grace.

He drew her skillfully into his arms as someone put on another tape.

She felt herself falling under the spell of his potent magnetism, prey to all the old familiar longings she had tried so hard to deny. They found themselves beside the sliding glass doors when the music ended, and Quinn led her through, out onto the open-sided corridor that led to the unfinished part of the building. "Come see my home," he invited.

He showed her through a jungle of rafters and joists, studs and empty window frames.

"Watch that two-by-four," Quinn warned just as Grace caught her shin on it. She doubled over in pain and Quinn scooped her up, holding her against him.

"Oh, my, you are tantalizing," he whispered as he planted tiny kisses along her throat. "When are you going to send me another love letter?"

The words ricocheted around in her mind, as the glass doors slid open and they were approached by at least half the party. Quinn warned his guests about the various hazards. "Poor Grace has already lost a leg to one of my braces."

Grace was pretty certain that the auburn-haired girl had been leading the pack when they had come through the door and scented their quarry.

The party broke up soon afterward, but not before Edward had invited her to attend the opening of his one-man show in Atlanta the following weekend.

Grace was acutely conscious of Elliot's disapproving eyes on her as she tried to come up with an excuse. And then the phone rang and Margaret hurried in to answer it. She summoned Quinn.

Grateful for the chance to escape, Grace said a hasty goodnight. With her arm hooked securely in Elliot's, she hurried out to the familiar safety of his car.

Gradually her thoughts polarized on two facts; she was inescapably in love with Quinn Donovan, and he was the last man on earth she could trust with the keeping of her vulnerable heart.

He was too experienced, too sure of his own compelling attractiveness, too free with the casual endearments to be anything but an older, far more dangerous version of Don Franklin.

EDWARD CALLED the next morning, suggesting that they meet for lunch.

"Lunch," she repeated vacantly. "Sure. Why not?"

They ordered catfish sandwiches at the restaurant, and Grace found herself unexpectedly telling the young artist all about her work for All Seasons. "Tight little renditions, ticky-tacky jingles," she minimized self-consciously, and he insisted on seeing them for himself.

Actually Grace always carried a copy of The Valentine in her purse.

"I like your drawing—this old-fashioned-looking valentine thing, especially," he told her. "Who inspires such palpating sentiments? My freewheeling brother? You two raised a few eyebrows when you snuck out on the party last night. Poor Maggie was fit to be tied."

"I guess if anyone has the right to be upset, she does," she murmured, and waited for a rebuttal.

"Could be. He took her in five years ago and gave her a job, straightened out the mess she had made of her life." Edward shrugged. "Quinn has this overgrown sense of responsibility. He was landed with a king-size load of it before he was even out of high school. Our old man bowed out, and Mama, bless her, wasn't up to dealing with a houseful of little blessings on less than nothing." She felt almost guilty for allowing him to continue. "He hung around a construction site. Learned in the saddle. Before he was done, he had put us all through school." Edward's face reflected something of the admiration he felt for his brother, and Grace swallowed around the constricting lump in her throat.

"He waited until the last one of us was launched before he finally got his degree." A fleeting frown passed over Edward's attractive young features. "He didn't have much time for his own pleasures back in those days. I seem to remember a girl—Allie, or something unusual like that," he mused, and then shook his head in dismissal of ancient history. "I was too wrapped up in my own affairs to pay much attention at the time. If Maggie loves him, it's no more than he deserves."

For a long while they just sat there, staring into the shaft of afternoon sunshine that filtered through the climbing plants in the window.

*

SHE COULD still back out. Just because she had promised Edward she'd be there... Then Quinn phoned just as she was hurrying out the door to school and offered her a ride to Atlanta on Saturday morning. "No point in taking two cars," he reasoned. "Besides, I haven't had time to ask how your battered shin is. You managed to get away before I could even speak to you the other night."

"You were busy."

"And you were suddenly in a terrific hurry," he drawled "I'll pick you up about nine, then. We'll stay over and come back early Sunday afternoon. We'll have all the time in the world to talk on the long drive, and there are a few important things we have to clear up between us.''

With that enticing proposition dangling before her, she was lost. And almost for school.

If she had had trouble concentrating on her classwork before, she now found it impossible. Her sigh of relief at the class-break buzzer was plainly audible.

There was a blue truck pulling into the parking lot on the other side of the new dorm site. A QD truck. Another sigh gusted out into the empty classroom as Grace watched Quinn swing out of the cab.

A girl in pink overalls cut across campus to waylay Quinn as he strode onto the building site. Carly Johns, her brash red hair bouncing, had dashed up to stand panting before him, and while Grace watched, the girl talked and Quinn listened intently. His lips moved once, his distinctive brows lifted momentarily and then he placed his large, shapely hands on each side of Carly's face and kissed her on the forehead!

Grace wheeled away from the window. She entered the corridor just as Quinn came in the east door. He called out to her, but she had caught a glimpse of Elliot, and she dashed off after him.

''Elliot! I haven't seen you lately,'' she greeted him.

''Not since the party...'' His voice trailed off, and then, gathering determination, he plowed ahead. ''I certainly hope I didn't foster any false impressions that day—'' He broke off.

Grace impulsively reached up and kissed Elliot's soft, slightly pink cheek.

Grace turned away, her eyes unconsciously sweeping the crowded hallway. She was in time to see a towering, Stetson-topped head disappear through the east door.

By Saturday morning she was ready to prove her immunity both to Quinn and to herself.

She closed the door and locked it behind her when she heard the sports car crunch onto her shelled driveway. Quinn met her halfway across the front porch, a scowl on his face. He hooked her bag with a single finger and led her down the shallow steps, and only then did she see the slender, shapely arm resting on the passenger window.

"Will you have enough room in the back?" Quinn's voice was laced with what sounded like impatience. "Maggie gets carsick. She didn't think you'd mind."

By dint of a few extraordinary contortions she managed to insert herself into the minute space available.

By the time they reached Atlanta, Grace wondered if one could develop claustrophobia in a matter of a few hours. Dense fog was punctuated only by the hazy gleam of slowly moving traffic as Quinn homed in on the hotel nearest the gallery.

It was an older hotel with a richly appointed interior. Margaret claimed to be starving, and Quinn looked queryingly at Grace.

"Not for me, thanks. I'm going to soak the kinks out of my bones and then nap awhile."

"Come *on*, darling," Margaret insisted. "She's certainly old enough to look after herself, and I want to go shopping before tonight. There's a fantastic jewelry store right here in the hotel, and you haven't bought me my valentine yet."

Grace went to her room and took a nap until a soft rap on her door aroused her. She wriggled upright to scowl at the door and yanked the bedspread loose, swirling it about her like a king-size sari. "All right," she grumbled, opening the door.

He sauntered in, looking exhausted. Evidently a shopping trip with his girlfriend-secretary wasn't among the more restful ways to spend an afternoon.

"Did you find Margaret a proper valentine?" she sniffed and then could have bit her tongue. It was exactly the sort of snide remark a jealous woman would make!

"She seemed to think so. Aren't you going to ask what brought you?" he inquired with mild curiosity.

Her head came up, sleep-clouded eyes searching his face warily. "Why should you bring me anything?"

"Why shouldn't I?" He shifted his weight and dug into one of his pockets, coming up with a small, domed leather box. The look he leveled at her was totally inscrutable as he handed it to her.

She swallowed convulsively, acutely conscious of his enigmatic gaze on her as she flipped open the small box. It was a pendant. Suspended from a flat, supple chain with a small gold cage encircling a heart fashioned of some strange, dark stone. The deep blue surface of the small heart gleamed with tiny flecks of gold.

"Lapis lazuli. Your stone. Didn't I tell you once that your eyes were the color of lapis?"

She looked up—right into the trap of his smiling eyes. "Quinn, I can't accept this. I mean, it's lovely—it's the most exquisite thing I've ever seen, but you know I can't—"

Like quicksilver, his mood reversed to poorly concealed impatience. He hunched his shoulders and wheeled away. "I'll buy you a box of fancy chocolates, then! Will your silly, hypocritical principles allow you to accept that?"

She caught him just before he reached the door, stumbling on the enveloping folds of the bedspread. "Quinn, wait!" She tugged the spread up.

"I've waited a little too long as it is! I should have taken the bait the first time you threw it out, only it took me a while to discover who you were!" His hands closed over her shoulders. And then, as if he were confused or had remembered something unsettling, he shook his head. "I keep forgetting," he muttered under his breath, "that it wasn't you who sent me all those love letters," he grated.

Bewildered, she searched his narrowed eyes for a clue. "I sent you *what?*"

His eyes slid away. With a soft oath, he captured her mouth. His hands were everywhere, moving over her back to curve beneath her hips, stroking her satiny flanks. He found her breasts, crushing them softly with trembling restraint, and then he held her away, emitting a groan of raw agony. "Hell, Grace, are you deliberately trying to drive me over the edge? Look at you!"

She did. He had stepped back, raking a trembling hand through his unruly hair, and Grace swayed as he removed the support of his powerful arms. She took one stricken look at her own nakedness and closed her eyes.

"You'd better lower the voltage for that pasty-faced boyfriend of yours, or one of these days you're going to blow out his circuits!"

Her eyes were still closed tightly when she heard the door open and then close again, and the soft snick of the lock released the tears that could no longer be held back.

BY THE TIME she had dressed Grace was in an almost unnaturally calm frame of mind. It was interrupted by Margaret's voice calling through the door. "Grace? Are you ready yet? Quinn's in a rotten mood, so I wouldn't advise keeping him waiting."

Grace opened the door. The other woman was stunningly overdressed in dark green satin harem pants with a gold lamé halter and jacket. In her ears were enormous, barbaric cubes of gold, studded with small, dark green stones. Emeralds?

"Like them? An early valentine."

"Lovely. They match your outfit beautifully."

"That's what Quinn thought," Margaret retorted smugly.

Grace's eyes moved involuntarily to the small, domed box on her dresser, and Margaret, following her gaze, reached for it, flipping it open. "Oh, aren't you going to wear yours? I told Quinn it would be embarrassing not to have something for you, since you happened to be our guest this weekend. Don't tell me you don't like my taste in costume jewelry. I thought it was so cute!" Her small laugh rippled out into the tense atmosphere.

With the unnatural calmness that had accompanied her

every action for the past half hour or so, Grace lifted the fragile chain from its bed of white satin and fastened it on, feeling the coldness of the metal and stone steal the warmth from the intimate valley between her breasts. She gathered up her gloves and purse and led the way out.

In the brightly lighted gallery Edward extricated himself from the small group of well-dressed patrons and hurried to meet her. He was leading her across the room to a grouping of small silverpoint drawings when they were intercepted by a tall, heavyset man who had evidently been sampling the liquid refreshments.

"This is absolutely the biggest load of hogwash I've seen this side of a pig farm, Eddie baby."

Grace almost lost her grasp on the slender stem of her wineglass. The young artist laughed and clapped the offender on the shoulder. "You'd be the expert on that subject, you ol' son of a gun. Grace, this lecherous sot is my good friend Farnum Taylor, the Fourth. As if the first three weren't enough, his folks had to go and commit the ultimate folly. Folly, meet Grace Spencer—artist, poet and all-around inspiration who braved the fog to be with me in my moment of stark terror."

Farnum, who, to Grace's amusement, actually answered to Folly, accompanied them on their tour of the show. Someone claimed Edward's attention, and Grace and Folly moved on. The talk gradually shifted from art to other topics, and Grace was grateful not to be left on her own while Edward held court.

Through a break in the crowd she caught sight of Quinn. He seemed to grow more morose as the evening wore on, and more than once she felt the impact of his lacerating gaze as she laughed at some outrageous remark of Folly's. Margaret was never more than three feet away from him, which made it all the more surprising when the tall, auburn-haired woman slipped quickly into the lady's lounge behind her.

The door closed quietly and Margaret heaved an overdone

sigh. She flopped on a pink leatherette sofa and said, "Is Folly giving you a lift home tonight? He told me he planned to drive back tonight and get an early start, and I'm sure he'd love to have company on the long drive home."

"Yes, but the fog...." Grace said doubtfully. "I don't think..."

"Folly could find his way through solid concrete," Margaret announced. "Besides, you'd be on your own tomorrow. Quinn and I usually sleep late when we manage to slip away for a weekend." She laughed and the sound rippled unpleasantly across Grace's nerves. "But if you don't mind hanging around on your own—we usually have breakfast in our room."

Our room. *Our* room! The words rang in Grace's head. She forced her voice into a semblance of carelessness and said, "Oh, then don't worry about me!"

The way back to the main gallery led directly past the bar, and Grace helped herself to a fresh drink as she passed. Arranging a brilliant smile on her face, she turned to locate Folly and proceeded to walk blindly into Quinn. The wine sloshed over the rim of her glass.

"You're overdoing it, Grace."

"Yes, Mr. Donovan, whatever you say, Mr. Donovan. Go to the devil, Mr. Donovan." The words were sweetly spoken, and then she turned and wandered off, her head at an uncomfortably high angle.

"You were saying?" Folly questioned, coming up behind her to drape a heavy arm across her shoulders.

"I was saying I'd give anything to be able to get back to Brunswick tonight instead of hanging around until Quinn feels like leaving tomorrow." There! She had committed herself; the next move was up to Folly.

Four hours later she was telling herself bitterly that she *ought* to be committed! Somehow, though, the nightmare trip came to an end. It had been a night out of time, an experience

Grace could hardly believe she had undergone as Folly deposited her bag on the doorstep.

"Gotcha here safe an' sound, huh? Rain or snow, hail or fog, ol' Folly always delivers. Say—you couldn't come up with a cuppa coffee for the road, could you? Those last few miles are killers!"

Closing her eyes on the urge to scream, she said, "Sure, if instant will do."

The house was thoroughly chilled. Grace went out to the kitchen in her coat and put the kettle on to boil. She went back into the living room to strike a match to the wad of newspapers in the bottom of the stove. She found, to her consternation, that Folly had removed his leather topcoat and his shoes and was stretched out under her granny afghan on the yellow sofa, sound asleep.

"Oh, rats!" She wheeled away, leaving the fire unlighted, and switched off the kettle. Coffee could wait. There'd be no point in even trying to wake him now.

She ought to have her head examined for accompanying him, she jeered. She went to her room and crawled wearily under the covers.

Sometime later she awakened by the sound of something falling, followed by a stream of highly original profanity. "Where the blasted devil is the bathroom?" Folly cried pathetically.

"Oh, Folly, stop screeching. It's on the back porch!" She got up and made her way out to the kitchen to plug in the kettle…again. She was actually whistling tunelessly under her breath when Folly lurched back into the room.

He cast her a speaking look. "Just get some coffee in me and I'll see if I can make it out to Jekyll. I've got to fly a blooming plane back and then go on to Cincinnati before tonight."

She was handing him a steaming mug of black coffee when the back door burst open and Quinn appeared, looking almost as wretched as poor Folly.

Of the three of them it was Folly who recovered the use of his tongue first. "Howdy, Quinn baby."

"Would you mind telling me exactly what's going on here?" Quinn enunciated slowly. Each word was released as carefully as if it were riding on a bed of TNT.

"I'm getting my head put back together, and this little angel here—what was your name, honey?" the seated man asked plaintively.

Grace blinked in disbelief.

Before she could protest, Quinn lifted the other man and frog-marched him toward the front door, collecting his coat and shoes as they went. He opened the door, ejected the foolishly grinning Folly and tossed his belongings after him.

Then he turned to Grace. It took only one glance at the implacable set of Quinn's jaw to assure her that escape was out of the question. No five-star general she had ever met carried himself with more of an air of command!

With two great strides he was standing in front of her.

"Do you have any idea of what went through my mind when Maggie told me you and that—that lush had left together in that fog? God!" His eyes closed momentarily, then opened to move over her in an anguished sweep. "Woman, you need a keeper!"

It was the wrong thing to say. She took a deep, steadying breath and then began to speak—grimly, flatly. "Let's get something straight—I don't answer to you. I don't answer to any man, not ever again. If you were worried, then I'm sorry. I didn't know he was in such bad shape. I'm sorry. I ruined your weekend for you by barging in where I wasn't wanted in the first place, and then, when I tried to back out and leave you two some time together, I only made matters worse! So sue me! I don't need you telling me when to stand and when to sit down! I grew up with that sort of male domination and I'm not about to take any more of it!"

At first, when Quinn repeated her words, she didn't recognize them. "Our weekend? Just whose weekend did you think it was supposed to be, Grace?"

"Yours. Yours and Margaret's, and there's no supposing about it!"

He raised a hand to his forehead, massaging the furrows that had suddenly appeared there. "Margaret." He sighed, and something in the resigned way he said the name brought a tight fist to close sickeningly around her stomach.

"There's something you need to see. Maybe after, we can talk without the fireworks." He smiled at her tiredly.

*

MOLLIE TROTTED around the house to greet them as Grace followed Quinn to the door. Since she had last seen his place, the windows had been installed in the main house.

He crossed to one of the built-in cabinets that formed the storage wall and removed a sheaf of papers.

She lowered her eyes to the crisp copy. *"Rose pink are your lips, my love, Iris blue, your eyes. Forget-me-not, for in your hands, My happiness yet lies."* The words, written in her distinctive handwriting and initialed with the small GBS, were flawless photocopies. "From your Secret Admirer" was written in blue ink. Oh, Lord!

She set it aside and read another. The signature, this time, was a skillful copy of her own first name. "Yours lovingly, Grace."

With numbed fingers she reached for yet another one and read the familiar lines. *"Daisies have a secret; Roses have one, too. Listen with your heart, my dear, They'll tell you I love you."*

Dropping the paper onto the small pile, she closed her eyes. All the secret glances, the quickly hushed giggles among the girls at school, came back to her. With a low, anguished groan her thoughts turned in another direction.

Quinn must have thought she was desperate for any man's attention!

"You do know that I had nothing to do with giving you these, don't you?" she muttered.

"After a while it occurred to me that the real author wouldn't have mailed me photocopies—unless she had a heart like a boomerang." His grin was almost up to his old standards. "But when Ogleby forwarded your letter about the sunken bathroom, I recognized the handwriting. You make your *G*'s in a unique way. Back when the first one came, I was amused. That was the secret admirer version. When they kept on coming, one or two a week, I was intrigued, and I was determined to find out who sent them. By the time I got the note from Ogleby, I had—well, you might say, run into you a few times, and I was more intrigued than ever. In the first place you hardly seemed the type. All hedgehog prickles—you certainly didn't seem to think much of me at close range. Even so, I couldn't figure out why you seemed to blow hot and then cold."

"Oh, Lord," Grace mumbled, hiding her face.

"For the life of me, I didn't know whether I was coming or going." He tipped his chair back at a perilous angle. "The thing was, I'd erected this...well, you might say, a barricade, over the years. Oh, I like women as well as the next man."

He grinned that overwhelming grin of his, and Grace felt her defense systems shutting down, one after another. "But, you see, something happened when I was still pretty damp behind the ears. I stuck out my thick neck and had it chopped off by a little gal I sort of fancied at the time. Figured after that I'd be better off playing by a certain set of rules."

Desperately Grace tried to marshal all the reasons why she couldn't afford to succumb to his spell.

"Only I hadn't figured on anything like you." He took her arm and urged her body toward his.

"Honey, I want you. And before you open that stubborn

mouth of yours, I'd better make something else clear to you.''

The stubborn mouth was open, all right—hanging from its hinges.

"My family are all scattered around now, busy with their own affairs, but that doesn't mean they aren't my family. I'm building a home large enough so that if any of them ever need a bolt hole, they'll have it. I want 'em to feel free to get together here on Christmas and Thanksgiving. My lady will have to accept the fact that just because I love her to the ends of the earth and then some, that doesn't mean I love them any the less.''

Grace couldn't have spoken then if her life depended on it.

"So you see, Grace, it has to be a wholehearted commitment. I can only ask you to make the effort—if you care for me enough.''

Somehow she managed to get the words past the lump in her throat. "If I *care* enough! Oh, Quinn, don't you honestly know?''

"Honey, if I did I wouldn't have gone through what I went through last night.'' Grace caught a glimpse of the agony he referred to before the control came down over his melting dark eyes, and it staggered her. "I dumped poor old Maggie out on her front stoop and came charging out to your place breathing fire!''

It was all she could do not to wrap her arms around his waist and bury her head in the strength and security of his arms. Not yet, though—a vestige of wariness held her back from committing herself fully. "About Margaret,'' she began.

"Margaret.'' He sighed. "My whole weekend began to go sour when Margaret invited herself along. And then you rejected the special valentine I had made for you by a goldsmith in Savannah.''

Her lapis heart!

He laughed in half-rueful embarrassment. "Nothing worked out the way I'd planned it. There were all these other fellows hanging around you—I saw red, and believe me, sweetheart, it wasn't valentines! I'd felt like taking your old boyfriend, Rand, apart that day when I saw you kiss him."

She had to break in then. "I saw you kiss Carly just before—"

"Carly Johns? Grace, the poor tad was in tears. When that poor little redhead owned up to sending the poems, I kissed her to keep from spanking her."

His hands were tracing patterns on the sides of her neck. Grace tried to control her crazy impulses. There were one or two things that had to be cleared away.

"Quinn, are you sure there's nothing between you and Maggie? A man doesn't normally give his secretary emeralds unless—"

"Emeralds! You mean those green glass things she picked out? Well, as a matter of fact, I felt a little embarrassed because I had had the heart made for you—I was planning on it being an engagement present. If she'd offered to take herself off somewhere, I'd have bought her the store." He grinned, slowly releasing a button on her blouse.

The last of her doubts drifted into nothingness. "Oh, Quinn, when it comes to loving, you've met your match. As big as you are, I'm not sure you're big enough to handle all the love I have for you."

The gauntlet was down. He picked it up. "Starting now, you're going to prove your words. That ought to take a couple of decades, at least, and then we'll need a few more for me to prove mine, so we'd better not wait around too long to get started. There's no waiting before or after a marriage license in the state of Georgia, you know."

His hands were making slow, soothing movements on her body that were anything but soothing! She raked her fingernails down the powerful muscles of his back, delighting in his immediate response. "Say it, Quinn—you haven't told me yet.'' With every look, every touch of his hands, he was telling her, but she needed to hear the words.

When her beseeching eyes moved past his aggressive chin, past the stern, yet tender mouth, the sensuous brush of his mustache and the proud thrust of his nose, to the melting warmth of his dark eyes, he whispered, ''Listen with your heart, beloved.''

EAST OF TODAY

Dixie Browning

As a beginning to a new venture, the day hadn't been all that promising, Kate admitted to herself as she left the Realtor's office. The eight-hour drive would have put a damper on her usual ebullience without the flat tire, the spilled coffee on her brand-new yellow wraparound, and now this!

Sorry, the secretary had said, but Mr. Elliott was in Florida at a convention. She could pick up the key from Mrs. Greyville at the main house.

What main house? From the instructions, she would have trouble enough locating the bridge to the privately owned island where she *thought* she had leased the only house. Mr. Elliott had assured her he had the ideal location, and since it was away from the village of Hatteras, she should have all the room and privacy she needed. The house was old, he had said, but the rooms were large, and he had arranged for four single beds in each of the two big bedrooms, plus one in each of the smaller rooms.

She found the bridge and paused at its crest to view Coranoke Island for the first time. Perfect! Low and marshy on one end, wooded knolls over to the north and a sandy shoreline with a tall, gaunt house that had not seen paint for generations, if ever. It reminded her of an elderly spinster who lived in the apartment house she had just vacated, and she dubbed her summer home the Gray Lady. Fitting, too, as it belonged to a family called Greyville.

The sandy road split soon after leaving the bridge, and she had no trouble determining which was the main house. A large, shingled home with well-kept gray trim and deep porches furnished with brightly cushioned redwood, it crowned a wooded knoll, sheltering under tall loblolly pines, enormous live oaks and smaller bay trees.

So delighted was she with its appearance that she quite

forgot to be disappointed at her lack of privacy on the island as she knocked on the paneled door.

After a minute she knocked again and looked around for a bell. None was in sight but there was a car in the garage, an impressive gunmetal-gray sedan, so she knew someone must be home. She wandered around the back and, turning a corner, heard a soft, teasing giggle. Following the sound, she saw a bikini-clad girl with red-gold hair and a terrific tan throw herself across a figure in a huge hammock and begin to tickle and tease in a manner that brought a flush to Kate's face.

"Uh—excuse me," she began, and the girl twisted around to stare openmouthed at Kate while her partner tried to regain his feet.

A hammock is no place for sudden moves and Kate watched, amusement lifting the tiredness from her clear, gray-green eyes at the sight of that tall, somehow forbidding-looking man playing footsies with his wife.

Unfortunately, he saw her look, and he was *not* amused as he disengaged himself from both blonde and hammock to stand before her. His tanned body reflected perfect physical condition, and not even his untidy dark blond hair could rob him of a certain air of authority. One dark, slashing eyebrow lifted in his rather aquiline face. Kate suddenly wished she had not gone poking around in strange backyards. She turned to the man's wife, unwilling to suffer any longer the scrutiny of his hard amber eyes.

"Mrs. Greyville, at the Realtor's office said you'd have the key to the other house. I'm Kate Brown—I've leased it for the season, you'll recall." Before the words had faded, Kate was wondering what sort of mistake she had made. The other woman's expression combined surprise and a sort of sly amusement, and she cut her wide, china blue eyes at her husband as if inviting him to share in the joke.

But the man only glared at Kate, his hands resting insolently on hips left bare above low-slung homespun jeans, and his gaze left none of her untouched. He would have towered above her own five foot six even on level ground, but standing above her on the porch, he had an unfair advantage, and Kate, who had driven four hundred miles, suddenly ran out of patience. She had sunk almost all her savings into this venture, the lease being the largest part of it, and she was in no mood now to play games with some petty tyrant.

"The key, if you please," she snapped, staring right back at him.

"Mrs. Greyville isn't here, but if you insist, I'll see if I can locate the key. I don't suppose you'd consider finding other accommodations?"

"Of course not! I was told that this was the only place suitable for my needs on either island and I paid a whacking good sum for it. I assure you, I have an official, airtight lease, and I'm not about to give it up and start all over again!"

He turned and slammed into the house while she waited. Uncomfortably aware of the scrutiny of a pair of rather vacant-looking blue eyes, she studied the distant shoreline until she was drawn to return the stare. The girl was certainly rude, but except for a petulant expression she was remarkably pretty.

No telling who she was, Kate mused as her anger slowly drained away and she heard her reluctant landlord return. She accepted the grudgingly proffered key with mumbled thanks and stalked away.

The Gray Lady, for all its unprepossessing appearance at the edge of the Pamlico Sound, suited her purposes admirably. She had carefully selected her applicants so that the sexes fit evenly into the two large bedrooms, more like dormitories now. The living room would be perfect for an indoor studio. The bathroom was ancient but adequate, and the kitchen was something from a Victorian nightmare, but she had no doubts that Annie could cope.

At the end of the lush row of oleanders that bordered the drive to the other house, Kate saw a discreet sign announcing the house as Bay Oaks. Well, unless her directional knob was out of kilter, Gray Lady was west and Bay Oaks was east, and never the twain should meet. She had come far enough east, anyway, settling for this drawing card of the Cape Hatteras National Seashore Park.

THE WATER was deliciously hot, and she soaked thankfully in the claw-footed old tub, wondering what Iola and Frances were doing now. She must remember to call her sister France. Now that she had decided to go for a stage career, the name Frances Brown had been examined for star quality and was found lacking.

Kate sighed and squeezed a sponge full of scented water over her shoulders. She missed them already. Iola, her mother, had been divorced since Kate was fifteen and France nine and they had more or less raised each other since. Kate had been the most practical of the trio, and she had worked to augment her mother's small annuity and to put herself through college. Iola added to their tight budget with the occasional sale of an article, for she was a freelance writer of the freest sort.

France was almost twenty-one now and truly beautiful. She resembled their mother with her blond hair and brown eyes. Kate was the plain one, with her unremarkable features and average coloring. That more than a few men had found her worth pursuing did nothing to change her mind about her own appearance, nor did it bother her that she lacked her sister's beauty. She possessed a marketable talent, and a practical business head, and by the end of the summer session, Kate intended to have saved enough to send her sister to England, to audition at the London Academy of Music and Dramatic Art.

She allowed the water to gurgle away while her mind touched on another factor in her decision to strike out on her own. Hal Brookwood.

With a mutter of impatience, she dried herself with a thick towel and stepped into her yellow lawn pajamas. They smelled faintly of a wildflower sachet she favored.

Almost too tired to sleep after making ten beds, Kate suddenly remembered that her last meal had been a hamburger and coffee early that afternoon at Manteo. She had yet to shop for groceries but there were still two of the hard-boiled eggs she had brought from home and possibly a little coffee in her thermos.

She had just peeled both eggs and sat at the red Formica-topped table in the kitchen, when the door opened to admit her landlord.

"You *are* Mr. Greyville, aren't you?" she asked, intent on getting to the bottom of it all before chastising him for not knocking.

He crossed the kitchen uninvited and pulled out a chair, swinging it around, then dropped into it. "Right. Cameron Greyville, Miss...Brown? I just now discovered the details of your lease from my grandmother, and since your light was still on, I thought we might discuss it."

Still indignant at his late intrusion, she was totally forgetful of her own casual attire, and she glared at him balefully.

"Look, Miss Brown. The agent evidently misplaced my last instructions, which were *not* to rent the house this season. I intend to spend a great deal of time here, and I need peace and quiet. I tried to reach him tonight but was told he'd gone off to some convention."

At least he seemed in a more amenable mood, Kate thought wryly, intent, no doubt, on talking her around. He looked as if no one had ever dared say no to him.

"I can arrange for you to have accommodation at a motel for the entire summer for the same amount you would have paid for this old place," he told her. "Shall I make the call?"

The eyes she remembered as golden brown looked almost black and completely expressionless.

"Sorry. It wouldn't suit me. And I've had the agent replace the bedroom furniture with cots and store the living room things to make way for my tables. The place is perfect and we're all set to start."

"We? I thought you were alone, Miss Brown. It is Miss?"

His glance touched her hand and her fingers clenched involuntarily.

"Day after tomorrow, Mr. Greyville, there will be nine others besides myself staying here," she informed him. She might not be *Mrs.* Kate Brown, but she was sure enough Kate Brown, A.W.S., and that signified her hard-earned inclusion into the nation's most prestigious watercolor society.

She was unprepared for his explosion. "Nine! Good Lord, why?"

"Ten including myself, Mr. Greyville, and what do you mean, why? Because they're paying good money to spend two weeks down here, studying watercolor with me. Then they'll leave and another group will take their place. Why else would I need a place this size?"

"Studying watercolor!"

Her small store of patience ran out. "Look, I explained to your Mr. Elliott..."

"He's not *my* Mr. Elliott!"

"Well, it's hardly *my* fault if you can't keep up with your own property! I leased this place in good faith for a legitimate business venture, and I don't *think* you'll find a loophole, Mr. Greyville, no matter how badly you want me out of here. And now, if you *don't* mind, I'd like to go to bed!" It was only then that she realized she had been sitting there in her thin cotton pajamas, and it must have dawned on him at the same time, for she felt his glance drop down to her throat and the roundness below. Once more she felt hot color rise to her face.

This was getting to be ridiculous! Already she had blushed more in one day than she had in the past fifteen years.

"Why couldn't you have stayed home and taught your painting classes?" he demanded.

"Because to attract people who are willing to pay top prices, you have to have more than one drawing card."

"The island being one," he sneered, "and I suppose *you're* the other?"

"You're darned right I am!"

"At least you're open about it. I've yet to meet a woman who didn't want to know, first, how much she could get and, second, how little she could give in return!"

Which seemed to Kate a harsh judgment for trying to make a living. "Does that go for your little hammock mate?" she asked sweetly.

"That, Miss Brown, is none of your business."

"Well, all I have to say is that any poor fool of a woman who's interested in you would *have* to be after your money, because you obviously don't have anything else to offer her."

She flinched from the flaring of his nostrils and the sparks that shot from his eyes, but before she could make an apology, he had turned on his heel and left, slamming the door behind him.

Long after she crawled wearily between the sheets, she was aware of something tingling in the atmosphere that hadn't been there before. It was the feeling of expectancy one senses sometimes before a severe electrical storm.

KATE AWAKENED early the next morning completely restored. She pulled on a pair of white jeans and a coral bouclé top and hurried outdoors to greet the day.

There were gulls wheeling, and a fresh breeze off the water made her wrinkle her nose in delight at the tantalizing blend of odors. She was determined to explore her surroundings before heading for the grocery store in Hatteras. This was her last free day for the next two weeks.

She came to a small, weathered wharf and admired the reflections of the two boats moored there—one a sleek new fiberglass runabout, the other a wooden skiff. She might be able to borrow it sometime. It would be fun to explore the coastline.

"Hello there," called someone from behind her.

Turning easily, she saw a tiny gray-haired woman in orange pants and a wild-print smock. She was carrying a trowel in one hand and a basket in the other. "I heard you'd arrived.

Hope you didn't have any trouble getting in. I was at a garden club meeting. Look.'' She held out her basket. ''Bottlebrush. It's Australian. Going to try it in the shelter of the house. What do you think?''

Bemused, Kate held out her hand.

''So you're Kate Brown, huh? Will you come up to the house for some coffee? I haven't had mine yet—wanted to get these seedlings out.''

The other woman had begun walking back in the direction of Bay Oaks, but Kate held back doubtfully. She didn't think the owner of the island would welcome an intrusion at this early hour, although after last night she owed him one.

''I don't think I'd better, Mrs....Miss...''

''Oh, call me Dotty. Cam says I am—dotty, that is. Cam is my grandson. Cam Greyville.''

''Oh. Then you're Mrs. Greyville?''

''Dotty Greyville. Coffee now? Don't hold back on Cam's account. He won't bite while I'm around, and that so-called secretary of his won't be up until someone tosses a stick of dynamite into her room.''

''Yes, well, all the same, I think I'll stay out and enjoy the morning a few minutes more before I head for the grocery store,'' Kate said.

Dotty dropped onto a lichen-covered bench under the oaks and Kate followed suit, amused to see a collection of gems that would have paid her salary several times over on the gnarled, dirt-covered hands. They fell into a discussion of Kate's plans and then Dotty went on to talk about her grandson. ''Stays up there in New York as long as he has to, then he slips away down here where he does his real work. He's the chief design engineer for Greyville Electronics. He loves it down here—says it's the only place he can hear himself think—but that pink-haired popsie comes trailing after him every chance she gets, and Lord knows how anybody can concentrate with her and her radio around.''

''She's awfully pretty,'' Kate ventured.

"Humph! Her type's easy enough to find, but he's not the marrying kind, thank the Lord."

"You don't want him to marry?" Kate asked curiously, dismayed at her own interest.

"Not one of those, I wouldn't. How'd you like to be shut up in the house for a long rainy spell with a pink-haired, half-naked female who talks baby talk? You'd see Miss Bebe Conlon hightailing it back up north if ever the bottom fell out of Greyville stock, and don't think Cam doesn't know it. His feet are planted firmly on the ground."

I'll just bet they are, Kate thought grimly. If she ever saw a man who looked as if he could hold his own against any odds it was Cameron Greyville. She decided later on, when she was putting away enough food for the first few days after spending an alarming amount of money for groceries, that she was going to like Dotty Greyville very much. The old woman with her pixie haircut and outspoken opinions was something of a tartar, but then, Kate never had cared for namby-pambies.

*

THE NEXT morning Kate was up again before six, looking forward to a few hours of glorious solitude. She had mentioned the skiff to Dotty yesterday and got permission to use

The skiff handled well, and Kate managed to work her way to a shoal she had spotted earlier. She rolled her pants legs up before jumping out to haul her boat up onto the hard sand. It was far heavier than it looked, but she gave it a shove and secured it the best she could.

There was not a whole lot to see. Overhead a single gull protested the invasion of his privacy and she grinned up at him. "You, too? Fie on you!"

She walked on, her grin fading. So far, except for Dotty, she had found scant welcome here. It took time, of course,

to become established in any new neighborhood, but tha
Cameron Greyville was the most aggravating man, with a
arrogant manner. Hard to imagine his being Dotty's grand
son, but then again, like didn't always breed like.

She concentrated for a while on the colors, painting in he
mind, arguing with herself as she sat on the sand and gaze
across the Sound to the invisible mainland.

It was some time before she recognized her name among
the ambient sounds—and the impatient buzz of a distant out
board motor. She searched the horizon before she saw tw
figures on the wharf of Coranoke. One was waving and th
other was Cameron Greyville. She would have recognize
that lean, powerful build anywhere—and the man beside him
looked familiar, as well.

Hoping that she was mistaken, she turned toward the skiff
only to see it drifting away. Darn! She should have though
of tides, but it hadn't occurred to her that the water coul
rise so much in such a short time.

The air was suddenly rent by an angry roar and she looke
up, startled, to see the runabout heading for the shoal. Ther
was only one man in the cockpit.

"Jump in," Cameron ordered, giving her barely time t
settle before peeling off to circle the skiff. He scooped u
the bow line and made it fast to a cleat behind him.

The ride was completed in utter silence, if one discounte
the roar of all that horsepower. Kate was glad to see Hal'
friendly face, even if he was one of the reasons she ha
needed to get away from home.

"Hello, Hal." She climbed out of the runabout, ignorin
his outstretched hand. Cameron didn't offer to help he
"What are you doing in these parts? I thought you'd be a
tied up at the store." She suffered his kiss with more warmth
than she would have had not Cameron Greyville been eyein
them with that infuriating condescension.

She had met Hal Brookwood three years ago and he ha
been her most persistent admirer. She dated him occasionally
They had met when she went into his bookstore to buy a

supplies. Lately, though, she had sensed a more serious note in his attentions and she had been glad of a legitimate excuse to end the light relationship.

"I left things in good hands. Sal Turner is working out even better than I had hoped. Anyway—" he looked at her with heavy significance "—I missed you." There was a spaniel look in his large, dark eyes, and she hated herself for not caring more.

They strolled back toward Gray Lady. Kate felt as if eyes were burning into her back, but when she paused to scoop up her shoes and glanced back, Cameron had already gone. Hal was distinctly put out when she told him he would have to find a room at a motel in Hatteras because her students and her housekeeper were all due today and there just wasn't any more room.

The first couple came just after lunch, and then cars seemed to roll across the old wooden bridge with a paradelike regularity.

By dinnertime everyone had arrived except Annie. Two women from Virginia were veterans of many workshops, and there was an enthusiastic beginner and a gorgeous would-be fashion designer, Stella Wright, who turned full batteries on to the only male under forty. Kate watched with amusement as they sized each other up.

Tony Palani had roared across the bridge in a red Aston Martin. Dark and good-looking, he soon evaluated the group, setting his gaze speculatively on Stella, as he made himself at home.

They were putting together a meal of cold cuts and salads when Cam appeared in the doorway to tell Kate she had a phone call. He stood there, looking the group over derisively, his eyes finally returning to Stella, who was leaning back in chair sipping a tall drink while the others fixed the meal.

Kate followed Cam across the clearing between the two houses. "She's not still hanging on, is she?" she called out suddenly.

He waited for her to catch up. "No, there's an operator

number for you to call. What makes you think it's a woman?''

"Oh, well, I just assumed it was Iola—my mother. She didn't say?''

"No, she didn't, but, as a matter of fact, it was a woman I suppose with loverboy on the scene the odds were cut down.''

"You never quit, do you? For your information, Hal is not my loverboy,'' she snapped. "Not that it's any of your business!''

Dotty greeted her with an invitation to dinner.

"Thanks, Dotty, but I've got the whole crew over there improvising something since our cook is late getting here.'' She waited for the operator to connect her, and then she was speaking to Annie.

"What happened?''

"Oh, Katie, I'm flat on my back in Forsyth Memorial, and I could kick myself up one side and down the other! Here I've gone and let you down, and I was looking forward to this summer so much!'' It seemed that Annie had climbed the foldaway ladder to her attic and attempted to bring down a trunk single-handed. She was now undergoing treatment for a slipped disc and would be out of commission for no telling how long.

After assuring her that there was no problem on this end, Kate invited her down to recuperate whenever she felt up to it, but they both knew there was little chance of that. She hung up the phone and turned away dejectedly. How in the world would they manage? Catering to eight people was a full-time job, and Kate could only hope to find someone locally.

As she passed the open doorway of the living room, Dotty asked if it had been bad news.

"'Fraid so. The woman who was to cook and keep house for us won't be able to make it, and my classes start tomorrow. I don't suppose you know of anyone I could hire? I can handle the laundry myself if I have to.''

"Maybe your good friend will stay and lend a hand," Cam suggested. "He looked the sort to turn a hand to anything if the rewards were sweet enough."

"I'm afraid that won't be practical," she retorted, turning toward the front door.

"I'll see you out," Cam murmured.

"That won't be necessary, thanks."

"It's as good a time as any to speak to you about your...artist friends."

The pause was somehow insulting.

"I came down to the island for peace and quiet, and I'd appreciate it if you'd restrain the freer of the free spirits among them. Let's not have any going and coming at all hours, especially the Latin-lover type with the sports car. Dotty sleeps on this side of the house, and I won't have her disturbed."

"Is that quite all?" Kate said tightly.

"No. While your crew looks harmless enough, keep in mind that this is a pretty conservative area and any wild parties or outdoor life classes—unadorned, that is—won't go unnoticed. You might find yourself asked to move on. A word to the wise."

By this time Kate had come to a slow simmer, and she turned to face him squarely. "Now you listen to me, Mr. Cameron Greyville. I don't know who gave you the right to make snap judgments about people, but you're absolutely wrong about my friends. From what I've seen of *your* taste in companions, you don't have any room to talk!"

"And now who's making judgments, Kate Brown? Just keep them away from this side of the island, do you understand?"

"Oh, but..." The protest broke from her before she could stop it. "Do you mean we can't even paint from the knoll or the grove on the other side? The best views of Hatteras are from there and I had planned..."

"I'll just bet you had, Miss Brown. I can see the avaricious gleam in those cool, deceptive eyes of yours when you look at my place, but you leased the old house. Everything else is out of bounds! And, while I think of it, stay out of my boats, too.''

"Gladly, Mr. Greyville! I don't even care to breathe the air in your vicinity!''

Kate had gotten over the misfortune of losing Annie's services by the time she reached Gray Lady. Cameron spelled trouble, and she was not sure just how to get around his edict, but no one in her right mind would expect her to keep eight adults shut up indoors for two weeks. She wasn't sure of her legal boundaries, but she would not relinquish any of her rights without a darned good fight. Even the thought of it brought a militant brilliance to her eyes.

THE FIRST class was conducted just over the bridge on Hatteras. Kate was able to size up the widely varied abilities of her students and consider the best approach to teaching them.

Among the middle range were two students who promised to become problems. Stella could probably have achieved exhibiting status but for a bone-deep inertia that spilled over into every aspect of her life. Her two interests, in seeming order of importance, were men and fashion, and that presented her next problem—Tony Palani.

Tony was good-looking in a dark, flashy way, and he made quite sure everyone realized the extent of his—or rather, his father's—wealth. He had immediately set his sights on both Stella and Kate, and he let it be known that he had a great deal to offer his lucky final choice.

As far as painting was concerned, he was an accomplished hobbyist who depended more on his charm than on any real ability, and Kate was afraid that long before his two weeks were up that charm was going to wear terribly thin. Hal was still in residence, having moved into Annie's room, and when he volunteered to help with the chores, Kate had little choice but to take him up on his offer. Actually, she really needed his help, for if teaching alone didn't drain her energies, there was the perpetual fetching of missing equipment and whatever else had been left behind when they trooped out to location.

Of course, they wouldn't have to go all that far if Cameron Greyville weren't such a beast about it. The best parts of the island were going to waste while her little troupe had to trudge a mile or so in the hot sun or pile into cars to go even farther afield.

It only served to underline her feelings about men in general. She found them totally unreasonable. Either they claimed to be wasting away from unrequited love and wanted her to give up her career and devote herself to making them happy or they expected her to hop into bed with them with no commitment on either side. There had already been a few hints of the latter from Tony, and the classes had hardly begun!

Hal departed early Wednesday morning after promising to try to make the trip again over the Fourth of July. Kate nodded in resignation. No matter what she said, he would come anyway. He was convinced that she loved him.

She saw nothing at all of Cameron, but Dotty strolled over one morning to look over the shoulders of the painters, and she volunteered a few comments that indicated familiarity with the medium. She made some ribald comments about Bebe Gonlon's taste in music when a breeze brought the tinny sound across the bridge. "She's hanging on a lot longer than usual. I'm wondering how long Cam's temper is going to hold up," Dotty said.

"We're treated to a free daily concert, with the wind in this direction every day this week," Kate said. It was as close to a complaint as she dared come, and she only hoped Dotty would repeat it where it would do the most good.

On the first day of the second week, Stella was absent from the afternoon class. She had skipped a few of the evening sessions to go out with Tony, but today he was very much in attendance, his good-looking face a little sulky.

By the time dinner was over and they were clearing the tables for the evening critique session, Stella had still not returned. They were well under way with an avid discussion when they heard a car pull up out front. Kate looked up from her demonstration to see Stella and Cam enter.

"We went out to dinner," she announced. "Hope you didn't wait for me."

"No," Kate replied coolly, flipping over the paper she had been demonstrating a masking technique on. "Did you have a nice evening?" She sounded peeved, and she could have kicked herself!

Stella thanked Cameron sweetly for the dinner, then promised to be on the wharf at eight-thirty the next morning.

So much for art lessons, Kate thought sourly. For a girl like Stella Wright, there was no contest between slaving over a hot drawing board and hanging around with an attractive man.

Tony made the most of her defection by concentrating on Kate. His previous attempts at flirtation had been diluted between the two of them, but now she had to put him in his place several times a day.

It was the next to last night, and the evening critique had given way to a flurry of matting and hanging. Kate had posted several notices in Hatteras for their one-day exhibit. It was a windup of the session, and she planned it mainly for the fun of seeing public reaction to their work.

Exhausted after a day of trying to impart enough to the students to keep them going on their own, Kate had wandered out to the bridge to watch the stars reflected in the ripples below.

"Stargazing?" Tony asked from behind her.

Kate turned and gazed at him warily. "No, just needing a few minutes alone. I run out of steam about this time every day."

"It does get to be a bit much, doesn't it?" he agreed, leaning over the rail beside her. "Now, if we were to do it all over again, I'd insist on choosing my roommate." He nudged her shoulder and picked up one of her hands, playing idly with her fingers before she snatched them away.

"Not now, Tony, please. I'm not in the mood for one of your verbal passes." She moved away.

"Then we'll move on to the action," he said, snaking an arm around her and pulling her against him, overcoming her resistance with a surprisingly wiry strength. When he crushed her arms against his chest and buried his face in her throat, she raged, "Tony, stop it!"

"Come on, honey, don't be like that. You haven't had any loving since Brookwood left, and you must be as hungry as I am."

She kicked at him and lost her balance. He took advantage of that to cover her mouth with his hot, eager lips. Finally, she decided to cool his ardor by remaining impassive.

But the kiss went on and on, and she felt her stomach churning. There was nothing more repulsive than being mauled by someone she didn't care for, and Tony Palani had rapidly descended to someone she actively despised. She was still standing frozen in his embrace when the headlights swept around the curve to the bridge approach. Tony's face left hers as the gunmetal Mercedes passed within a foot of where they were standing.

Cameron was at the wheel, his face a sneering mask, and silhouetted beside him was Stella Wright.

THE DAY of the open house began with showers and cleared just before lunch. They had chipped in and bought the makings for punch, popped gallons of popcorn and cubed pounds of cheese to go with the assortment of crackers.

The paintings were only matted, but they looked good. By careful selection, it had been possible to include several from each student, and everyone was in a cheerful mood.

Everyone except Tony, that was. He was still sulking after having struck out the night before.

More guests showed up than Kate had dared hope, and there were even a few sales to brighten spirits. At about four-

thirty, she sensed attention pull away from the exhibit and
the refreshment table, and she leaned over to see Cameron
at the front door, his hand on Dotty's shoulder.

Dotty hurried over and spoke to several of the students,
but Cameron remained aloof. Kate wondered in spite of herself how such a mean, hateful soul could be housed in such
a magnificent body.

"It's delightful, Kate," Dotty exclaimed, coming over
with a cup of punch in her bejeweled hand. "The show, I
mean, although this punch isn't half-bad. What is it, anyway?"

"Nothing you'd ever recognize, Dotty."

They laughed together. Dotty expressed an interest in one
of the watercolors of Bay Oaks, and then Stella and Tony
converged on them from opposite sides of the room. Tony
was under the influence of something more than innocent
punch. Kate braced herself for unpleasantness.

"Hello, Dotty," Stella drawled. "Haven't seen you around
lately."

"No, but then, I try to stay out of the way whenever Cam
has a heavy load of work to get done," Dotty answered
smoothly, her small eyes snapping.

Stella shrugged off the innuendo, and sniffed when Tony
draped an arm across Kate's shoulder. "Did I tell you, Stella,
that I've decided to stay over for the next session?"

Kate gasped. "But you can't. It's all filled!"

"Oh, no, it's not. Did I forget to give you the message?"
He looked at her in mock consternation. "Sorry, sweetheart.
Greyville told me but I clean forgot. The kid from Richmond
won't be coming. He had to have an emergency appendec-
tomy, and that's a refundable cause for dropping out, so I've
decided to do you a favor and stay on," he said with a sickening leer.

Kate would have given twice the tuition just to wipe that
look off his face. She was determined to have it out with
him, but not here in front of an all-too-avid audience. She
couldn't help but be aware of the other two women as she

stood there in Tony's casual-appearing embrace. Stella looked knowingly amused and while Dotty looked sympathetic enough, she was unable to keep that slightly wicked look of speculation from her eyes.

Only Cameron's reaction was hidden from her, and she would not turn to face him. She fancied she could feel the heat emanating from his body behind her and so was doubly shocked to hear the front screen door slam and see him stride past the window on his way back to Bay Oaks.

*

TRUE TO HIS threat, Tony stayed on, and Kate could come up with no grounds for turning him away. She did need the money, for even though Annie's salary was saved, she had not counted on the high cost of the meals.

Tony's staying also meant that she did not have the two-day respite between sessions. Everyone was packed and gone by nine on Saturday morning. She had counted on having a quiet little break, but Tony insisted on taking her sight-seeing, and she found herself agreeing weakly. Maybe she was more tired than she thought.

They ate in one of the better restaurants on Saturday night, after dropping off a huge load of laundry, and Kate had to admit it was nice to enjoy a meal she hadn't prepared. They had reached the dessert stage when Cameron and Dotty walked in. Dotty led her grandson across the room to their waterfront table, ignoring Tony's frown as she greeted Kate warmly.

"Won't you join us?" Tony asked reluctantly.

"Oh, but you're just finishing," Dotty protested.

"Nonsense," Cameron insisted, drawing up two more chairs. "I'm sure they'll enjoy another coffee, and we'll have the advantage of a good table." He looked lean and handsome and somehow pleased with himself, and it occurred to Kate that such a man could be infinitely dangerous.

They parted finally, with the excuse of having to collect the laundry plus a few groceries, and it did not occur to Kate until they were on their way back to Coranoke that tonight she would be alone in the house with Tony. She felt suddenly vulnerable, especially since Tony's attitude had deteriorated since dinner.

They pulled up in front of the house. "I'll get the laundry and you can carry the groceries," she said.

"Are you asking or telling?"

"I'm asking, but it wouldn't hurt you to offer. You certainly consume your share of them." Not very gracious, but she couldn't help it.

"Seeing as how I'm paying through the nose for it, you shouldn't complain."

"You know, Tony, you're really not a very nice person, are you?"

"Once you get to know me better, you're going to love me," he told her with a crooked smile. He reached for her, but her hand was on the door latch.

"You're disgusting! I think you'd better take off, Tony. You haven't paid for the second term, and I've found it necessary to limit the enrollment." She was out of the car and reaching for the boxes in the back when he caught her, and she slapped out at him angrily. "Tony, behave yourself!"

He had come around the car so swiftly that he caught her by surprise, his arms circling her waist from behind. She tried kicking, but it didn't work.

"Calm down, sweetheart. You know you've been counting the hours today just like I have." He lifted her by the shoulders and turned her to face him. She swung at him just as the headlights appeared, blinding them for a instant.

"Oh, good Lord, Tony, am I going to have to call the sheriff?" she exploded angrily.

"What would you charge me with? I haven't done anything you haven't been inviting me to do, have I?"

"You're an utter swine!" she yelled at him, jerking from his grasp. She turned and began to run, not caring about the laundry, the groceries or anything except getting away from those clutching hands. Unfortunately, he put out a foot, and she went sprawling headlong into the sand.

"They all fall for me sooner or later," Tony quipped, leaning over to lift her up, but she kicked out at him again.

"Go away, will you? Just leave me alone!" Tears of pure rage burned her eyes.

"You heard what she said. Get!" came a familiar gravelly baritone, and Kate clenched her fists. Was it inevitable that Cam should witness every mortifying encounter she had with Tony?

She felt herself being lifted up from under her arms and then Cameron was inquiring with a rough tenderness if she were all right.

"Fine. What did you expect?" Embarrassment made her sound shrewish.

Cameron's hands dropped from her shoulders. "If I'd expected a little common politeness I'd have been damned disappointed! Go on in to your little friend," he sneered, and turned to go.

"Wait. I'm sorry." She was struggling to keep her voice level. "I'm really sorry. And—and I do thank you, Mr. Greyville. Of course, I could have handled the situation, but even so—"

"Handled the situation? If you had even a grain of sense, you'd never have put yourself in that position in the first place."

"Thank you for those words of wisdom, Mr. Greyville," she blurted. "Just think, if the whole world knew what you know, no one would ever get themselves in trouble again."

"You and that mob of yours. Just tell them to keep away from my side of the island." He was towering over her again, and she thrust her chin out belligerently.

"You didn't object to one of them," she told him with mock sweetness. "I noticed that as soon as your little top-ten tootsie moved out, you filled the vacancy with Stella Wright. Too bad she had to leave, too."

"Too bad is right. At least she knew how to behave like a woman instead of a frustrated, bad-tempered shrew who—"

Kate didn't allow him to finish. She swung wildly, and Cameron stood with mocking insolence and took the blow squarely on the cheek. Then he reached out and jerked her against him with a punishing force as his mouth came down on her outraged protest. She seethed as his hands began to move over her body with an insulting thoroughness, but as the kiss changed into something less aggressive and more subtly seductive, she found her anger draining away. It was then that his kiss broke the barrier of her determination and invaded the warm, soft depths of her.

By the time he had finished, Kate was shaking, and he put her away from him abruptly, retaining the grip on her shoulders before turning her in the direction of Bay Oaks. "Go and tell Dotty to pour you a stiff drink," he ordered peremptorily.

"I can't do that. The groceries... Tony—I don't even know where he is."

"I'll take care of all that. Now go and do as I said."

CAMERON returned some twenty minutes later and, without speaking to either of the two women, poured himself a stiff drink and tossed it back. Then he poured another and sat down. Only then did he look at Kate. "You're welcome to stay the night if you'd care to, but Palani won't be bothering you anymore."

Kate was stunned to realize that she wanted nothing so much as to snuggle into the comfort of this rambling house and forget all about her classes, forget everything except the unqualified friendliness of the old woman and the strength that emanated from Cameron Greyville.

Feeling oddly more threatened now, she made herself stand. "In that case, I can only thank you, but I'll go along now. He...it was just that Tony caught me off guard," she prevaricated. "Thank you again," she blurted, hurrying to the door before either of them could rise.

Tony's car was gone and so were his belongings. In the kitchen the boxes were stacked neatly on the table.

The next morning Kate was awakened by a sound that was all mixed up with a dream and she lay there, blinking awake, as the door opened. Cameron Greyville stood there.

"Are you absolutely insane?" she demanded, sitting up in her thin white nightgown, her dark brown hair tumbling over her tanned shoulders.

"I knocked, but when there was no answer, I was afraid— well, I can see that you're all right now."

"Get out of here!"

"I want to speak to you, before Dotty gets here."

"Look, have you any idea what time it is?"

"Pipe down!" He crossed the room to sit at the foot of her bed. Kate drew the cotton bedspread up under her chin.

"You play a marvelous outraged virgin, my dear, but that's not what I've got on my mind at the moment." His eyes roamed her form clearly outlined beneath the light covers. "Dotty has a bee in her bonnet about taking your course. With Palani gone, there's a vacancy."

"So?" she demanded suspiciously.

"So…let her come, and don't be too critical of her efforts. I want her to enjoy herself without worrying too much about coming up to your standards, if you have any."

"Mr. Greyville, I *do* have standards, and I'm sure Dotty will fit comfortably in the class. I happen to like *her* very much."

"The inference being that you find her grandson less palatable," he jeered.

"Exactly."

"You know, Miss Brown, I find it remarkable that two males in the past two weeks have been willing to risk your thorns in search of any possible nectar," he mused.

"My love life, Mr. Greyville, is my own affair," Kate retorted. "For your information, I find men remarkably easy to do without altogether. They're a bunch of pompous, opinionated, arrogant—''

"Don't choke on your own wrath, Kate, darling. I suspect you're throwing out a Freudian challenge.''

"Get out!'' she raged.

"If I get too bored this summer, I might even take you up on it,'' he promised, closing the door behind himself.

THE SECOND session began smoothly with a more or less harmonious group. It was a younger group, on the whole, with a social worker, a kindergarten teacher, two housewives, a retired minister and two jaded-looking men who told her they were on sabbatical in order to "find themselves.'' Dotty was a delight to have. An added bonus was her permission to use the land nearer the other house.

By the second day, the group had settled down to a good, working pace, and Kate had resigned herself to doing most of the chores, as usual.

On a morning when the thermometer threatened to blow its top, she herded her charges to the other side of Bay Oaks to the shady grove of trees.

They were trudging back for lunch when Cam called to her from the house. "Call came for you half an hour ago,'' he told her.

"Why didn't you call me? I wasn't that far away,'' she snapped. The heat was making her short-tempered.

"Out of sorts, aren't we?'' he murmured maddeningly, looking cool and unfairly handsome behind the screen door.

Kate felt the trickle of perspiration down her back and she felt grubby and mean and unattractive and ridiculously close to tears.

"Don't you want your message?''

"Oh. Well, tell me, then.''

He opened the door and she found herself drawn into the inviting coolness of the hallway.

"Woman by the name of Iola—your mother, I believe— said to tell you that France has tossed her job and that they're coming to spend the rest of the summer at the beach with you. You're to expect them sometime after dark.''

"Tonight? Are you sure? They couldn't. I told her—'' She broke off in dismay.

"Bad news? You don't want them? A little too late for that, I'm afraid, but really, Kate, your mother sounded like a delightful person to me. Still, you're the best judge of that, I guess.'' He finished off a drink and asked if she'd like something cool. "You look as if you could use it,'' he said.

"Thanks,'' she muttered, "but I've got to fix lunch for my group.''

"Let them fend for themselves for once. You can't wet-nurse a bunch of adults all day and be effective as a teacher. Come on. There's shrimp salad, and I'll open you a beer to go with it.''

She allowed herself to go along with the tide, and when he pointed her toward the bathroom with a terse order to wash up, she obeyed with unnatural meekness.

Eileen Greer, the daily, whom Kate had seen several times in the grocery store at Hatteras, smiled at her when she emerged, and directed her to the porch where Cameron and Dotty waited.

"I feel guilty,'' she admitted, accepting the chair Cameron offered. "They're over there at Gray Lady making do with cold cuts while I'm here being served a feast.''

"Gray Lady?'' Cameron's thick brows lifted.

"Oh, it's just a silly name I gave the house when I first got here. It looked so much like a woman I know. You know how things sometimes make you think of people.''

She accepted a serving of delicious-looking shrimp salad and slices of melon, and they all did justice to Eileen's talents in the kitchen. Dotty managed to put away an amazing amount, considering her size and the fact that she interrupted every other bite to remark on something.

"And now,'' Kate said finally, "if I may use your phone, I'd better see if I can line up some accommodations for my improvident family.''

"I wouldn't think of it, Katie," Dotty said.

Kate was taken slightly aback. "Well, of course there's a pay phone...."

"What my grandmother means, Kate, is that we'd be delighted to have them stay here," Cameron said. "There's plenty of room."

"Oh, that's out of the question," Kate protested, but she was no match for the Greyvilles.

KATE MADE it through the rest of the session by filling every hour as full of activity as possible. If she had allowed herself time to think, she might have sat down and wept.

Her family, true to form, had arrived in style. France had blown her severance pay, plus the last of Iola's quarterly check, on a trade-in. The old Ford might not have made the trip, but the disreputable Spitfire was the height of insanity. Her mother—that dreamy, impractical divorcée who at the age of forty-nine wore floating chiffon to do her lick-and-a-promise housework and used an injured knee shamelessly when the occasion arose to get all sorts of preferential treatment—traveling across the state in an open sports car with a stagestruck all-but-teenager! But they had settled into Bay Oaks with the ease of old family friends.

It was no surprise that Dotty and Iola hit it off at once, for they were both complete originals, but to see France hanging on to Cameron's every word was a bit much. Of course, he fell for it hook, line and sinker. Few males could resist France's voluptuous little figure, contrasting, as it did, with her blond curls and melting chocolate eyes.

"I'M GOING TO run into the village to get some milk," Kate said abruptly on the Saturday evening when her class had left. She had dined at Bay Oaks at Dotty's insistence, largely ignored while the two women talked of common interests and France played up to Cameron.

"Hmm? What's that, dear?" Iola murmured.

"If you're going into the village, I'll take you," Cameron remarked, laying aside his newspaper.

"Why don't *we* go, Cam? We could take my car with the top down and Kate wouldn't have to bother," France pleaded.

"Read that article on the money market while I'm gone, pet, and then you'll understand what I was getting at, hmm? Ready, Kate?"

They were outside before Kate could come up with an excuse not to accompany him, and he steered her over to the gunmetal Mercedes. Once seated, she tucked her apple-green skirt closely around her as if it might offer some protection from him.

He climbed in but didn't close the door immediately. Instead he turned to study her face intently in the dim interior light.

"Aren't you afraid of drawing mosquitoes?" she snapped.

"You're more afraid of the light than you are of the darkness? I wonder why?" he persisted in a soft tone of voice.

He shut the door and then his hands were close over her shoulders. Before she could do more than utter an outraged protest, his mouth closed over her own and he hauled her across the console so that she fell awkwardly against his unyielding body. She remained absolutely still while his kiss threatened to rip the very soul out of her. When he pulled his mouth away to curse softly, "Kiss me, damn you," she felt a tiny thrill of defiance. When his fingertips lingered on the racing pulse at the base of her throat before dropping to her breasts, she crumpled. When she felt the inflaming touch of his thumbs as they brushed the aroused nubs of her nipples, she groaned and opened her mouth to his plundering tongue. Overwhelmed at her own response, she pushed against his chest, then shook her head frantically in rejection of her own frightening desires.

"What's the matter?" he murmured. "Don't you like what we can do to each other?"

She struggled away from him. "Leave me alone!" she demanded. "Let me go!"

"Quit acting like an outraged virgin, Kate," he provoked, his hand finding her breast again with unerring accuracy. He cupped the throbbing roundness with one determined hand as he forced her to face him once more.

"Why didn't you bring my sister if this was all you were thinking about? She's obviously besotted with you!"

"Now, is that any way for a woman your age to look after her younger sister's welfare?"

His hand was having an irresistible effect on her aching breast, and his warm breath played on her overheated face. Kate could hear the sound of her own blood as it rushed like a tidal wave through her veins. "D-don't make fun of me, Cameron. I'm not in your league and we b-both know it," she whispered.

"And what is my league?"

"Stop it!" The words were torn from her, and she heard the tears in her own voice even before she felt the cool wetness on her cheeks. She sat rigidly in the darkness, while the man beside her played on her traitorous body like a virtuoso, and she was unable to stop him even when her nerves screamed at her that she was in danger. That the danger was only half-understood made it all the more frightening, and she shut her mind to the stunning pleasure his skilled, persuasive touch was bringing her.

"Katie, Katie, why can't you relax and just let nature take its course? You want me and we both know it, so why pretend?" His mouth came closer and he insinuated the soft little words against her stiff lips with a light touch. Then, with his mouth still hovering a breath away, he taunted, "Why not, Katie? Why not?"

Because I love you, you fool, she screamed silently, and it would kill me to be another in your lineup of momentary distractions!

"I hate you, Cameron Greyville!" she heard herself saying in a voice she hardly recognized. "I hate you for making me feel this way," she whispered in a choked sound that tore through the brittle tension.

"No, you don't, Kate," he replied tiredly, moving away from her. "But you've left it too long now, I'm afraid. You'll never be more than half a woman, and soon that half will grow so embittered that you won't even be able to smile at a man without cracking your shell." He started the engine. "And to think I believed you were only waiting for some poor fool to awaken you. There aren't any Prince Charmings anymore, Kate. It's an extinct species, I'm afraid. So go on back to sleep in your castle and let the briars grow up around it."

Before she could get her breathing under control, they were at the store.

"Shall I get your milk?" he asked in a clipped tone.

"Please," she replied huskily. "A gallon, please."

He slammed the door. Kate sat there in the neon-fractured darkness, watching the summer people with huge, unseeing eyes.

Cameron dropped her off at her own place, and she let herself in with leaden motions. By the time she was ready for bed, her mind was safely encapsulated within the narrow confines she allowed it, ticking off items against the arrival of tomorrow's class.

A WEEK passed during which she hardly saw her family. Cameron left the island each night soon after dark. Sometimes he was alone and sometimes France was with him; once, he took all three women in his household. Kate watched them disappear over the bridge with a bitter longing in her eyes before she turned to the woman beside her and began explaining how to paint convincing reflections.

She continued to use the shady grove on the other side of the Greyville house. If Cameron wanted to rescind permission, then he would have to tell her himself. She had spoken to him only once since that disastrous night. He brought over a letter that had been put in his own box at the post office by mistake and was as impersonal as if she were a transient renter on his property.

Which was nothing less than the truth.

ON THE NEXT to last day of the session, she sent her group on to the house for lunch and wandered down to the beach beyond the shady grove.

Impulsively she turned and began to wade out into the shallow water. She wore old sneakers with white shorts and T-shirt, and the warm water crept over her ankles, her calves and up to her knees. It occurred to her that she would enjoy a trip to the ocean and a brisk, refreshing dip in the Atlantic. As long as she had been here, she had yet to swim in the ocean. It just hadn't occurred to her to take off an afternoon and go swimming. There had been no one to go with her, and she didn't relish going alone.

She was wading back toward the shore, her eyes on the water as she tried to avoid submerged hazards. Not until she was in ankle-deep water did she dare to look up again, and when she did she halted, her heart leaping painfully.

"I wondered if you were trying to wade all the way to Engelhard," Cam remarked. He was standing at the edge of the water, his legs braced apart—long, tightly muscled limbs whose tan was modified by the coat of crisp, dark hairs— and his hands planted on his hips above low-riding white shorts. There was something so masculine about him that Kate was embarrassed at her own reaction. As a result, when she spoke, her words sounded sharper than she intended.

"What do you want?" she asked ungraciously.

He held out a hand. *"Pax,"* he said, and she was compelled to wade closer until she touched her reluctant palm to his. "I've brought an invitation to lunch. When we didn't see you go back to Gray Lady, it occurred to me that you might be needing a break. You're going at it too hard and heavy, Kate. Why don't you readjust your schedule so that you'll have more time to yourself?"

She bristled, but when she would have withdrawn her

hand, he gripped it more tightly. "I can't shortchange my students, Cameron. They're paying for so many hours a day and they'll get it."

"But do you have to throw yourself into it quite so whole-heartedly? Nobody can put out and put out indefinitely without either breaking or having the quality compromised."

"What would you know about teaching art?" she demanded fiercely, and this time she succeeded in pulling her hand away.

"Nothing, but, Kate, what I've said goes for any enterprise. You're driving yourself too hard, and you're getting as gaunt as a scarecrow. Not even that lovely tan can cover up the shadows under your eyes. You look haunted, Katie." His voice took on a tender note that threatened to undermine her, and she answered it with a rueful smile.

"All right, you've made your point. I'm deteriorating badly. So I'll consider a different schedule, but only because it just occurred to me that I want to go swimming at least once while I'm here—lower myself under a cold wave and stay there until the sun goes down."

"I'll take you one day next week, if you like. Now, how about lunch with your family and Dotty? Before you refuse—" he grinned "—I'll be busy in my study, so it will be strictly a hen party. I'm afraid your mother thinks you've been neglecting her lately."

*

ON SATURDAY morning, before the arrival of the next group, Cameron sent word by Dotty that he was going surf fishing and wanted to take Kate along. "You'll love it," she declared. "I went with him once on one of his nighttime expeditions and it's another world."

What the devil—why not? The summer was already half over and there were so many things she hadn't done. Unfortunately, she *had* done the one thing she shouldn't—fall in love with a man who considered her some sort of joke. That was enough to insure that she look elsewhere for her next workshop location.

But while she was here, she may as well try it all. So, according to Cam's instructions, she wore shorts and took along a jacket. When she climbed into the front seat, she found a very disgruntled France glowering at her from the back.

"What are Iola and Dotty doing tonight?" she asked.

"Going to a meeting of some sort, I believe," Cam told her. Trust Iola to get involved in local activities on a summer visit.

They parked at the end of a gravel road and trudged over the high, soft dune. The soft, damp wind held tantalizing hints of exotic shores thousands of miles away. The moon was three-quarters full and it played tag with dark, silver-edged clouds, illuminating the breakers in a beautiful, mysterious way.

"It's absolutely magic," Kate said, turning impulsively to where Cam was rigging tackle onto three rods in sand spikes.

"Holding a rod and reel gives you an excuse to spend time enjoying it without feeling like a damned fool." He smiled.

"Well, I can think of better things to do, but under the circumstances…" France let her voice trail off.

"Done any fishing before?" Cameron asked Kate as he baited her double rig with shrimp.

"Not much. Lake fishing, mostly."

While he tended to France, throwing out her line for her, Kate edged as close to the creaming breakers as she dared and let fly. She backlashed, cursed softly, and backed up, untangling as she went, finally cheating and reeling in the line over the worst tangle. Then she waded out and cast again. It might not go far, but since she couldn't see, what difference did it make?

"I'm going back to the car. You two can stay here drowning in shrimp as long as you want, but my skin's tender, and something's about to eat me up!" France declared loudly.

"I haven't felt a thing, have you, Kate?" Cam asked, taking France's rod.

"Not a thing. Guess I'm not very sensitive," she replied, pushing away an uncharitable feeling of glee. After all, France *did* have a lighter complexion.

"We'll be back before long. Nothing seems to be biting tonight—at least underwater. Play the radio or tape, if you'd like." Cam tossed her the keys.

After a while, a snatch of music drifted over to the surf, and Kate hummed along with a half-forgotten song about never loving again. Cam appeared at her side, reeling in to check his bait.

"Bored?" he asked.

"Nope. I don't think I've ever been bored in my life, and— Cam!" she screamed. "Something's happening!"

"Well, hang on, don't panic. I checked your drag and it's fine. Reel him in."

"But, Cam, he's reeling *me* in! Take it—you do it!" she cried, trying to hand off her rod to Cam, but he backed away, putting his own rod into a sand spike in order to coach her along. But she was getting deeper and deeper into the surf, the water breaking about her hips. Cam was right behind her.

"You've got plenty of line, Kate, so let him run."

"But that's just it," she wailed. "I had a backlash and I reeled in over it and... Oh, no!"

What happened then was never quite clear. There was a loud snap and her foot slid down an embankment. The next thing she knew, she was being pummeled and rolled by thundering tons of water. It only occurred to her much later that her life had not flashed before her eyes; the only thing she could think of was Cam.

And then she was being pulled apart, her arm grasped and held, and she felt herself being dragged back up onto the hard-packed sand, flung down on her face and pounded. She never quite lost consciousness, but she was beyond telling Cam that her ribs were fragile and that she had been scraped over every inch of her body, so that when he turned her and began to breathe into her mouth, she was more aware of gravel digging into her skin than she was of his mouth on hers.

The next few hours were a kaleidoscopic nightmare. She had insisted on walking into the house on her own two feet so as not to alarm Iola and Dotty, but when France reported the Spitfire still out, Cameron scooped Kate up in his arms, took the steps as if she weighed no more than a child, and laid her on top of an elegant brown spread on a king-size bed.

"I'll ruin it. I'm all wet and sandy. And you should have left me at my own place. Cam, please, won't you..."

"Please, won't you shut up? France, fetch your sister something to put on."

"Which room is hers?" France had yet to spend more than five minutes at Gray Lady. Cam muttered an inelegant phrase and ordered her to look after things until he got back.

"Are you really hurt bad, Katie?" France asked.

"Of course not, silly," Kate croaked. "I just got the wind knocked out of me and swallowed gallons of sand and salt water. Just let me lie here for a few minutes, and then I'll go home. Look, France—don't tell Iola, all right?" Kate coughed and asked for a tissue. "Lord, I feel awful. I must look terrible."

"You do," France told her. She touched Kate's hair and then brushed her hand on the seat of her shorts. "Well, if there's nothing else I can do for you, I'd like to get a bath and put lotion on my bites."

"You ought to know better than to wear so much perfume. It attracts them," Kate said, wishing her sister would leave.

"Maybe I'll get used to them after a while. They say if you stay down here long enough you don't even notice them," France said.

"How long are you planning to stay?" Kate implored.

"Honestly, you can't stand it, can you?" France said, her dark eyes flashing. "You weren't fool enough to think you had a chance with Cam, were you? The only man who ever looked at you twice was that stodgy old Hal Brookwood. I'm Cam's guest and you're just his tenant, so if anybody leaves, it won't be me!''

With an exasperated sound, Kate sat up and swung her feet to the floor. Her head rocked and she lifted a hand to her forehead. "Look, France, this is obviously a man's room—Cam's, I guess—and if he put me in here, it means that the other rooms are all filled up, and it's just not fair for you and Iola to move in on somebody you don't even know and stay the whole summer long. Don't you realize that they might have other friends who'd like to drop in for a week or so? There's no room!"

France shrugged her beautifully formed shoulders. "Look, it's too late to cry over spilled milk now. Cam and I *did* meet and, what's more, we like each other—like each other a good deal, as a matter of fact. We have an understanding, Cam and I. He'll do whatever I want, and if you're nice to me, then I might...I just *might* get you a rent reduction." Her smile was in no way reflected in her innocent-looking eyes.

Kate was across the floor in less time than it took to consider the action. She shook the younger girl, although her own strength was only up to a token effort. "Now you listen to me, Frances Brown. If you dare do anything stupid and get yourself in trouble, you'll have me to answer to, not Iola! You've caused her enough grief in the past, and this time— you behave yourself or you'll have me to deal with!"

"Stop it, you hateful old thing!"

France's cry came just as the bedroom door opened to admit Cam, a light green nightgown draped over one arm and a glass of amber liquid in his hand. France let out a wail and launched herself at him, tears flowing down her becomingly flushed cheeks. "Cam, make her stop it. She's being perfectly dreadful to me!" She buried her face in his chest, causing the drink to slosh alarmingly.

"What's been going on here?" he asked mildly, resisting the younger girl's efforts to pull his ear down to her mouth as she whispered at him.

"She says she doesn't want us here. She says I have to go and take Iola with me, and she's just saying that because she's jealous. She's always been jealous of my beauty, Cam, ever since I was a little girl, and now she wants to get rid of me and I don't want to go. Please say you won't send me back to that hateful old job where I melt because they're too cheap to use the air conditioner."

A bubble of mirth arose in Kate's throat and she dropped down onto the bed again as laughter overcame her. Her head was splitting, her throat was raw, but it was so funny, such bad theater, that she howled. And then the laughter changed to something else, and her face crumpled, and she sat there with her hands hanging limply at her sides and cried openly.

There was a flurry of movement seen dimly through shimmering eyes and then she was lifted up and cradled against a warm, hard wall that rocked with the rhythm of a heartbeat. "Hush, Katie," Cam murmured. "Hush now, it's not important."

The sobs slowed and finally ceased, and she sniffed, then hiccuped. "Oh, Lordy, once I start these, it takes forever to get rid of them," she wailed.

"Well, you've already had your scare, so I'll have to try my own favorite remedy on you."

"What's that?" she sniffed weakly, looking up at him. He was leaning against the headboard and holding her against him, her sandy, wet hair spread out over his shoulder. She knew the answer to her question as his mouth closed over her own and she hiccuped once and then her arms wound around his neck and she gave herself up to the powerful medicine of his lovemaking. And when she felt his hands at her buttons, she could only shrug and help him ease the garment from her shoulders. Her shorts came next, and he eased them down over her legs without ever breaking contact with her throat, and his downward trail of kisses.

"It'll probably take a fish scaler to get all the gravel off your skin," he murmured, scratching lightly against her midriff to loosen the tiny grains. He held her breast and picked the small shells off deliberately and Kate turned away from his overpowering nearness.

"You shouldn't be here," she protested weakly. "You shouldn't see me this way."

"Your inhibitions are showing, Katie darling," Cameron whispered, trailing the backs of his fingers down her thigh, making her acutely aware that she wore only a pair of nylon pants and a lacy bra.

He lowered his face to her throat again, finding all the most sensitive places and between tiny, nibbling kisses, Cameron teased her, telling her that her hair looked like seaweed, that there were few openings for mermaids this season, but even though his words were light, she could sense the rapidly increasing tension in his own body and his amber eyes were strangely dark and intense. He made no attempt to hide the state of his arousal, and when he spoke, his words were torn between deep gasping breaths and shaken with the pounding of his heart. He licked her throat.

"Hmm, salty—sandy, too," he whispered, "but delicious." His hands moved again and she was released from the constraint of her bra and it felt so free, so fine, when his lips moved to the gentle hills of her breasts and conquered them, teasing the straining tips with his tongue.

"Ahh, Cam, please," she groaned, hardly knowing what she was pleading for.

"Kate, darling, I must have you." He uttered the words in a voice that was hardly recognizable as he fumbled with his own clothing.

Borne along too far, too fast on the tidal wave of passion, Kate heard nothing until she felt Cam stiffen and draw away slightly, and then she heard the front door slam and Dotty's voice calling out to see where everyone was.

With a half-stifled cry of pure frustration, he lifted himself from her. "Kate, I'm sorry. I had no intention of allowing things to get out of hand."

Her very nerves screaming, she forced herself to reply flippantly, "Oh, that's all right. At least my hiccups are cured.

Now, if you don't mind, I'd like to put on my clothes and get out of here.''

All her senses unnaturally alert now, she could hear France's voice and Dotty's and Iola's, and she knew it would be only moments before the invasion. "Please," she entreated.

"Kate, let me help you into the bath. You need to wash that sand and salt off you." He half-lifted her from the bed and she jerked her arms away from him.

"You've helped me quite enough. What did you do with my shorts?" She pulled the corner of the bedspread over her as a protective shawl, for all she wore now were her damp nylon panties. "And stop staring at me like that. It's not the first time I've been kissed, believe it or not!"

"Stop trying to be so tough, Kate. We'll continue with this another time."

"Oh, no, we won't!"

When Iola called nervously through the door, he told her to come on in. "She's shocked and she took a pounding, but basically she's all right," he told the anxious woman.

Kate still had a part of the bedspread caught up around her bare shoulders, the rest of it trailing across the bed. "It's all right, Mama," she said, "I just got in over my head, that's all." In more ways than one, she added silently.

IN SPITE OF A strong compulsion to return to Gray Lady and her own stark little bedroom, Kate was glad to fall into Cam's king-size bed after soaking away part of her aches and pains. She awakened the next morning to find herself stiff and headachy, but infinitely better than she had been.

When awareness of her emotional ordeal began to surface above her physical complaints, she did her best to ignore it, but there was no avoiding the knowledge that Cam had come very close to seducing her last night—with her full cooperation. Now, to her utter shame, she regretted the interruption. Just a few more minutes and she would have known what it was like to be made love to by a man who had come to mean more to her than any living creature.

It was lust, not love, she reminded herself, but all the same....

Snap out of it, you silly old fool! she whispered fiercely to herself. He saved your neck once last night, but Dotty and Iola saved it the second time. That would have been a fine state of affairs—you in bed with the man who, for all you know, might end up your brother-in-law!

Dotty came up with a dress for her to put on and reported no sign of any students so far, and, after dressing, Kate descended the stairs with a slow, awkward gait.

Cameron emerged from his study as she reached the bottom step, and his tawny eyes missed nothing. "All better now?" he asked, his searching look seeming to signify more than just her physical well-being.

"Fine and dandy," she replied brightly.

"If you have a minute, I want to talk to you about canceling out on this session." He reached for her arm and she jerked it away.

"You what?"

"You heard me. You're in no condition to teach, Kate, but you insist on driving yourself. You can call them now and probably reach most of them before they set out, and if you refund the fees, they'll sign on elsewhere and everyone will be a lot better off."

"Well, thanks a lot. That's a real vote of confidence, Mr. Greyville. You may be my landlord, but that's *all* you are! Nowhere in my lease does it say that you can give me orders on how to conduct my business." She came down the last step and brushed past him. "Thanks for the use of the bed," she said over her shoulder as she stalked off into the blinding, relentless sun.

THE STUDENTS came on schedule, a mixed group again, but Kate didn't doubt her ability to mold them into a working unit. She did reschedule her afternoon class to a later hour, and since that made the nightly critique and demonstration session late, she made it peer critique instead, leaving her free to relax while her students discussed one another's work.

On the last day of classes she took her gang to the grassy stretch alongside the wharf. She had seen Cam's car drive off soon after class began and had not noticed it return, and she thought it might be a good time to drop in and see if Iola and France wanted to go to Manteo and Nags Head with her tomorrow. Dotty, too, if she was interested.

Slinging her gear into the canvas holdall, she set out, head down, face shaded by the brim of her straw hat. She could hear Dotty's tuneless whistling from the garden, and from an open window upstairs came the sound of France's radio.

She rounded the corner, swooping to inhale the fragrance of a window box of nasturtiums and phlox, and straightened to see a tangle of bare legs dangling from the porch hammock.

"Were you looking for me, Kate?" Cam asked laconically.

Another head popped up at that and she found herself staring back at Bebe Gonlon's petulant prettiness.

"Are you still here?" Bebe demanded rudely.

"Are you back again?" Kate said, just as rudely.

Cameron threw back his head and let loose a rich chuckle, pushing the red-gold blonde away. "Ladies, ladies, there's room enough in the hammock for both of you. Care to climb aboard, Kate?"

"I was looking for Iola. Don't let me interrupt anything," she insisted, turning to leave.

"Kate?" The one word, spoken softly, stopped her in her tracks and she turned to see a look on Cam's face that baffled her completely. It was almost as if he had reached some conclusion that satisfied him immensely and had just now had it confirmed.

*

HAVING arranged to take France and Iola to Manteo and Nags Head to do the galleries and browse the shops, Kate was outside rinsing the salt from her windshield before the sun had even cleared away the morning haze. She heard the front door at Bay Oaks and looked up in time to see Cameron, a bag in each hand, standing on the porch with four women.

Iola waved and then France, with a hesitant look at Bebe, threw her arms around Cameron's neck and whispered something in his ear—or at least it appeared that way to Kate.

She closed her eyes for just a moment. Oh, how it hurt, in spite of all her fine resolutions to act her age, to resign herself to having no part in Cam's life, and smile when it killed her to watch him treating France and even Bebe with the casual affection she coveted so much. Not that that was all she wanted from him, but it still looked good from where she stood on the outside looking in.

Kate dragged them, unwilling, through the galleries, and they insisted on spending equal time in the shops. It was when they were on the way home that Iola mentioned the extension course she had signed up for at the high school. Kate turned to her in dismay. "What on earth for, Iola? Those things last at least six weeks, don't they? Good Lord, I thought you were only here for a short visit." She continued in desperation. "Besides, France will be leaving for England pretty soon. How on earth will we get both cars back home?" Iola could do short stints behind the wheel but with her bad knee long drives were out.

"Oh, you needn't worry about me, Kate. Cam and I have already made our plans," France said from beside her, with a secret little smirk.

"What plans?" Kate demanded.

"Never you mind, fusspot. We didn't tell you because we thought it might upset you—we know how you are—but

Cam's going to take care of me and then you'll be free t
do your own thing.''

Kate took a deep breath and as they were nearing Cora
noke bridge, she said, ''I think you'd better tell me just wha
your plans are, Frances.''

''Sorry,'' her sister replied. ''I promised Cam I wouldn't.'

''But I'm your sister,'' Kate agonized. From the back sea
came a gentle snore. Iola was asleep.

''Just a hint, then. Pretty soon you won't have to wea
yourself out trying to keep up with me, so you should b
happy. Lord knows, you've complained often enough.''

That hurt. Not so much as the idea of France and Cam
together, but enough to make her duck her chin into her colla
defensively. ''I only hope you know what you're doing
France. I don't want you to get hurt.''

''Oh, don't worry about me. Cam's a marshmallow,'' he
sister said airily.

''I'm surprised you'd allow your marshmallow to spen
the day with Bebe Gonlon, then. She obviously has a swe
tooth, too,'' Kate remarked.

''Oh, he took her to Norfolk to the airport. I'm not worrie
about Bebe. She's been after him for ages, but he only pu
up with her because he feels sorry for her. Her father worke
for Greyville and he got in trouble with the law. Now he'
doing time, and Cam feels responsible. Well, he's not, bu
you know Cam.'' She shrugged. ''Anyway, he says she's
good little secretary, but when she gets on his nerves, he ju
tells her to trot her carcass.''

''Frances Ann, I don't know where you pick up slang lik
that,'' Iola said sleepily from the back. ''Kate never talke
that way and nor did I.''

They pulled up before Bay Oaks just as the sun sank int
the Pamlico Sound.

THE NEXT morning Kate decided to explore Ocracoke, th
next island south of Hatteras. She invited France to go wi

her, but the younger girl said something about having her hair done for a party, so Kate shrugged and turned away.

The ferry ride was exhilarating, and Ocracoke was a charming town built around a silvered, bowl-like harbor accented by clusters of boats. Kate drove around, then parked and walked, following the narrow, sandy roads bordered with picket fences that enclosed thickets of yaupon and oak, yucca and oleander. The day passed pleasantly enough.

Maybe I should be wearing a Vacancy sign, she thought with a flash of humor, after a second woman with three children under five asked her if she knew where a rest room was. Feeling in need of a quick wash herself, she decided to drive back up the beach to the facilities at the ferry landing.

She got within a quarter of a mile of her goal, having stopped a while to watch a herd of Ocracoke's famous Banker ponies, when she felt a lurch. A flat tire! There was nowhere to pull over, and she watched helplessly as car after car sped past on its way to the ferry.

Well, darn! Fifteen minutes later, she sat in her car and faced the unpalatable truth. It was almost dark, there was no traffic at all now, and she had no idea how late the ferries ran. And her spare was flat.

Not that it would hurt her to spend a night in her station wagon, but she felt terribly alone here on the north end of the highway miles from anywhere. She hadn't even had the foresight to bring along a flashlight!

For perhaps twenty minutes she sat there staring at the hazy horizon. Then, as one winking white light seemed to grow into several and they were bracketed by a red and a green, it dawned on her that another ferry was approaching. While her car was stuck on Ocracoke, she was free to cross the inlet. Surely she could get a ride as far as the Coranoke bridge.

Even in the warmth of the July night she felt chilled, and she crossed her arms over her breasts as she jogged along the pavement. She was almost at the slip when the ferry eased into position and lowered its ramp. As cars crawled off the

ramp and picked up speed on their way south, she stepped
well off the highway. One of the cars screeched to a stop just
past her and began to back up again. It stopped beside her
and Cam got out to demand what the hell she was doing
hiking along the highway alone in the middle of the night.

Not until they were crossing the inlet on the way home
after having secured a promise from a service station that the
tire would be replaced and the car delivered to Coranoke
before ten the following morning did he speak to her again,
and then she'd just as soon he hadn't.

"If you ever go off like that again without letting me
know, I'll have your hide!" he informed her in a blistering
tone.

"Now, just a darned minute there, buster! Where I go and
what I do have absolutely nothing to do with you, and you'd
better get it through your thick head that just because you've
got something going with my sister, and my mother seems
to have latched on to you like a barnacle, there's no way
you're going to start telling *me* what to do! No *way!*"

"Are you quite finished?" His voice was dangerously
mild.

She nodded. "I just wanted you to understand that I don't
need you. I don't need anyone."

"You didn't need anyone to mend your spare. You didn't
need anyone to remind you to take along a flashlight in your
car for emergencies...."

"I could have called someone, and—"

"Shut up!" He reached for her and jerked her across the
seat, and she steeled herself against giving in to him, when
by all rights she should never speak to him again. But then
where Cameron Greyville was concerned her good sense flew
out the window.

It was a punishing kiss, a kiss of anger and frustration, and
Kate's mouth felt bruised even as she sought more of whatever it was he was offering her. When her hands went from
his chest to slide around his neck and entangle themselves in
his thick, alive hair, he groaned and lifted his mouth for just

an instant. "This time, woman, there's no escape for you—not until I'm good and ready," he promised her, and when his mouth covered hers again, it was a piercing, bittersweet invasion that was an act of possession in itself.

With a surge of desperate strength, Kate twisted her head aside. "Cameron, stop it! Don't do this to me. It...it isn't fair," she wailed softly. "You talk to me as if I were an idiot, and then you treat me as if—" She broke off with a gasp as his hands slipped up to weigh the ripe fullness of her aching breasts, his thumbs stroking the engorged nipples through her thin tricot bra. She despised herself for letting him use her in this casual, devastating way—this potent male animal whose virility could not resist a challenge, and she, Lord help her, was no challenge at all, did he only know it!

Her yellow knit top was no barrier to his discovering hands, and when she felt his hard, smooth palm on the cool satin of her thigh, she stretched herself out invitingly, and it could have been the center of Tokyo instead of a dark ferry in the middle of Hatteras Inlet, for all she cared. The delicious shuddering quicksilver that rippled through her body left her devastated, limp and helpless against his inflamed passion.

There was a sudden lurch, and they both became aware of the changed tenor of the engines as the ferry swung around to engage the ramp. "Even here there's no privacy. Never enough time," he said with a sigh.

The engine roared into life and they rolled off the ferry and headed for Coranoke. With trembling fingers, Kate combed through her hair and straightened her clothes and wondered if she looked as totally devastated as she felt.

"Will you be needing a car before ten?" Cam asked tersely.

"Not that I know of," she replied.

"If anything comes up, you're free to use the Spitfire."

"Oh, are you taking charge of France's possessions now as well as her life?" she flung at him.

He didn't dignify her gibe with an answer, and Kate felt

thoroughly ashamed of herself. He had that right, if anyone did. After all, they'd soon be endowing each other with all their worldly possessions. She muttered an apology under her breath and he dismissed it with a brief nod.

"I'm taking you straight home. Your mother has been worried about you," he told her.

"That I doubt!"

"You never give up, do you? A real tough case. Whether you know it or not, both your mother and your sister care a great deal for you, and when you run off this way and worry them, I can only think you're totally indifferent to their feelings." He had pulled up in front of Bay Oaks.

She said very quietly, "I think, if you don't mind, I'll just go home. I've had a pretty full day and I'd like to get an early start tomorrow. So tell Iola—"

"That's another thing...why do you call her by her given name? Are you so afraid of showing affection for anyone? *Damn*, Kate!" He opened his door with a snort of disgust and she did not wait for him to help her out. By the time he caught up with her, she was almost at her own front door.

He held her by her upper arms and she thought he was going to kiss her again. She swayed slightly toward him, but he only shook her and released her, telling her harshly to go to bed.

*

IF IOLA had been worried about her the day before, there was certainly no sign of it when she and Dotty stopped by the Gray Lady on their way to the library the next morning.

"We're having a wingding tomorrow night, Kate. Eight-thirty, and wear something special. It's a celebration!" Dotty called out.

"A celebration of what?" Kate asked.

They glanced at each other and Iola said, "Well, that's not our business to tell, Katie, but you'll know soon enough."

As if she didn't already know deep in her heavy heart, she thought.

AT FIVE the next afternoon Iola came scurrying across to Gray Lady. Someone had driven up hurriedly only moments before and Kate supposed that things were getting into full swing over there.

"Need anything?" she called out.

Iola panted dramatically and then, one hand to her bosom, told Kate that Dotty had had an attack and that the doctor was there.

After the first few moments of shock, Kate tried to think what to do, since both France and Iola tended to fall apart in emergencies. "I'll come back with you. There may be something I can do to help. Do you know how serious it is?" The thought of losing the dear little woman struck her as inconceivable!

After seeing the ambulance off with Cam following in his own car, Kate settled down to phone the guest list and explain the circumstances. France was up in her room and Iola was lying down after Kate had begged a sedative from the doctor for her. She'd probably have to stay over here tonight, but Cam would no doubt be staying at the hospital.

After all the calls were made, Kate fixed supper for them, using things that had been prepared for the party. Now she sat alone in the kitchen with her third cup of coffee.

Cam had called earlier from the hospital to say that Dotty was out of immediate danger but that they were taking her to Elizabeth City and that he'd be along after a while to throw a few things into a bag, and would she wait there, please. France, struggling to hide her disappointment, had already gone back up to her room.

IT WAS almost eleven forty-five when Cam returned. He looked so utterly drained that Kate went to him instinctively, holding out her hand. He took it, placed it on his forehead for a brief moment, then dropped it to kiss the tips of her fingers.

"How is she?" Kate asked.

"She's amazing. The last thing she said before I left was not to let the vol-au-vents go to waste because they wouldn't keep."

A strangled laugh escaped Kate's pale mouth. "Oh, Cam, she's priceless! Tell her we put away five for supper and France accounted for three of those." He may as well know about France's healthy appetite, since he'd soon be supporting her. "I gave Iola the sedative, and she's doing fine."

Cameron had loosened his tie, and his shirt was unbuttoned almost halfway to his belt. Kate resisted an impulse to run her hands inside the opening and feel that warm, hard body, to offer it all the comfort she could give, but instead she poured him a cup of coffee. "The calls are all made, the food put away, and I fixed a plate for you," she told him.

"Good. I'll just run upstairs first and wash up. I'll pack a bag, and I want to see France. Be down in a minute."

THE NEXT DAY had thirty-six hours in it—all of them empty. It dawned on Kate that she had another class due in, and the idea seemed so irrelevant that she laughed aloud. The sound brought Iola hurrying in from the garden, where she was tying up chrysanthemums. "What is it?"

"Nothing, Mother." Kate sobered. "I just remembered that I have a class due in this afternoon. It had completely slipped my mind."

"Oh, Kate, no! Look, sweetie, I don't think Cam will want you to go on with your classes. I mean, not under the circumstances. Can't you turn them over to someone else?"

"Oh, Iola, be practical for once. Even if I could afford to, you just don't go about canceling classes that have been scheduled for months—not when people have gone to the expense of traveling all this way."

"Well, Cam's not going to like it," Iola warned, hitching

up her aged chiffon negligee to tie a sneaker after removing her work glove.

"He can just lump it, then," she replied tartly. "Look, just because Cam seems to have adopted the pair of you doesn't mean that I don't have a career to think of. I'm going over to Gray Lady now and fix a cold supper for the new group. In fact, why don't you move over there with me? There's plenty of room—well, Annie's room, at least."

"Katie, how can you? Here Cam will be coming back any minute now and you want him to walk into an empty house? You know, in some ways you're totally unfeeling, Kate."

"Oh, Mother, I'm not unfeeling. You know how much I care for Dotty, and...and Cam, too, but he'll have France with him, and I think they'll prefer to be alone."

"France? Why on earth should he... Has he called? Did they miss connections?"

"What connections? And no, of course he didn't call, but— Well, I mean, after all..." Kate stammered to a halt. No one had informed her officially of the relationship between Cam and her sister, although just why they had to make such a production of it, she couldn't say—unless France was determined to make a big entrance, sporting a ring the size of a headlight.

Iola assumed an infuriating little smirk, confirming Kate's assumption. "Well, it's certainly not my place to tell you, Katie, dear, but let me just say this, in case you get upset at the way we've handled things. Cam knows how you overreact sometimes when anyone tries to help out. You see, I told him all about Daddy...."

"You what? I do *not* overreact! You know very well that I've done all I could from the day Daddy walked out because you always said I was the strongest one of the family, and now you tell me that—"

"There, you see? You're at it again. Darling, France is twenty-one years old. She's old enough to look after herself, and in some ways she's a lot more capable than you are, and I..."

Kate's stricken eyes turned blindly away and her mother stumbled to a halt. Finally, Iola mumbled something about letting Cam take care of it, and soon Kate was alone again.

THE NEW GROUP came all at once, and when the first two carloads of chattering women pulled up in front of Gray Lady, Kate had to brace herself to greet them with any enthusiasm at all. Summer was on the downhill slope and so was she, she decided as she showed them where to stow their gear.

By seven-thirty she had them all fed, and the rooms buzzed with the echoing sounds of eight voices. Iola had joined them for supper but had returned to Bay Oaks, and Kate had promised to come over before bedtime. She could leave the porch light on for Cam when she did.

The light, southeasterly wind rustled the leaves of the oleanders so that they sounded like rain as Kate crossed the dark area between the two houses.

Her mind was on alternative plans for tomorrow's class in case it did rain, and when she looked up into the porch she almost tripped on the bottom step. "Cam?" she inquired softly, her voice sounding uncertain.

"I left the light off on account of the bugs." He appeared at her side and took her arm, and she pulled away as if burned by his touch.

"I can manage, thanks. Where's France?"

"Probably boarding a plane for England about now."

The words rocked her back on her heels. "What did you say?"

"I said, pro—"

"Never mind, I heard you, but, Cam, why?" They were on the porch now and he led her over to the swing.

"To get the feel of the Continent, I believe was the way she put it, before her audition."

"Oh, don't be so maddening. Where did she get the money?"

"I gave it to her," he answered.

Kate's automatic response was explosive, but she managed to choke it off. "You might at least have told me," she muttered.

"We didn't tell you because we all knew exactly how you'd react."

"You mean you've all discussed me, talked about..." She bit her lip. "You have some kind of a flattering impression of me, don't you?" she accused bitterly. Her face was beginning to crumple.

"Kate, if things had gone according to my plans, we wouldn't be sitting out here getting ready to fight again, I can assure you, but—"

"Oh, of that I'm certain! It's just too bad that you're not halfway to England with my sister. What will you do—fly over as soon as... Oh, Cam! Dotty! I didn't even ask!"

"She's fine," he told her with a laugh as he dropped an arm across her shoulder and pulled her stiff body against his. "Dotty's just fine. She'll be coming home next weekend. I've made arrangements with Eileen to live in and look after her for a few weeks."

"If you need an extra hand, I can pop in between classes," she offered.

"You'll have your hands full, I hope—getting ready for something else," he told her.

When she didn't reply, he turned to look at her. "Well, aren't you going to ask me what I mean?" he teased.

"If you want me to know, I assume you'll tell me," she retorted primly, and he laughed again. She decided she'd better go inside before she did anything foolish. "Iola... I told her..." she began, and he pressed a finger across her lips.

"Kate...Kate Minerva Brown, will you marry me as soon as it is legally possible and put an end to this inept, mismanaged courtship?"

"This...will I...?"

He sighed heavily. "There, you see? I try the direct approach and instead of a simple yes I get a 'this' and a 'will I.' Your family warned me."

"Cameron Greyville, just what in the devil are you talking about? If this is your idea of a joke, then I...then you..." Her voice wobbled off and to her horror she heard a noisy sob escape her.

"Katie? Darling, what is it? Have I hurt your feelings? I didn't mean to be clumsy about it, but, sweetheart, I've never done this before. These past few days have been such a strain, it's a wonder I didn't just say to hell with it and drag you off to the nearest preacher."

She was unable to prevent a watery smile, but her voice wasn't up to replying, and when he turned her so that she lay half across his lap, she burrowed her face in the warm, clean-smelling flesh at the throat of his open shirt.

"Katie? What's it going to be, love—wedded bliss or a life of glorious sin? I'll go either way, whatever it takes to make you finally and completely mine." He caught her chin and lifted her face, glowing warmly down at her in the soft, starlighted darkness. His lips touched the corner of her mouth, then slid lightly over her lips to the other corner, and when she would have caught his head and put a definite end to his tantalizing butterfly kiss, he shook his head. "No more until you give me an answer, Katie Minerva. Iola says you do, France says you don't and Dotty says I'm a fool if I let you get away. Well? Do you? Will you?"

"Oh, Cam, I love you so terribly much I'll do anything you want me to. I thought you knew—although I hoped to heaven you didn't."

"But why, precious? Why couldn't you have given me a hint instead of acting like a blooming little cactus whenever I tried to get near you?"

She leaned away from him. "Ha! As I remember it, every time you got near me you tried to...well, you know!"

He threw back his head and roared. "I tried to what? If you mean I did my best to make love to you, then let me remind you that you were only one step behind me every time."

Before she could protest, he proceeded to demonstrate, and

by the time he lifted his mouth from hers, she could only nod weakly. "You win," she said.

"No, darling, we both win—although I'll concede that I'm the bigger winner. After all, once I made up my mind to have you, it was only a matter of time."

"How could I have been fool enough to fall in love with such an insufferably smug creature?" she crowed, covering the hand that had crept up to cover her breast—the breast that covered a heart that was full to overflowing. "When did you make up your mind?" she asked.

"Somewhere between the first and the second kiss," he growled against her throat. "But once I tried to do something about it and almost ran afoul of that armor you wear, I had to back off and try a bit of strategy. For one thing, I knew I had to get your wacky, lovable, but dependent family off your back so you wouldn't reject me and do the martyr bit. I couldn't have handled a second rejection from you, love. It seemed to me that it would be easier to solve all your problems and then sweep you off your feet, only things got all fouled up along the way."

"Poor Saint George," she cooed. "And here I was trying to keep a stiff upper lip and learn to call you brother-in-law. Did you know that?"

He didn't, and by the time she had elaborated, he felt another demonstration was in order. "Your mother explained to me, darling, about your father and his lady friends," he told her much later.

"That was why I didn't dare let myself trust you. Mother went right on loving my father even when he practically paraded his...his girls in front of her, but I could never share you. Never! It hurt me too much every time I saw the way you were with Bebe and Stella and even France," she confessed. "Mother said some men could never be satisfied with a single flower when the whole garden was in bloom."

"Darling, the other women in my life meant about as much to me as the pictures in a seed catalog. France is a pretty scamp—spoiled, mischievous—although with a woman like

Iola for a mother, there's hope for her. You have no more cause for worry about any other woman than I have about Brookwood or Palani. There's only one Kate Minerva Brown—fiercely independent, warm and loving, with an overdeveloped sense of responsibility and an irreverent sense of humor—and she's mine, promised to me way back in the beginning of time.''

"You're right about one thing, at least," Katie told him breathlessly. "Whatever she is, she's yours." Her arms crept up around his neck, and just before his face blocked out the starlight, she caught a gleam of amber eyes that promised several lifetimes of enchantment.

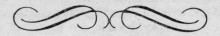

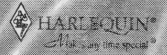

Receive *The Art of Romance* absolutely free!

This wonderful collection of
30 romantic souvenir postcards
will take you through a nostalgic
journey of illustrative cover art,
from charming Art Deco effects
of the early 1900s to the
crisper, more photographic
style of today.

All you have to do is collect two proofs of
purchase from any two TAKE 5 titles, send them in and
you will receive *The Art of Romance* absolutely free!
Harlequin will absorb all postage and handling costs.

Just complete the order form and send it, along with two (2)
proofs of purchase from two (2) TAKE 5 volumes, to:

TAKE 5, P.O. Box 9057, Buffalo, NY 14269-9057 or
P.O. Box 622, Fort Erie, Ontario, L2A 5X3.

NAME

ADDRESS

CITY   STATE/PROV.   ZIP/POSTAL CODE

(Please allow 4-6 weeks for delivery. Offer expires June 30, 2002.)

PROOF OF PURCHASE

TAKE5

T5-POP